PRAISE FOR CAROLYN RAE'S
Romancing the Gold

Romancing the Gold received a Top Pick and a 4 1/2 star review from Night Owl Reviews.

Night Owl Reviews gave *Romancing the Gold* a Top Pick and 4 1/2 stars. Here is what the reviewer said, "I absolutely loved the characters, and found myself cheering repeatedly for both Megan and Josh as they bravely fight through the South American jungle for their lives. This novel is a wonderful book that readers of most ages will absolutely adore. One word of caution: the love scenes are HOT! Which, in my humble opinion, made it even better."

OTHER BOOKS BY CAROLYN RAE

Hiding from Love
Witness Protection Series, Book One

Protected by Love
Witness Protection Series, Book Two

Tempted by Love
Witness Protection Series, Book Three

TEMPTED

by

Love

Witness Protection Series, Book Three

Carolyn Rae

Williamson Press
Hurst, Texas, USA

TEMPTED BY LOVE
Copyright © 2015 by Carolyn Rae

Williamson Press
Hurst, Texas, USA

ISBN: 978-0-9965873-2-7

Cover Art © by Charlene Raddon, Cover-Ops Cover Art
Interior Formatting by Author E.M.S.

Published in the United States of America.

Acknowledgments

With thanks to former U.S. Marshal Dub Bransom for information.

This book is dedicated to my critique partners, Pepper, Jan, Dorothy, and the DFW Writer's Workshop, and to NTRWA, DARA, Yellow Rose RWA, and for their help and encouragement as well as writing teachers, Donald Maass, the late Dwight Swain, the late Jack Bickham, and the late Rita Gallagher.

Chapter 1

U.S. Marshal Sheila Talbot glanced at her rearview mirror. That black pickup made every turn she did and stayed two blocks back. The hairs on the back of her neck prickled. It hadn't been that long since she'd picked up John Schmidt, her new witness, outside a McDonald's. The smell of French fries and hamburger lingered in the air. Her stomach rumbled, reminding her she'd skipped lunch to pick him up.

She cast a quick glance in his direction, and then looked back at the road. The pickup was still behind them. Obviously she'd been made.

He glanced behind them. "We've got a tail. Go right at the next street. And don't use the turn signal."

She stifled a retort, glanced in the rearview mirror, then sped up and pulled around the corner. She hadn't expected such an air of self-confidence in a witness whose life was in danger. Neither had she expected Schmidt to be so muscular or so good-looking, with white teeth accentuating his golden tan. But then, an ex-cop would be used to exuding an air of authority. However, he was turning out to be a bossy S.O.B. "Since when do you give the orders?"

"Turn into that alley there. It curves. We can be out of sight quickly."

Gritting her teeth, she cranked the wheel hard and careened

into the alley. She maneuvered the car along the curved pavement. At the next street, he said, "Turn left and head down the next alley."

"I don't see anyone following us now." Where did he get off acting like an expert? She knew he'd done surveillance and undercover work, but that didn't give him the right to order her around.

He leaned back in the seat. "Don't they teach you Marshals anything?"

That did it. She opened her mouth to tell him to shove it, but thought better of it. "They teach us enough." He grasped her arm. She shook it off. "Get your hands off me."

He pointed. "There. Turn into that alley."

She scowled, but turned where he indicated. Probably a good choice.

After emerging from the alley onto a street, she cruised past modest homes. "I'll pull into some driveway and park like we belong there until they pass."

"No way. We'd be sitting ducks."

"Duck is the word. He won't notice an empty car. Besides, I'm armed."

"Just keep driving."

Sheila gritted her teeth. If he bossed her one more time she'd…. Okay, deep breath. She wouldn't lose her cool. Not while they were being tailed. After that, he was fair game. "Look, I'm running this show." Her gaze darted to the rearview mirror, then to the road ahead. "Damn. There's that black pickup again."

He leaned forward. "Turn left here, then right at the next corner."

She'd picked up on the excitement in his voice right before she gunned the engine. "You're enjoying this, aren't you?"

A smirk flashed across his face, then disappeared. He pointed. "Go down that street. The sign points to a police station ahead. We can hide in their parking lot."

The neighborhood substation wasn't very big. Sheila pulled into a space between two blue and white Crown Vics. "Now duck down, and stay put until our tail passes."

He scrunched down in his seat.

Sheila settled low behind the wheel, but kept her eyes on the rearview mirror. At least Schmidt was following orders instead of giving them. "After half an hour our tail should give up. By then we'll get cramped sitting like this."

"So? Done it many times in Detroit."

Sure enough, the black pickup passed. With the tinted windows she couldn't tell if there were one man or two. A few minutes later, the same vehicle drove by again.

After unfastening her seat belt, Sheila sat there, wondering why Schmidt had asked to be in the Witness Security Program. He seemed able to take care of himself. His instincts had been right on target. He'd led her safely to the station, but from now on she had to show him she was in control.

Feeling safe enough to sit up straight, she asked, "How come you haven't applied for a job as a cop here in Texas?"

"It's a long story."

Judging from the scowl on his face, he didn't want to talk about it. "So why did you go to work in a bank?"

"I'm a CPA, and my uncle got me a job in the small town bank where he works."

Finally, after waiting until she was convinced it was safe, she backed out into the street. Keeping an eye on the rearview mirror, she took a roundabout way to the small office the agency had rented in a warehouse district and led him inside. She laid her briefcase on the desk and pulled out a sheet of the rules. After handing it to him, she motioned him toward the chair. "Look this over, Mr. Schmidt."

Ignoring the chair, he glanced at the rules and then slapped the page on the desk. "What do you mean I can't call my sister? Hard to trace one of those prepaid cell phones." Schmidt paced in front of the scarred oak desk.

"Sit down, please," Sheila said. He perched on the edge of the chair. Obviously, he wanted this discussion to be brief. She remained standing so he'd have to look up to her. With wavy chestnut hair and those amused brown eyes—except they didn't look so amused right now—a guy that good-looking probably talked women into going along with him. That wouldn't wash with her.

She raised her voice. "Even with a paid-up cell phone, you can't be sure someone can't access your phone records. You can talk to your friends and family if you use a pay phone and route the call through our office, or you can write them by sending the letters to our office."

He frowned. "Damn. I want to put those guys away as much as you do. Marshal Carson gave me a similar list—he said those were suggestions for keeping safe. Hey, I know how to be careful, but these nit-picking rules are ridiculous."

"Those rules are for your safety."

"Yeah, yeah. I know." He didn't seem to be worried about the danger he faced. In fact, he seemed more interested in looking at her. "Nice suit," he said.

Surprised, she met his gaze and saw only the look of an interested male. Obviously he wasn't taking her seriously. "Uh, thanks." It was nice to be complimented, but she had more important things to concentrate on. The aroma of his lime-scented aftershave wafted over her. The gray-walled room seemed close and too warm. Wishing there was a window, Sheila unbuttoned her suit jacket, exposing her white tailored blouse, and leaned forward. "You said you wanted protection if you were going to testify."

"Yes, but—"

She held up her hand to silence him. Emotion flashed across his face like wheat waving in a sudden wind. She hoped he wasn't having second thoughts. "You're doing the right thing. If you testify about what you found when you examined Dirk

Dobson's books for that import-export company, the government should be able to nail them all."

"I'll do my part to put those crooks behind bars, but I won't turn into a hermit. When I worked undercover, I might have looked like one, but I had a life when I got home."

The look on his face said restricting his activities didn't sit well. She tried to imagine him with long hair and baggy jeans. She thought about not being able to talk with her beloved grandparents or her friends regularly. Cut off from his family and friends, he must feel alone. "Look," she said, "just think of this as another undercover job."

Since the U.S. Marshal handling John had resigned under pressure, she'd been assigned to watch over him. Her supervisor and other Deputy U.S. Marshals in the Dallas Witness Security Division—all male, would be watching her. She'd be damn sure not to make a mistake with her first witness.

This man looked as if he could take care of himself in a fistfight, but she wouldn't let him or the government's case be endangered by carelessness.

She paused and took a deep breath. The ticking of a wall clock broke the silence. He was staring at her again. "Okay, listen up. Don't you realize how vulnerable you are? After you testify against Dobson, staying in the program will be even more important. Dobson's boss may be small potatoes, but he probably has men scouring Texas for you."

She pushed the stapled sheets toward him. "You need to know these rules backwards and forwards."

John glanced at the papers, and then leaned back in his chair. To a tune from "Oklahoma," he sang, "Don't call your folks again. Don't use a credit card." His deep voice boomed in the small room. He switched to the tune for "Hernando's Hideaway" from the movie, "Pajama Game." "Go to a new secluded place so no one there will know your face." He tossed the pages onto her desk. "Yeah, I get the picture."

He glanced around the small room. "Seems like the agency

could afford a better office for a professional like you."

"This isn't my office. It's a more isolated location—less likely someone will see you here. We rent space in this Dallas warehouse in case we need to interview high profile witnesses."

"I pulled off some good jobs as an undercover cop in Detroit, but when my name got in the paper, it became too hot there. However, I doubt the news reached here, so I wouldn't call myself high profile."

She wondered about the circumstances behind the reasons he'd left Detroit. His tone was matter of fact, but frown marks creasing his forehead indicated he didn't want to discuss that.

He shot her an inquiring look. "Okay, what's next?"

She tapped a pen on the desk. "Role playing. You'll be new in town. What if someone asks where you come from and what you do? How will you answer?"

Rising, he leaned forward and shook her hand vigorously. His grip was firm, but then he shot her a mega-watt smile and squeezed her hand before letting go, leaving her with an unexpected tingle.

She took a deep breath, hoping he wouldn't notice the effect he had on her.

"I'm John Schmidt, and I'm from Joisey." He mimicked the accent perfectly.

She frowned, trying not to laugh. "You have to do better than that. Use your new name. It's what you'll go by from now on."

"Ah'm Brent Broussard," he drawled and settled back in the chair with a lazy grace. "Ah'm from Georgia, where they sell peaches, and southern gals in pastel cotton dresses hand you a mint julep on a hot afternoon." He flashed that charming smile again. "I'll bet even you appreciate having doors opened and a gentleman offering his arm when crossing the street."

For a moment she could almost see herself being led onto the dance floor and coaxed into his arms with that come-hither grin. He'd be a smooth dancer, she was sure. What was she thinking? "Be serious," she said, straightening her shoulders and mentally admonishing herself to do the same.

He sat up straighter, took on a more determined look. "My name's Brent Broussard, and I'm from Detroit." He steepled his fingers. "Anyone trying to track me will have a hard time digging up background for a Brent Broussard in Detroit. I won't try to fake a southern accent. Hasn't been that long since I moved here."

"Folks around here would say you do have an accent, a Midwestern one. Now, what do you plan to do for a living?"

His brown eyes twinkled as he propped an ankle on his knee. "That's easy. I'm presently unemployed, but I'm looking for a job as a CPA."

"What about your credentials?"

"Carl Carson, the Marshal I was assigned to first, said I couldn't use them." Leaning forward in the chair, he crossed his legs and frowned. "Can't you reissue my license in my new name?"

Sheila shook her head. Must be hard having to start out again without credentials he'd already earned. "We don't falsify those documents. At headquarters in D.C. they make new ones for your identification, but that's all."

"If I have to work as a burger flipper, I'm not doing this." He rose, shoved his chair back, and headed for the door.

She frowned. His ego could be a problem. "Brent, come back."

He didn't answer. "John," she called.

He turned to face her.

"If you want to save your skin, you must answer to Brent. That's your name from now on. You can admit to knowing how to keep books, but you can't use any of your former credentials. Now sit down. Most people would love to be an actor. Here's your chance."

He turned the chair around and straddled it. "Yeah, but I

won't get big bucks for it like Mel Gibson."

"You won't see your name in lights either, and it better not be in the news. If Dirk's ex-boss, Sheldon, sends men to find you, you'll be dead before you can blink an eye."

His gaze met hers for a long moment. "Okay, let's get this game over so I can get on with my life." He spoke as if this were like an afternoon tennis match. He'd probably look great in a T-shirt and shorts.

Sheila adopted a no-nonsense expression. "This is serious. Read the rules again."

"Already did. Twice." He shoved them toward her. "So where are you sending me?"

"Mesquite."

"Where the hell is that?"

"It's a Dallas suburb."

"I'd rather stay in Dallas where there's some action." His grin suggested he'd like to include her in some of that action—dancing, maybe. She needed to stop thinking about what it would be like to be in his strong arms—to have those amber-flecked brown eyes concentrating on her. She straightened, her chin jutting forward. "The idea is to be as inconspicuous as possible."

"Lady, I know how to move around without being noticed. Done it lots of times, but what's there to do in Mesquite?"

"They have rodeos almost every weekend."

"So I go to a rodeo once or twice—I can only stand so much manure. What else is there?"

Sheila walked around the desk and perched on the edge. "Find an organization that interests you—since you sing, join a church and sing in the choir."

He tipped his chair forward. "So can I run into Dallas to see a play or listen to some good music?"

"Sure, if the bus runs near your place."

"You mean you're not getting me a car? Deputy Marshal Carson made me get rid of my Corvette."

"A red convertible is too noticeable, too flashy. You sold it,

8

didn't you?"

"I traded the Vette to my ex for a timeshare."

"Whose name is the timeshare in?"

"Hold your horses. It's in her maiden name. She took that back in the divorce settlement."

"You'll have to dispose of the timeshare."

"No way."

"They can harass your ex-wife and trace it to you." Sheila looked him in the eye. "You may not be too fond of her, but do you want to put her life in danger, too?"

His eyes darkened, and worry lines creased his forehead. "Of course not. I don't want anyone threatening her to get at me."

Apparently he had some compassion for his ex-wife. Her opinion of him went up a notch. She edged back to her chair and sat, then shook her head. "I'll arrange to have a real estate agent list the timeshare for sale. We'll sell it and keep the money for you." She pulled a form from his file. "All you have to do is sign the—"

He rose from the chair and leaned over the desk, his muscled forearms plainly displayed. "I'm not signing anything. Didn't even get to stay there before the marriage went sour."

"Sorry, sir."

He frowned. "Don't call me 'sir.' I'm not that much older than you." He propped an elbow on one knee. "I'll get a lawyer to draw up papers in my new name."

She shook her head. "Sorry, sir, but that's not a good idea."

"I told you not to call me that." He perched on the edge of the chair. "My name's John, I mean Brent." He was trying not to show it, but obviously the situation unnerved him.

"John's not your name anymore. If you hear someone say it, don't even turn your head."

"Okay, I get the message. Can't I at least sell my timeshare to one of my friends so I could stay there occasionally?"

"You don't get it, do you? You can't meet any of your

friends in person, not now, not next week, not even next year until we put those guys away."

"What happens if I don't stay in the Witness Protection Program?"

"It's called the Witness Security Program. We could try to set up your deposition with Dirk Dobson's lawyer, but they don't usually do that in federal court. If you leave the program, you'll be on your own. With luck, they might not find you for at least a week. Is your will in order?"

He swallowed. "Did you fax my letter requesting two months off to take care of family matters to my boss?"

"Yes, but—"

"I know. If the court date is postponed, I can say goodbye to my position at Suburbia Bank. Wish to hell I'd sent a subordinate to audit Bart Sheldon's company books, but we were short handed at the time. My boss wanted us to go the extra mile to get the business. Now I can't call my family without going through your office. This set-up stinks."

She sensed his frustration, but the only help she could give would be to protect him. Rising, she drew herself up to her full five-foot-eight inches. "Are you going to play ball or not?"

She watched his expression but couldn't tell what he was thinking—he must play a good hand of poker.

Had she come on too strong? What if he wouldn't follow instructions and got hurt or killed under her protection?

Brent drummed his fingers on the edge of the desk. It wasn't really hers, but his territorial action bothered her. How could she intimidate this guy without coming across as a bitch? Sure would help to have an experienced female Marshal in her unit to show her how.

He tipped his chair back. He was grinning—probably he'd tell her to take the Witness Security Program and shove it, but the look in his eyes intrigued her. She waited.

"Okay," he said. "I'll play your game, but—"

"This isn't a game," she spat out and then wondered what he'd been about to add. With a firm voice, she jumped in before he brought up anything else. "You'll have to do everything we say."

"You mean everything *you* say, don't you?"

"That's right."

"Don't you have to report to a supervisor?"

"Of course, but I run the show."

Was that a groan she heard? She stepped around the desk. "I've rented you a room in the home of an older widow. I'll take you there now."

He smiled. "I'll do everything you say if—"

"No conditions. You'll follow orders if you want to stay alive."

"But you didn't let me finish."

"You can tell me your idea on the way, but I may veto it." She pulled some keys from her purse. "Come on."

He flashed her a thousand-watt smile. "I'll make you a deal. My week at the timeshare condo comes up soon. Come away with me for a long weekend. You'd look great in a bikini."

His gaze roved over her, settling on her breasts, letting her know he liked what he saw.

"No way," she snapped, struggling to hold her ground. His gall blew her away. Did he think she was a pushover?

"Hey, I'm not talking about sex. Just want to enjoy the place at least once. We can go swimming and lie on the beach." His charming smile said if she showed the least bit of encouragement, he'd try to talk her into his bed. His intense look unnerved her. Hell, if that ever happened, she might find him hard to resist.

She glanced out the small window, then back at him.

His look turned serious. "We could spend some time talking about why your agency developed all those nit-picking rules. Must be some interesting stories behind them."

Sheila slammed the keys to the agency car on the desk.

"Being seen together socially with a witness isn't allowed. That could lead someone to you."

"Might take them a while to get there. It's in Hawaii.

Chapter 2

"You can't be serious. There's no way I'd take off with you to Hawaii or anywhere else."

He laughed. "Figured as much. Just wanted to see what you'd say."

"You're impossible." For an instant she imagined herself rubbing suntan lotion over Brent's broad chest and racing into the surf beside him.

If he could read her thoughts, he'd probably laugh. She suppressed a groan, wishing she dared ask for another witness for her first assignment. No—that would be admitting failure. Besides, her partner, Joe, was overloaded. Somehow, she'd master the situation—and Brent.

She picked up the keys. "Let's go."

Feeling his eyes on her, she locked the office door, scanned the area outside the warehouse, and strode to her car. He followed and climbed in.

Recalling the background reports she'd read about him being a track star in college, she asked, "Do you plan to jog in your new neighborhood?"

Brent met her glance and held it. He'd enjoyed baiting her, but now she seemed to be making small talk. He wasn't sure which he hated more, all these damn rules, or being told what to do by a bossy woman. He needed the protection so he'd play along—within reason. "I usually run every day."

She started the car. "Don't jog in the streets. Maybe you can join the YMCA or a health club—in Mesquite, not downtown Dallas."

"I see," he said. So she had a purpose behind her question. He watched her hands as she drove. One hand held the wheel steady, but the fingers of her other hand beat a tattoo on the rim. If he could keep her on edge, maybe she wouldn't be so controlling.

He didn't even take this kind of treatment from his mother, who kept telling him he ought to find a nice girl and get married. With blue eyes and long blonde hair rippling over her shoulders, Sheila had a great body, but she was definitely not his type.

After a roundabout trip with lots of sharp turns, she braked in a quiet neighborhood. The car jerked to a stop.

He started to ask how long she'd been driving, but thought better of it. After following her up the outside stairs to an efficiency apartment over a garage, he waited while she unlocked the door and handed him a key. Despite her tough talk, her hand felt soft. How would her hands feel on his body?

Inside, his new place consisted of little more than a sitting room with a bathroom and a tiny kitchen. It would do for a while. He didn't usually hang around home much, but with Sergeant Sheila, that might change.

She moved with seemingly effortless grace, setting down a sack of groceries, checking the peephole in the door, and testing the lock.

She turned to meet his gaze. "Do you have to keep your eyes on me every second?"

He leaned against the wall. "I appreciate your thoroughness."

"My partner suggested this place, but it's my job to make sure it's safe."

After throwing his suitcase on the daybed, he unpacked. He noticed her staring at his cotton briefs printed with Detroit Lion helmets as he set them in a drawer. Bet she wondered if he were a football fan. Just let her guess. He certainly wasn't going to open up after the way she'd ordered him around.

It was bad enough the way his father ruled the roost when he'd lived at home. He'd had more than his share of belts applied to his backside. His sister, on the other hand, had always got away with murder. Sometimes she even convinced their parents he was to blame for something she did.

Thank goodness she'd grown out of that. He'd even given her money so she could stay in college after their father had told her to stop wasting time and get a job.

He hoped Sergeant Sheila wouldn't spell out the rules again. Oh, he'd be careful—after all, he faced danger from that shady bookkeeper he was going to testify against—but he wouldn't let her run every minute of his life. He'd seen the way she looked at him. Maybe if he made a play for her, she'd stop trying to control his every move.

She walked out on the landing. As she leaned over the railing with faded, peeling paint, he got a tantalizing view of her long legs.

The railing wiggled when she shook it. He stepped closer to see for himself. "Shouldn't you have checked that out before you picked this place?"

She turned abruptly and bumped into his chest. He grabbed her arms to steady her. Inhaling her perfume, something fresh and flowery, he fought against the urge to pull her against him, see if the rest of her were soft like her hand. She had a startled look, as if he'd caught her drooling over an expensive dress in a shop window. She was attracted to him all right, but she'd never admit it.

Sheila backed away from Brent, careful not to bump into the railing. No sense in giving him the idea she was interested in him. Not used to feeling a sudden attraction to a man—she preferred getting to know a guy slowly—she drew in a deep breath. This would never do. She had to concentrate on business and ignore how he made her feel. Besides, men who went in for flashy cars or gambled a week's salary in a poker game didn't appeal to her.

She wondered if that were a one-time occurrence. Remembering Rodney, she doubted it.

Brent must have seen the look of surprise on her face because he stepped back. "Sorry," he said. "Railing could be rotten. I didn't want you to fall."

"Thanks. I appreciate your concern." She brushed past him and mentally shrugged away the jolting awareness of his sturdy thighs against hers. Should have been more careful on this postage stamp porch.

She met his gaze. "This landing is rather conspicuous. When you go out you should—"

"I know," he interrupted. "Survey the area before venturing out. Isn't that what you were going to say?"

She nodded. Damn the man. Was he trying to impress her by being one step ahead? Obviously he was intelligent, but to keep him safe she needed to have him firmly in hand.

Adopting a business-like expression, she took one more look around, then stepped back inside. "Don't stand out here long enough for people to get a good look at you."

Brent walked in and settled onto the corner of the brass daybed, now made up like a couch. He rested his arm across the back. "If you've checked everything out, why not sit down." He smiled invitingly as if expecting her to sit beside him. With that ruffled slipcover, the day bed seemed more appropriate for a bedroom. She met his gaze, and then turned away. Surely he wasn't trying to make a move on her.

Sheila stepped into the kitchenette. The widow who owned this place must have converted a walk-in closet into this tiny kitchen. She made sure the hood above the stove worked and checked the wiring. She stocked the small cupboard with cans of soup and ready to eat food. He probably didn't cook much, but he wouldn't starve.

As she stepped out of the kitchenette, he lay on the daybed, his ankles crossed. He was watching her again. Suddenly self-conscious, she straightened. "I know it's not much of a place, but you should be safe here."

"This place will cramp my style. I couldn't bring a woman here. I'd have to take her out for dinner by candlelight and dancing somewhere nice or maybe for a picnic out in the country. But I suppose I'll have to wait until I can find a job and buy a car."

"That's right. We don't have the funds to buy cars for witnesses." She wondered what it would be like to walk through the woods beside him with birds singing and crickets chirping. Would he hold her hand?

Forget it, she told herself. No time for that—and definitely against policy. Besides, after losing your heart to a man you'll never see again and all the trouble afterwards, you don't want a boyfriend. She blinked back unwanted wetness. No sense in dwelling on the past.

He stood. Although he was just few inches taller than her five-foot-eight inches, she had to look up to meet his eyes.

Unnerved by his sexy grin, she said, "The rent is paid for two months, and here's some cash." She handed him an envelope of bills. "This will have to last until you get a paycheck. Since you're an accountant, I assume you know how to manage money. We don't have the funds to support you indefinitely. Don't apply for a credit card. They're too easy to trace."

He frowned. "If I can't use a credit card, I'll have to get a temporary job, then save up and pay cash for some beat up old clunker."

"That's right." She handed him a cell phone and a piece of paper with the number written on it. "This is for emergencies. It's registered in the agency name. We'll pay the bill, but don't call any of your friends and family with it. For those calls you must use a pay phone and route them through my office." The tones of the Star Wars theme sounded. "What's that?"

"My cell phone. Hello?" He listened, then frowned. "Who the hell is this?" He scowled, then clicked the phone off.

"What was that all about?"

"A threat."

"Who was it?"

"Some man who called me before. Didn't recognize the voice."

"What exactly did he say?"

"You won't live long enough to testify. We'll find you."

Sheila reached for the phone. "Do you have caller ID?"

He nodded.

"Get the number."

He pushed some buttons. "It says, 'out of area.'"

"Give me that phone. I'll see if someone at the agency can trace it. You can use the other one to call me."

He slapped it in her hand. He smoothed his brown hair, then gripped the arm of the couch. "Any more instructions?"

"Just be sensible, and keep a close eye out for anyone who acts strangely."

"I'll try to blend in as you say. If I land a part in a little theatre play, I'll send you an invitation. You'll see what a good leading man I can be."

With his looks, he'd probably have a good chance at that. "Better try out for a minor part."

"Where's the challenge in that?"

"We don't want your name or your picture in the papers."

He frowned. "All work and no play will make Brent a dull man."

"Better a dull man, than a dead one." Sheila yanked the door open and stepped out onto the porch.

He followed, but stayed in the doorway. Halfway down the stairs she turned back. "Don't stand in plain sight. You make too good a target."

"Just watching until you get in the car. Since you'll be coming to check on me, I'll say you're my sister so the

18

neighbors won't think anything's unusual and mention it to nosy strangers."

"Good point."

His gaze raked over her. "On second thought—we don't look much alike."

"Well, I'll only be here to check on you during the week. That won't be enough to attract much notice." Thank goodness for that. The way he put her off and attracted her at the same time was unnerving. If he got even an inkling she were attracted to him, she'd be mortified.

She wished now she hadn't picked the name Brent for him. This man wasn't anything like the other Brent she'd known, but she'd had to come up with a name quickly when requesting another set of identity documents after his other alias might have been compromised by a former Marshal.

He grinned. "Okay then, I'll say you're a girlfriend."

"I'm not your girlfriend."

"Shouldn't I pretend you are to cover up the fact I'm hiding out? I could even take you out to dinner sometime—you know, to talk over your investigation of the threats against me."

She didn't even want to think about that. Brent would probably hold her hand and feed her a line as long as her arm about liking the way she looked. "We're not supposed to be seen together. You'll get information on a need to know basis."

He scowled. "But it's my neck that's on the line."

"True. But I'll keep you abreast of any new development."

He grinned, his gaze dropping to her breasts.

She smothered a gasp. Should have phrased that differently. Why did her first witness have to be such a pain in the ass? "The only reason I'll come here is because it's my job to keep you safe."

She turned and strode down the stairs, her chin jutting out. The nerve of him. A man wouldn't put up with this. Of course, Brent wouldn't act this way with a man.

"By the way, Sheila."

She turned. "What now?" she called over the racket of a garbage truck next door.

"Aren't you going to answer your phone?" It jangled from her purse.

"It's probably the office, and I won't be able to hear outside." Taking the stairs two at a time, she raced back up into the apartment.

It was Alice, the receptionist at the office. "You didn't answer at your desk so I called you on your cell phone. Think you'd better talk to this Rodney. He insists on speaking to you. Want me to transfer the call?"

"Go ahead."

That's all she needed, another difficult man to deal with. She'd set him straight about when to call her. "Hello, Rodney, don't call me while I'm at work."

"Sheila, baby, I need your help."

"Don't call me baby, and I don't want to hear any sad stories. You need to stand on your own two feet and deal with your problems."

"But," he whined, "you're a Marshal. I've got this little gambling debt I can't pay off right now, and I'm being pressured to come up with the cash. Can't you lean on the guy or something?"

"So, act like a man and get a loan."

About to sever the connection, she noticed Brent watching her. He whispered, "Old boyfriend?"

"Not exactly."

"Wait, don't hang up," came the voice from the phone. "The guy I owe said he'd forget the debt if I'd find out the name of the man who's going to testify against him. Doesn't someone have a right to know who his accuser is?"

"I'm not telling you anything."

"But you'd know who it was, wouldn't you?"

"Even if I did, I wouldn't give out that information."

"What if I tell you who's asking? Then you can tell me you

aren't guarding the witness he wants to know about, and I'll be off the hook. This guy keeps pushing me—says he wants the money or the information."

"What guy?"

"He's asking for his brother, Dirk. Think his last name is Dobson or something."

Sheila swallowed a gasp. Dobson, the bookkeeper for Bart Sheldon's little crime empire—Dobson, the man who took the fifth rather than testify against his former boss, Dobson, the man whose two sets of books Brent had audited.

"So," Rodney asked, "is that guy in the witness program?"

"What makes you think I'd know? I don't handle witnesses now, so don't call me about that again." She turned off the phone.

Brent's look was accusing. "You lied to him, didn't you?"

"He was asking for your name and if you were in the Witness Security Program."

"I see," he said, but his eyes seemed to accuse her of poor judgment for being involved with Rodney. She gritted her teeth. Rodney was none of his business.

She dialed the receptionist at the office. "Alice, from now on, just let me know that he called, but don't put him through. And don't give out any information. You could get in trouble if you let anything slip to the wrong person."

"Okey dokey, but I'll keep an eye out, I mean an ear out for that Rodney person. I'm pretty good with voices so I should be able to pick up on his."

"Just be sure you don't mistake a legitimate caller for him. And I wouldn't say 'Okey dokey' any more, if I were you. Sounds unprofessional." Sheila disconnected.

"Not much of a man, is he, asking to borrow money from a woman?" Brent asked.

"That was a private phone call. A gentleman wouldn't be listening."

"It's the only way I learn anything around here. By the way, about the landlady, what's her name?"

"Mrs. Stewart. I'd introduce you, but this is her day to play bridge. You can say 'hello' to her later."

"What did you tell her about me?"

"Nothing. I pretended I was your girlfriend."

He grinned. "See. There's a good reason for you to act like one. She'll probably tell all the neighbors about the pretty woman I'm dating."

She stared at him. Why had he said she was pretty? Oh, yes, part of his act. Well, she'd ignore that. She stepped out onto the porch. "I hardly know you. I wouldn't feel comfortable acting as your girlfriend."

"I can take care of that." His friendly grin slid under her defenses. He grasped her hand, his gentle touch disarming. She told herself she wasn't afraid of him. He might be obstinate about his protection, but he'd act like a gentleman, wouldn't he?

She tried to pull her hand away, but his grip was firm. Before she could stop him, he pulled her into his arms and kissed her. His lips were gentle at first, then changed. It was as if he found her mouth so irresistible he couldn't move away. Worse yet, she was having trouble doing that very thing.

Then he deepened the kiss, shaking her with its intensity. He made her feel wonderful, but she couldn't do this, not with him of all people. She tried to push away, raised her arm to slap him.

He grasped her hand in his and brought it to his mouth. He placed a soft kiss on her knuckles. His tender lips spread a comforting warmth through her. "You're softer than I thought you'd be. Why do you keep trying to be so tough?"

He smoothed a lock of hair from her forehead, his touch like warm spring raindrops. "You just haven't met the right man to awaken your capacity for passion."

Her insides still trembling, she pulled her hand away. No telling what he'd do to shore up that mistaken impression.

Chapter 3

He met Kathy, the girlfriend of former Deputy U.S. Marshal Carl Carlson, in a Denny's restaurant. She'd called after visiting Carl in federal prison. Kathy was a looker all right, with platinum hair, bright red lipstick, and a well-filled out sweater with a low vee-neck.

He eased his big form into the booth and sat across from her, trying not to stare at her tits. Not smart to make a move on Carl's girlfriend. His old friend had a jealous streak as wide as a football field. He could have someone watching.

Kathy leaned forward, giving him a better look at her cleavage. She shoved a piece of paper toward him. "This is from Carl."

He scanned the page, taking in the address of the U.S. Marshal's office in Dallas, a description of the receptionist, Alice, and two unfamiliar names at the bottom. "So what's he want me to do?"

A waitress stopped at the table. He ordered coffee and two doughnuts for each of them, which arrived immediately.

Kathy waited to speak until the waitress left. "Carl wants you to make a play for this Alice and see what you can find out."

He wolfed down the first doughnut, then the second and licked his fingers. He pointed to the two names written at the bottom in a hurried scrawl. "What about them?"

Kathy moved a long red nail to the name John Schmidt. "Carl and Bart Sheldon want you to keep this witness from testifying. If he does, the Feds might lay extra charges on Carl and Bart and give them more jail time. Carl wants you to put the fear of the devil in that snitch or take him out if you have to. This here's his real name. Carl claimed the agency's probably changed it by now."

With dainty fingers she put her second doughnut on his plate. "You take this. One's enough for me."

"Thanks." He took a bite and savored the sweetness. He pointed to the name Sheila. "Who's this, and how come there's no last name?"

Kathy shrugged. "I forgot her last name, something beginning with a 'T' I think. I wrote these down in a hurry, 'cause visiting hours were over, and the guard was hustling Carl back to his cell."

"What's she got to do with anything?"

"She's the Marshal who was given Carl's old assignment— protecting the witness who'll testify against his friend, Bart Sheldon, and his bookkeeper, Dirk Dobson."

"I see." He took another long look at her exposed cleavage. He raised his eyes to meet hers. She didn't seem to mind. In fact, he bet she enjoyed his ogling.

He snatched up the rest of the doughnut she'd given him— he shouldn't eat it, but…. "So Carl wants something done to make this Marshal look bad."

She frowned. "You already talked to him, didn't you? I gave up my standing appointment at the beauty shop to meet you. If he told you all this, why on earth did he ask me to meet you?" She threw her half-eaten doughnut on the table, then rose. She shoved her coffee mug so hard the liquid sloshed onto the table, barely missing the doughnut half. "I'm out of here."

He rose, towering over her as he grasped her arm.

She winced. He smiled at the look of alarm in her eyes. She'd listen now.

He shoved her back down in the seat. "I can't visit Carl in prison. I have a record, and he knows it. Just figured that's what he'd want after being forced out of the U.S. Marshals Service."

Had Carl had told Kathy that witness could send his brother to jail? "Did Carl tell you anything more?"

Kathy shook her head. "That's all I know. Let me go." She tried to pry his hand loose. "I'll be late at the beauty parlor."

He pointed to the paper. "Write your phone number down before you go." He released her hand.

She scribbled some numbers and sashayed out of the restaurant.

He snatched the paper, stuffed her half-eaten doughnut in his mouth, and threw some bills on the table. "Temperamental bitch," he muttered. Rubbing his forehead, he headed for his pickup. Crap, a sugar headache was all he needed now. Shouldn't have touched that third doughnut.

❦

Sheila leaned back in the driver's seat and glanced at Brent. He didn't seem nervous about spending Thanksgiving at her grandparents' house. In fact, he'd looked pleased when she asked. She didn't have the heart to let him spend it alone so far from home, but she couldn't tell Grandma why she was bringing him.

The only trouble was, she'd never brought a man there to dinner before. Grandma was sure to think he was someone special. Turning her attention to the road, she hoped there'd be no embarrassing questions.

Brent touched her arm, startling her. "Sorry," he said. "Didn't mean to scare you. How come you picked a name without asking me what I'd like? Carl Carson let me choose one."

No point in telling him she suspected a leak at the agency.

"In the interest of caution, D.C. headquarters wanted a new driver's license and a new social security number for you. I had to pick a name on the spot."

"I see."

He didn't say much for the rest of the trip.

After forty-five minutes on city streets and three freeways, she finally reached Fort Worth. With the nagging feeling that a black pickup was following her, she exited the freeway and took several turns through Fort Worth's city streets. As she made her way back to the highway at the southern city limits, she was pretty sure she'd lost the guy.

Heading out of Fort Worth on 35W she saw even more vehicles like the one she'd thought was following her. Pickups were the vehicle of choice for Texas men. Maybe the driver of that black one had just been going in the same direction.

By the time she turned off on the road to Cleburne, traffic had thinned. No suspicious vehicles tagged behind. She breathed easier. "We're almost at my grandmother's house, but on the way back, I'll give you more tips on how to respond to possible questions and how to watch out for your safety."

He glared at her. "We covered that already. Give me credit for a little sense. If there's anything else I need to know, just lay it out. It's my life that's on the line. Don't need a damn keeper to pound things into my head."

"Good. We haven't the manpower to babysit you 24/7."

"So, how many people does it take to make someone disappear?"

"Headquarters does the IDs, and then each witness is assigned to a team of two Deputy Marshals. I'm the only one, except my partner, who will know where you live, where you work, and how to contact you." She parked outside a modest, ranch-style house. "We're here."

Brent walked around the car and opened the door for her. His irritation seemed to have dissipated. As he strode beside her on the narrow sidewalk, so close he invaded her space, his lime aftershave washed over her. With that gleam in his eyes, there was no telling what he'd do or say.

She straightened and stared straight ahead, not wanting to let his amber-flecked brown eyes penetrate her soul and see how much he bothered her.

As she raised her hand to lift the doorknocker, he leaned against the front door, even closer now than he had been coming up the walk. "Something's been bugging me. Why did I get reassigned to a different Marshal, and why did headquarters think you needed to change my identity again?"

She hesitated, not sure how much to tell him. Carson had left the agency under a cloud. She banged the door knocker. "Carson's no longer with the agency. In the interest of caution, I redesigned the plans for your safety."

"Was he fired for messing up?"

"I'm not allowed to discuss the reasons he left." There'd been rumors about a leak somewhere. "Shhhh. I hear footsteps. Someone's coming."

Her grandmother, petite and feminine in lemon slacks, matching silk blouse and high heels greeted them at the door. "Good to see you, dear." She hugged Sheila and held out her hand to Brent. "Nice to meet you. I don't know why Sheila has kept you a secret. I'm always glad to meet her boyfriends."

"Brent is just a friend. I brought him to dinner because he has no family nearby. I'm lucky I still have you two, now that Mom and Dad are gone."

Brent smiled. "Thanks for letting me come on such short notice. I count myself lucky to have such a charming hostess."

Her grandmother beamed. "Oh, get on with you. Flattery will get you anything." She held out her hand for Sheila's purse. "Let me take that. I don't know why you insist on carrying such a heavy pocketbook."

Sheila held tight to her purse. "I'll put it up." Grandma would be alarmed if she saw the gun inside.

"You'll have to excuse me," her grandmother said. "I need

to check on the turkey." She gestured toward the couch. "You two have a seat and make yourselves at home." She turned and headed for the kitchen.

Sheila glanced around. As always, everything was impeccably clean and neat. The muted red and gold plaid of the comfortable couch and love seat was repeated in matching draperies and the mat framing the oil painting of Sheila's late mother.

From the kitchen, grandmother called out, "Harold I need your strong arms to lift the turkey out of the oven. Would you be a dear and come do it?"

"Hold your horses, Mary. I'm coming," said Sheila's grandfather in his halting tones. A few seconds later he made his way down the stairs, then stopped at seeing Sheila and Brent in the living room. Sheila introduced Brent.

Her grandfather shook hands with him and said, "So, this is your young man. Glad to meet you, Brent."

Sheila glanced at Brent, who smiled without seeming embarrassed in the least. "He's just a friend, Granddad. I didn't want him to have to spend Thanksgiving alone." She sat back down on the couch, hoping he'd drop the subject.

"Sheila dear, do you still plan to make a career as a U.S. Marshal?"

She nodded. "One of these days I intend to be promoted to Supervisory Deputy Marshal."

"Well, I'm sure you'll do fine, but I don't really understand what exactly it is that you do."

"Sorry, Granddad, it's classified."

"Can't even tell your family? What if you were a janitor? Would they let you reveal that?"

"If I worked as a janitor, it would be an undercover job, and I couldn't talk about that either."

"Harold, are you coming?" her grandmother called from the kitchen.

"Oh, all right," her grandfather grumbled good naturedly as he headed to the kitchen.

Sheila turned toward Brent. "Have a seat."

"Your grandparents don't seem old-fashioned. They haven't even asked my intentions."

Sheila laughed. "I don't think they expect me to get serious about someone yet. They understand I'm focused on my career and haven't much time for dating."

She studied his expression, wondering if he'd think her odd. However, all she saw was an interested listener. "I need to concentrate on my job 24/7."

"Surely a little social life wouldn't hurt."

"I'm the only woman in the Witness Security Division. I have this crazy, nagging feeling that if I screw up, I'll get fired or transferred to a less interesting position." She bit her lip, wondering why she'd told him her deepest fear.

He leaned forward. "If you were good enough to get this job, why would you worry about losing it?"

"I finished training with a top rating. I'm as good or better than any of them, but as the last one hired, I could get laid off if funding is cut."

"Why would you volunteer for a risky assignment where a man's superior strength and experience are called for?"

Sheila clenched her fists. "Are you suggesting I'm not capable just because I'm a woman? I have a black belt in karate, and my marksmanship scores are the highest in the agency."

"I'm impressed. How many other witnesses have you taken care of?"

She hesitated, then leaned back on the couch. "Actually, you're the first."

Leaning forward, he frowned. "That hardly fills me with confidence."

"Look, I've been a Deputy Marshal for over three years, and I know my job." She rose and walked to the window. After a quick glance at the manicured lawn and shrubs, she turned back to face him. "I know how to place a witness so he fades into the background, so those who want him stopped aren't likely to find him—that is, if the witness follows my instructions and doesn't do anything rash."

Her grandmother stepped in the room and announced dinner was ready.

Brent rose. "Let's go. We don't want to keep our hostess waiting." A mega-watt smile brightened his face, making her insides quiver. Maybe after she got to know him better, he wouldn't affect her like this.

She walked beside him into the dining room. Crystal and silverware gleamed, and the aroma of turkey washed over her. On the buffet a pecan pie sat next to a pumpkin one, tawny brown against the shining mahogany surface.

At the head of the table her grandfather carved the turkey. It oozed golden juice as the knife sliced into it.

Brent pulled out a chair for her and eased it under the table after she sat. He smiled at her grandmother. "I really appreciate your including me for a holiday dinner." He glanced at the empty chair across from him. "Someone joining us?"

Her grandmother looked anxious. "I'm expecting Sheila's brother, Rodney. I don't know what's keeping him."

Sheila hoped her grandparents wouldn't say anything more about Rodney. He'd recently received probation for a minor offense. She thanked her lucky stars that happened after she was hired at the agency.

Brent faced Sheila. "Would that be the same Rodney you spoke to on the phone a few days ago?"

When she nodded, he smiled. "I see," he said. Grasping her hand under the table, he squeezed it. Smothering a gasp, she yanked it away. He shifted in his chair until his arm touched hers. The warmth of his arm spread through his sleeve, heating her arm as well. She moved her chair a few inches away.

Brent sported a knowing grin. Damn him for making her uncomfortable in her grandparents' home after she'd done a favor to bring him here. She wanted to ignore him, but that wouldn't be very hospitable.

Her grandfather frowned. "We're not waiting for Rodney. Bow your heads for the blessing."

After "Amen" was said, she felt Brent's ankle against hers. She glared at him.

He moved his foot away, but didn't miss a beat. "Excuse me," he said in low tones, then added, "When do I get to meet your brother? Is he coming later?"

Her grandfather sighed, sliced off some turkey, laid it on a plate and passed it to Brent. "He's probably sulking in his apartment."

Sheila's grandmother chimed in. "Harold, dear. I wish you wouldn't speak of him as if he were a child. He's a grown man."

"Why the hell doesn't he act like one? Seems more like ten - years old than twenty. Take away his place setting."

Sheila's grandmother shook her head. "He may still come, and Harold, dear, please don't criticize him in front of a stranger. Sheila did the best she could to raise him after Cindy and Louis were killed in that terrible accident."

Brent said, "Perhaps I'll be more than a stranger one of these days."

Now he'd gone too far. How could she refute his statement without explaining his situation? She took a bite of mashed potatoes. Smothered with rich amber gravy, it didn't taste as good as usual.

Although his ego could probably stand it, she couldn't say she'd never be interested in him. That would be rude and hateful—even if they were alone. And she wouldn't stoop to hurting his feelings in front of others.

He was grinning with that sensuous mouth of his. Why was she thinking about his mouth? She didn't even like him, but she had to admit he exuded a virile sensuality. Heaven help her if he figured out she wasn't immune to him.

Grandmother beamed. "I'd hoped by now that Sheila might get married and settle down. I do so want to have great-grandchildren."

Sheila gulped, remembering the baby she was forced to give away because she had no job and her parents wouldn't pay for college unless she did. Unlike grandma, her mother had never seemed to like children. Sheila had always resented it when her mother would shoo her friends into the playroom and send them all outside when they got noisy.

After the accident that killed her parents, Sheila had tried to make Rodney's friends feel welcome, although she probably should have tried harder to discourage some of his wilder ones.

Grandmother had a dreamy look. "I'd adore getting to hold a tiny baby again and seeing your smile on its face. You had such a lovely smile when you were little."

Brent leaned forward. "It's still lovely. Be nice if she smiled more often."

How could she smile with grandmother saying things like that and Brent making her nervous? She hoped Grandma wouldn't say anything more. She didn't want Brent knowing her secret. Although she'd called her friend Darla to be sure everything was all right before leaving work yesterday, she couldn't help wondering if she'd made the right decision. Blinking her eyes, she tried not to think about it.

After sticking that tracking device beneath U.S. Marshal Sheila Talbot's car yesterday, following her to that house in Bedford had been a cinch. Now that he knew where she lived, he could check on her any time. Piece of cake.

That had been almost as easy as fooling Alice, the receptionist at the U.S. Marshal's office, into thinking he was an Office Depot salesman. He'd given her a package of Post-it notes and a discarded catalogue he'd picked up from outside the door of another office in the building. She'd told him they got everything through Government Services Administration.

Hoping to find out Sheila's last name, he asked if Sheila handled the ordering.

Alice had looked at him kind of funny, then said, "No."

He'd had to play up to her and take her to lunch at the deli in the office building before she'd let it slip that Talbot was Sheila's last name. When Alice mentioned Sheila's brother liked to gamble, that was an unexpected stroke of luck. He'd figured Rodney Talbot, the guy Sheldon had assigned him to lean on for a percentage of the gambling debt, was probably related. Later, when he pumped Rodney for information about Sheila, he'd learned she was indeed his sister and she drove a blue Mustang. Jealousy oozed from the guy's pores. Too bad Rodney didn't have the smarts to realize out he could afford one if he gave up gambling—but that wouldn't be good for business.

This morning he'd headed toward her house, but picked up her car on Highway 183 bright and early heading toward Dallas. After a frantic exit and U-turn, he'd managed to catch up with her and stay far enough back so she wouldn't notice him. Surely she wasn't going to work? But if she was going to pick up the witness, he could find out where she'd stashed him. Then he'd come back later and surprise the man.

This was a hell of a way to spend Thanksgiving morning. He sighed. His folks probably wouldn't miss him, but he'd sure miss turkey with rich brown gravy and all the trimmings.

Good thing he'd come early because he might have missed Sheila, and that tracking device only worked for a limited distance. And as far as she'd driven after picking up that dude in Mesquite—he hadn't been able to follow her so easily on the highway. He wasn't sure if this was a boyfriend or the witness. He'd figure that out later. Right now he needed to keep on her tail.

He was beginning to think she was heading for Waco, ninety miles south of Fort Worth, when she turned off on a two-lane state highway. After watching her Mustang pull into a driveway, he parked his black pickup down the road.

He grabbed a pair of sweat pants from behind the front seat of his truck and stepped outside. Yanking them on over his jeans, he hoped no one would pay any attention to someone jogging out here in the country's chilly air. When he got to the house, he slowed down as if he were winded. Through a picture window he saw four people standing beside a dining table loaded with turkey and other dishes.

One couple looked too old to be Sheila's parents — probably relatives of some kind. The other man could be a boyfriend, a relative — or her witness. He passed the house, turned around, and then made a slow jog back past the house and looked in the window again.

He didn't see Rodney. Perhaps he wasn't welcome after hitting up them up for five hundred dollars to pay part of his gambling debt to Sheldon. Or maybe the lazy bum was actually working at some restaurant to earn the rest.

Smiling and chatting, the people inside looked to be in good spirits — except the visitor. His face looked a bit strained. If that guy was her boyfriend, he wouldn't be dumb enough to wear jeans and a sweatshirt to eat with her folks. But if he were the witness, he wasn't dressed in a suit like a bank officer.

Rodney appeared, wearing neatly pressed pants and that gray cashmere sweater he was so proud of, but not his heavy gold bracelet. Maybe he'd hocked it.

Damn, how had he missed her brother's arrival? He watched Rodney hug Sheila and the older couple, then sit down and load up his plate. That loser could pack away food and still stay as thin as a fence slat.

At that moment Rodney glanced out the window and frowned. Uh oh. Lowering his head and lengthening his stride, the jogger sped up. Wouldn't do for Rodney to recognize him. No use making anyone suspicious. After all, his face bore a striking resemblance to his half-brother's. And Dirk's picture had been in yesterday's paper. He hoped Dirk wouldn't get convicted at his trial. He'd do what he could to keep that damn bean counter from testifying. His brother wouldn't take well to prison life.

He owed his brother a lot for getting him out of a jam and introducing him to Bart Sheldon. Bart offered a good piece of the action for someone to lean on a patsy with a big gambling debt.

He liked the satisfying feel of flesh beneath his fists when he pounded sense into those deadbeats. They always coughed up the dough then if they could get it. So far Sheldon hadn't come right out and asked him to off anyone, but if he could take out that witness, they couldn't pin much of a case on Dirk.

Back in his truck, he turned on the radio and listened to a Dallas Cowboys game, keeping his eyes ever watchful of Sheila's blue car. At half time they were losing. Disgusted, he turned it off and stepped outside. A squirrel scampered by. He picked up a rock.

The squirrel dropped in its tracks and lay writhing on the ground. Damn, his aim was good. He got back in his truck and turned on the game again. Hot dog, the Cowboys were ahead. He bent his head to hear better — couldn't turn up the volume — didn't want to miss Sheila when she left.

He almost didn't see her pulling out of the driveway, but managed to follow far enough behind not to be noticeable. Gently, he patted the burlap sack beside him, then pulled his hand away after feeling something sharp. Now all he needed was a lonely stretch of road.

Not many cars were on the road as Sheila turned onto the highway, giving her a chance to savor the gold and brown leaves on the trees. Though a blue norther had blown in, chilling the air, with Brent beside her it seemed warm and cozy inside.

She'd gotten up from the table, hardly remembering how

she got through dinner. The only thing she recalled tasting were the pumpkin and pecan pies. After telling her folks she needed to take Brent home, she'd hurried him out to the car.

She glanced in the rearview mirror again. That black pickup had been following her for several miles. She turned off at the next junction, planning to double back after a mile or two. The black truck followed.

After seeing a gas station, she pulled in next to a pump. When the pickup kept on going, she drew a sigh of relief.

Brent asked, "Would you like me to get out and fill your tank?"

She shook her head. "I don't need gas. It looked like that black pickup truck was following us."

"You must be paranoid. There are more pickups than cars on the roads around here."

She backed up, turned around, and headed the way she'd been going before. If that guy were following her, she'd outfoxed him. She gunned the motor and drove back toward I-35. She hadn't gone far when she saw another black pickup behind her — or was it the same one?

Chapter 4

"Damn," Sheila muttered, gripping the wheel even tighter.

"What's wrong?" Brent asked.

"That black pickup's following us."

"Better head for the police station in Fort Worth."

"I intend to," she snapped. He must think her an idiot. She stepped on the gas. The truck sped up. Her pulse pounded. She took a deep breath to calm herself.

Hands gripping the wheel, she glanced in the rearview mirror. The black truck stayed behind. So obvious. Lousy tracker was probably trying to intimidate her—or worse, ram her or run her off the road. So far he'd done nothing. No sense calling the cops.

"Write down his license number, Brent."

She kept her eyes on the mirror and the road ahead. Paper rustled. A pen scratched. He'd obeyed. Good.

She entered an underpass. The truck started to pass her on the right. She let up on the gas. Instead of passing, the pickup edged closer. The center concrete divider and bridge support columns loomed perilously close. The other vehicle bumped the side of her Mustang, shaking her whole body. The scrape of metal against metal clanged in her ears.

"Damn you," she shouted and hit the brake. She felt like ramming him, but that would be stupid. The truck edged past. She slowed even more.

"Look for an exit," Brent said. "We need to get away."

She scowled. "That's obvious."

She watched for road signs. If she could pull off at the last minute while the truck kept on going, she'd be free. No exit signs appeared. She slowed. The pickup did too.

She glanced at Brent. "Recognize the driver?"

He shrugged. "Can't see well enough to tell."

She glanced at the driver. He had both hands on the wheel. At least he wasn't holding a gun. She stepped on the gas. Her Mustang pulled ahead by a yard and then two. "Got any other enemies you didn't tell me about?"

"Besides Dobson? Not that I recall. But he could get someone to do his dirty work."

She pushed down harder on the accelerator. "What about gambling debts?"

"Don't have any."

At last she forged several yards ahead. The truck slid in behind. Knots twisted in her stomach. She tried to ignore them. "Any big winnings someone might want to recoup?"

He turned to look behind, then shook his head. "Last time I won big, there was a huge pot, but nobody had a lot at stake."

"I see." She wondered how often and how much he gambled. Would he gamble on his life just to defy her? She drew in a deep breath. Her mother always said you catch more flies with honey, but she wouldn't butter up Brent. His ego didn't need bolstering. Besides, he'd probably laugh if she tried.

At last the sign for Fort Worth city limits appeared. She let out the breath she'd been holding. She could head straight to the downtown police station or try to lose her tail on Fort Worth streets. She'd stay on the freeway as long as possible. At least there'd be witnesses.

The next exit came up. The truck tagged behind like a lumbering rhinoceros. She passed the exit up.

She could feel perspiration beading on her forehead and neck. A drop ran down between her breasts. She opened the window a crack, inhaled a breath of fresh air. Driving up behind a bus, she wrinkled her nose at its smelly exhaust.

"What if I decide to disappear before the trial comes up?" Brent asked.

That's all she needed. "We can put you under armed guards 24/7." She gripped the wheel tighter. "Stop talking. I need to concentrate on losing that guy." She glanced in the rearview mirror. The pickup was still behind.

"You can't just lock me up. I'll contact the ACLU. Bet they'd stop you."

What a stink that would cause. "Try that, and you'll be dropped from the program." She looked at the rearview mirror again. As if connected by an invisible chain, the truck kept an even distance from her.

However, it didn't do more than hang behind. More cars entered the freeway. Maybe he wouldn't try to ram her—too many witnesses around. But if he shot at them, they'd be sitting ducks—especially if he shot her tires.

An eighteen-wheeler blocked her way. Stepping on the gas, she zoomed around it. A van in front slowed, its signal light blinking. She jammed on brakes and swerved, barely missing another car.

The black pickup loomed in her mirror. Its teeth-like grill grinned at her, devil-like. A space opened ahead of the turning van. Stepping on the gas, she pulled in front.

"Man, you sure can maneuver this car," Brent said.

Surprised at his compliment, Sheila glanced at him. At least he didn't doubt her competency as a driver, but would he accept her orders and keep a low profile?

She didn't have time to think about it. The black pickup pulled alongside, passed, and then shot in front of her. She braked to avoid hitting it. Maybe he'd given up.

The driver threw something out the window. Then she saw what he'd dropped. It glittered in the sunlight—broken glass and spikes.

She swerved to avoid the prickly trail, not knowing if she'd run over some. Holding the wheel, she tensed, waiting for signs of a flat tire.

Nothing happened. She drew a sigh of relief and moved into the exit lane. He swerved to follow her and passed her on the left.

At the last minute she turned back onto the freeway, crossing over the little road bumps separating the exit from the freeway. That jarred her Mustang, shaking her.

Brent stared at her. "That was a cool move."

"I've lost him, probably not for long. Now for the police station."

On the smooth freeway, the car sped along. Thank goodness her tires were holding up.

Boom. The car jerked, hurtling toward a white Cadillac in the left lane.

She pulled at the steering wheel. Her car jerked from side to side, then crashed into the side of the white Caddy.

Now the police would come. Thank goodness her insurance was paid up.

With difficulty, she wrenched the wheel to pull over to the shoulder. Grabbing her purse, she got out. The white Cadillac had parked in front of her. A man in a suit, probably an Armani, got out, looked at his vehicle, and shook his head. A cool breeze disarrayed his blow-dried hair.

Scowling, he strode toward her. "What the hell were you doing? You drunk or something?"

She shook her head. "I think I had a blow out."

"You muscle car types are all alike. Probably running on bald tires. Too busy showing off to keep your tires in good condition."

She stepped closer. "They're only a year old, but the guy in front of me threw broken glass and spikes on the road."

"Yeah, right. I didn't see any."

She pulled out her phone. "I'm calling the police." The

wind picked up, chilling her. She pulled out a business card. "I have insurance with State Farm."

"Just give me the information." He crossed his arms in front of her, then tapped the fingers of one hand against his elbow. "And hurry up. I'm late for an important meeting."

She ignored him and pushed a button on her phone, already set to call the police. She reported the accident, said it wasn't serious enough to require an ambulance, and hung up.

She glanced back. The black pickup truck jerked to a stop beside the road about 100 yards back. Where were the authorities, now that she needed them? Brent opened the passenger door of her Mustang. "Don't get out!" she shouted.

The man in the Armani suit stood there, holding out his hand and glaring at her. After writing the name and number of her insurance agency on her card she handed it to him. "You'd better get back in your car. The driver of that pickup back there is the one who threw stuff on the road. He may have a gun."

The driver of the Cadillac stuffed her card in his pocket and glared at her. "Why do I run into all the nuts on the road?" He strode around his car and opened the door on the driver's side.

She followed him and tapped him on his shoulder. "Don't leave now," she ordered. "The cops should be here any minute, and I need your name and phone number."

Turning with a glare, he shook off her hand and slapped a business card in her palm. "Don't know why I should waste my time with a ding-a-ling who can't keep up her car."

She gritted her teeth. "I'm a U.S. Marshal," she snapped. "The insurance company won't pay your damages if there's no police report."

"They'll pay. I'll see that they do. And if it's not enough, I'll come take it out of your hide." He stepped toward her, his eyebrows moving closer together.

Brent opened the car door and started to get out.

Sheila dashed back and grabbed his arm. It was all she

could manage to hold him back. "Don't get out. That guy back there might have a gun."

"But this man's threatening you."

The man glared at Brent over the roof of his car. "Who are you, her husband?"

Brent shook his head. "Just a...a friend."

Sheila broke in. "He doesn't want to wait for the police."

Brent leaned across her. "Why the hell not? They should be here any minute."

Armani suit replied, "You going to make me?"

Brent wrenched his arm from her grasp and pushed his way out of the car.

"Get back in the car, Brent. That guy in the pickup could fire off a shot any minute."

Brent scowled. "Why aren't you calling for back up?"

"I already did."

Frowning, he grabbed the car door. "Do you have to order me around like you would a damn two-year old?"

"I'm responsible for your safety, damn it. Now get back in the car."

"And let this guy throw a punch at you?"

"He'll be sorry if he does."

The man glared at her. "I've half a mind to, but I don't hit women. I'm calling your insurance company tomorrow. If I don't get satisfaction — you'll be sorry."

Sirens sounded, but she couldn't see the patrol car. "Hold your horses. They're on the way."

She glanced back. The guy from the black pickup stepped out. Looked like he had a rifle aimed their way. She shoved Brent around the open passenger door. "Get in and duck." She grabbed her gun, pushed the door shut, and crouched beside the car just as a bullet whizzed over her head. With her arm steadied on the roof of the car, she pointed her Glock toward the driver. She hoped it would shoot accurately from this distance.

She got off one shot, but couldn't see where it hit. Another bullet hit her car's back window. It morphed into a crumpled mess.

Clenching her fist, she took aim again.

She heard another blast, and a sharp pain erupted in her arm. Before she could shoot again, the shooter jumped behind the wheel. His pick-up zoomed across the median and headed the other way.

The siren came closer. About time. Damn, they'd question Brent. Clutching her throbbing arm, she turned to face him. "Brent, make up a name and address. Police reports are public records. We can't have anyone knowing where to find you."

"I'll think of something." He glanced at her arm. "Did you get hit? If so, we need to call an ambulance."

"I think a bullet grazed my arm, but I don't need an ambulance. It's just a flesh wound." Trying to ignore the pain, she scanned the area. "That bullet should be somewhere around here."

Brent took hold of her wrist and inspected her wound. "Forget the bullet. We need to get your arm taken care of. Do you have a first aid kit in the car?"

"Yes, but let's talk to the police first." She walked around the front of her car as a patrol car screeched to a stop beside them, red and blue lights flashing.

A uniformed officer stepped out, notepad in hand. "Can I see your driver's license, please?"

"I'll give you my license, but first I need to report a drive by shooting." She pointed to the broken window and held out her arm. "He made a U-turn and headed south, but we got his license number." She turned to Brent. "Can you write it down for him?"

Brent scribbled something on a piece of paper and gave it to the cop. He walked back to his cruiser and spoke into his radio. Returning to them, he said, "Okay, headquarter's got someone on it. You okay, Miss? Shall I call Medstar?"

"No. I'll be okay as soon as I put a bandage on this." She held out her injured arm.

"If you're refusing an ambulance, you'd better see a doctor for that. Now, tell me what happened here?"

"This was just a fender bender. Talk to him first. He's in a hurry."

As the cop walked to talk to the other driver, she turned to Brent. "What name are you going to give him?" she said in a low voice.

"James Bond." He grinned.

"Be serious."

"That's a perfectly good name."

She groaned.

"I'll think of something."

"It better be good."

The officer returned and asked for names, addresses, and phone numbers.

Brent gave the name Jamison Bondell. He flashed her a sly grin, then listed an address in Irving. She admired his quick thinking in picking another town in case the street name wasn't a real one.

She pulled out her badge and gave the cop correct information for herself. When she reminded him to check on the license plate number for the black pickup, the officer glared at her, but said, "Yes, ma'am." He stood there, scribbling more notes.

Sheila said, "Might be a good idea to look for the bullet in the grass—for evidence in case you catch him."

The officer frowned. "Don't tell me how to do my job. You need to see a doctor."

After they got back in the car, Brent said, "Let me see your arm."

She held it out. Blood oozed from one end of a long wound. It was beginning to crust over.

He whistled. "Looks nasty. Where's your first aid kit?"

"In the glove compartment."

He opened it and pulled out the kit. Grasping her arm gently, he sprayed on disinfectant.

When she flinched, he said, "Sorry, but we don't know how many germs that bullet had on it."

Carefully, he applied a bandage strip over the area still oozing blood, then let go of her arm. "Let's go see a doctor."

"Not until after I get you home. First I have to change the tire."

"You know how to change one?"

"Of course. My dad made me learn right after I got my driver's license."

"I'll do it for you."

"What if the guy in the pickup comes back and shoots at you?"

"He wouldn't dare — not with the cop still here."

"Give me the key to the trunk."

She handed it over. "Thanks. I'll help."

After Brent changed the tire and put the ruined one in the trunk, she fastened the jack in place. Leaving the cop scribbling on a notepad, she headed for I-30 and Brent's apartment.

Brent touched her arm. "You shouldn't be driving with an injured arm."

"It's not that bad, and I know my way around Dallas and Fort Worth." She watched constantly for a tail, but didn't see one.

"How do you suppose he found us?" Brent asked.

"I don't know. I thought I saw a tail earlier, but when I turned off onto the road to my folks' place in Cleburne, there wasn't anyone behind us."

"What if he put a tracker on your car?"

"How would he know what my car looks like or that I'm handling your security?"

"Your Mustang's easy to spot. Could Carson have told someone what kind of car you drive?"

"He's not with the U.S. Marshal Service any more, and no

one else at our office except my supervisor, my partner, and the receptionist know you're assigned to me."

"But what if Carson resents you for taking his place and wants to cause trouble?"

She met his gaze. "Not likely. I wasn't responsible for his leaving. I don't think he'd take out his resentment on me."

"Better check out your car. The guy who followed us—I've run into his type before when I worked undercover. He might have tampered with your brakes, too."

"I'm no mechanic, but they seemed to work okay."

"Do you have a regular place you take your car to?"

She nodded. "But he won't be working on Thanksgiving." After stopping for a red light, she headed north, grumbling at the slowness of Fort Worth city traffic.

"You'd better pull off the road somewhere and let me look underneath."

She turned off I-35 onto I-30 and headed west. "Do you know what to look for?"

"My first car was used. I learned to fix a lot of things. Think I'd recognize something that doesn't belong."

"Don't think he'll find us if I pull into Trinity Park. It's not far." She took the exit for University Drive and drove along past the wooded, grassy area bordering the road.

He pointed to a sign on the opposite side, which said Botanic Gardens. "Drive in there and let me look."

She pulled into the entrance and parked beneath an oak tree with brown and scarlet leaves. Before getting out, she scanned the area for the black pickup, but saw none. Brent got out, checked under the hood, and bent over to look beneath the car. She stood guard.

"Can't see anything," Brent said. "Wish we could run it up on a lift."

"I'll take it in tomorrow."

Brent lay down on the pavement and inched his head underneath. "Found it."

"Can you pull it loose?"

"I'm trying."

Finally, he slid out from under the car with a small dark object in his hand. "Let's put this behind the fence at the entrance."

"How about behind some bushes so he'll have to hunt for it."

"Good idea."

Sheila got back behind the wheel. "Thanks for helping. I never would have found it."

Brent smiled. "Always glad to help a lady out."

She didn't like this at all. How could someone have put a tracker on her car without her knowledge? She'd parked her car in the federal garage. Even if someone snuck past the attendant, how would that person know which car she drove?

In a group where everyone was like a large family, she hated to think someone wanted her to fail with a witness, or even worse, was trying to endanger Brent. When she'd joined the Witness Security Program Division, they'd all seemed to welcome her. Some even offered to help if she needed muscle in a situation. Feeling confident of her ability, she'd pasted on a smile and hoped she'd never have to ask. Lately she'd felt more comfortable with them, but now she'd be on the alert. There must be more to this — some connection to someone outside the agency.

She moved her car closer to the entrance of the park, scanned the area, then ran to some gray-green bushes with lavender flowers growing behind the fence. She shoved the object beneath the verdant ground cover and wished it were poison ivy. After hurrying back to her car, she took off for Brent's place, constantly watching all the way for a tail.

Later, when she parked in front of his upstairs apartment, he said, "Come on up, and I'll clean your arm properly."

She shook her head. "I'll do it when I get home."

He opened the car door. "Don't bother to come up, then. I

have my key. By the way, I have to hand it to you. I don't know any women who would have kept their cool the way you did."

She smiled in spite of herself. "That's what I've been trained for. Although, until today, I really didn't expect things to get rough. You'll have to be very careful from now on."

He dug out his key. She reached for it. "I'd better unlock your door and go in first."

He pulled it out of reach. "That guy wouldn't dare come here after we reported him."

She glared at him. "After what's happened, you're not going in before I check out the place first. Give me the key, and stay inside the car."

He scowled, but slapped it into her hand. "Do you have to order me around like a drill sergeant?"

His comment stung, but she ignored it. She wasn't out to win a popularity contest. It was important to make sure he obeyed, whether he liked it or not. She got out of the car and walked beneath sweet gum trees ablaze with red and yellow leaves. A few brown ones crackled underfoot as she climbed the steps to his door.

After unlocking it, she reached in to flip on the light. Inside curtains flapped at an open window. Books, magazines and cushions lay strewn about. She checked for an intruder. Finding none, she raced back down the steps.

He was standing behind the open door. She gritted her teeth. Why couldn't he obey orders? She pushed him toward the car. "Get in. Your place has been ransacked." She ran around the car and slid behind the wheel. She drove around the corner and up and down several streets until she was sure no one followed. Parking in back of a McDonalds, she yanked out her phone. "I'm calling the police."

Chapter 5

Why didn't they answer the phone? This was a 9-1-1 call for heaven's sake.

Parked two blocks from Brent's ransacked apartment on a quiet tree-lined street, Sheila scanned the neighborhood of modest homes for suspicious persons or vehicles. Finally, someone answered.

She gripped the receiver. "I want to report a break-in at the upstairs apartment at 1205 Adam Street," she told the dispatcher. "The burglar may still be hanging around. The landlady's name is Mrs. Stewart."

"What's the occupant's name, ma'am?"

Sheila hung up, checked the rearview mirror, then started the car.

Brent stared at her. "Didn't they want more information?"

"Yes, but I'm not giving out your name."

"You're being paranoid. The landlady will probably tell them."

Sheila turned down another side street. "Somebody's giving out information on your whereabouts. Until I find out who, I don't trust anyone."

He shot her an incredulous look. "Not even the cops?"

Stopping for a red light, she scanned the area for suspicious vehicles. "You got it." Her stomach twitched. She'd eluded the guy in the black pickup, hadn't she? However, he or someone else had beaten them here. Were there two of them?

How long had that damn tracer had been on her car? Had someone followed her home? Come to think of it, there had been a black pickup parked nearby when she'd stopped at a drug store yesterday, but it was gone when she came out. She'd figured she was paranoid for looking for a tail when she'd left the store, but now she was glad she had. She was sure no one followed her home.

Brent touched her wrist. "How long's it going to take for them to check out my place?"

She pushed his hand away. "We'll call tomorrow. You're not going back until I know whether it was a simple burglary or something else."

"You taking me to a hotel?"

She shook her head. "After the Cowboys played this afternoon, there won't be much available. Besides, I want you away from Mesquite."

She searched her purse. Damn, she'd left her federal credit card locked in her desk at work. They'd reimburse her tomorrow, but she didn't have enough cash for anything but a seedy motel. Between buying stuff for her house and making a down payment on her Mustang, she'd maxed out her credit card. A cheap motel wouldn't have good security. She bit her lip.

"Where are you taking me?"

His comment interrupted her thoughts. "I have a new house in a wooded area. No one at the office has the address."

"How do they get in touch with you?"

"My cell phone."

"Where's your place?"

"North side of Bedford."

"Another suburb?"

Nodding, she turned her attention to the wheel, but couldn't resist stealing a glance at his handsome face. In the light from the street lamps Brent's square chin with its faint cleft looked determined. His full lips were clamped shut. Maybe he was finally realizing the extent of the danger facing him, enough to follow her orders.

He seemed to trust her — most of the time. That was a start.

He stared at her. "Taking a witness home — isn't that against policy?"

She checked the rearview mirror again. "Yes, but for tonight, it's the best option." Looking back at the access road, she watched for a tail as she entered the ramp to LBJ Freeway.

The freeway had plenty of traffic for a holiday. She checked again for a tail, but no one seemed to pay any attention to them.

Brent seemed restless.

"Can you help me look for a tail?" she asked.

He looked out the window, then turned to face her with an intent expression. "Carson, that guy you replaced, he acted friendly and concerned with my safety. Did he do something wrong?"

"That's classified."

He scowled. "He could be the biggest threat to my safety, and you won't tell me anything. That's horse pucky."

"Horse pucky?" She stifled a laugh.

"My mother insists I talk like a gentleman around ladies." He leaned forward. "You were great when that guy followed us in Fort Worth, but my life's on the line. Damn it. I have a right to know about Carson."

Checking the rearview mirror again, she hesitated. How much dared she tell him?

"You can't be with me every minute. Sooner or later, I'll have to protect myself. Carson seemed okay. What happened?"

"The others all liked him — couldn't believe he acted that way."

"What did he do?"

Carson had shot at a witness he was supposed to protect, but she wasn't going to tell Brent that.

She watched for a tail as she entered the ramp to LBJ

Freeway. "He violated the rules and endangered a witness. He's in jail now, but don't repeat what I told you."

"I get it. The agency's afraid people will lose faith in the program."

"We couldn't prevent the reporters from writing about it, but a visit to the editor encouraging him to keep the story off the front page did the trick. It got buried on page seventeen." She smiled.

"And I bet you were the one who talked him into it. They must have thought a woman could be more persuasive."

Blending into traffic, she bristled at his assumption she'd been chosen because of her sex. "After I explained how bad publicity would reduce people's confidence in the Witness Security Program—the editor was very cooperative. Page seventeen was even better than we'd hoped."

"You know..." He paused. "As a woman, you have some distinct advantages."

"What are you getting at?"

"Women are better at reading people. And I'm sure you were very good at persuading that editor."

His compliment encouraged her, made her feel as if she could handle things. Sheila bit her lip. She'd never thought of it that way. Unlike her father, there were times when Brent made her feel valued and competent. She knew she was competent, but it felt good to hear it affirmed by someone else.

"Do you suspect Carson leaked information about me?"

She nodded.

"Did you report your suspicions to your supervisor?"

She frowned. "He didn't take me seriously."

He put a hand on her arm. "Bet that pissed you off."

His warm touch jolted her, but she shrugged it off and checked the rearview mirror again. She didn't want him thinking she needed comforting. "Hey, I'm good at what I do. Got the highest marks during training, including marksmanship, and I test every six—"

"Shooting at a stationary target is one thing. It's my ass Dobson and his boss want to can. Don't want a rookie looking out for my safety if I'm going to be under fire. What's your supervisor's name? I'll ask for a more experienced Marshal."

A knot formed in her stomach. She ignored it. Here she'd thought he believed her competent. How wrong she'd been. "I wouldn't if I were you," she said in her most authoritative tone.

"You can't stop me. Take away my cell phone, and I'll use a pay phone."

She frowned and looked down the street she was passing. "You may be my first witness, but I'm not a rookie. Yes, I suspect a leak, but the less anyone—at the agency or anywhere else—knows about you, the better." She opened the window a crack and shot him a determined look. "For your information, you have to be a Marshal for three years before starting with Wit Sec."

"You look too young to have worked there much more than three years. Can you get someone you trust to replace you?"

"That's not done unless a Marshal endangers the witness."

"What about being tailed and getting shot at?"

She scowled. "I'm the one who got shot."

He shifted to face her. "But it could have been me, damn it."

"I kept you from getting hit."

He looked out the window. "I've been watching for a tail, but I haven't seen any suspicious vehicles."

He continued to watch as she turned off on a state highway, and then turned onto the two-lane road leading to her place in the woods.

She opened the window. Birds chattered in the trees. Driving through the gnarled branches of the post oaks lining the pavement always seemed to calm her after fighting traffic on the freeway. Glad she'd bought three acres of woodland to keep the trees around her, she turned into her private gravel drive.

Brent's eyes were closed and his body relaxed. A fine

lookout he'd been. His lips curled up in a smile, but his eyes stayed closed. He looked less contentious now, as if they might have a conversation without arguing.

Was this how he'd look in the morning waking up next to a woman? Sort of sleepy and vulnerable. Would he slide an arm around her and pull her close against his hard body, maybe kiss the back of her neck? She could almost feel his soft full lips caressing and nibbling. Her skin tingled from the thought.

Don't go there, she told herself. She jammed her foot on the brakes, jerking the car to a stop in front of her house.

Apparently startled, he sat up straight. "Where are we?"

"My place. Don't get out. I'm going to put the car in the garage, out of sight from the road."

"You think anyone has followed us?"

She shook her head. "I don't believe so. We should be safe for now." Tucked beneath the house, the garage sat midway down a hill. Once inside, she got out of the car and yanked the garage door down.

"Don't you have a garage door opener?"

She shook her head. "My new house needs too many things, and they all cost money. Come inside." She unlocked the door and led the way, hoping she hadn't left the place too cluttered.

Clunk. He must have knocked something over. She hoped it wasn't a can of paint. She flipped on the light.

A grimace flashed across his face. "Damn. Couldn't you at least keep the pathway open?"

"I'm in the middle of finishing up after the builder. I wasn't expecting guests."

Brent rubbed his shin. He scanned the kitchen. Several pieces of drywall leaned next to an open space framed by two-by-fours. "This place is only half done. What lousy builder leaves a place like this?"

"My brother, who's doing this to pay back a loan." She wasn't going to mention Rod's gambling debts."

Brent stepped around a bucket of paint and walked through the archway to the living room. He scanned the knotty pine paneling and the burgundy leather couch with its matching chair. "You've already got pictures hung. Looks like you've done a lot to make it livable."

Her bright smile softened her face until she was almost pretty. He didn't know why she attracted him. His type of woman was soft and clingy, one who deferred to his wishes. Oh, he'd ask a date's preference about food, but he'd pick the restaurant. He caught a glimpse of her full breasts straining against her blouse as she took off that mannish blazer she wore. If she were anyone else, he'd soon be curled up with her beside the fire. If she ever softened up, he bet she'd be one hell of a woman in bed, but it wasn't likely he'd find out.

She was rubbing her arms. "It's cold in here. I'll get some more logs and build a fire."

"Let me do that. Where's your woodpile?" He turned toward the back door.

"Behind the house, but don't go out there. The land's uneven and it's dark. You might fall."

"I'm no tenderfoot. Don't you have a flashlight?"

"Sure, but I'll get the wood. Someone might be hiding in the trees."

"Thought you said no one knew where you lived."

"That's right."

"And you didn't see anyone tailing us, did you?"

She shook her head.

"Where's your flashlight?"

She yanked open a drawer and pulled one out. "Here."

Brent grasped the flashlight, touching her chilled hands as he did. He shoved the flashlight in his jacket pocket. "Your fingers are icy. He covered her hand with his. "I should warm your hands first."

She seemed ill at ease and tugged her hand away. "We'll both get warm faster if you go get some logs." She pointed to a different door from the one they'd entered from the garage.

He released her hand and headed out the door. She was a challenge all right. He thought about trying to strip her defenses and get her so attracted to him that she was putty in his hands—like most women he dated. With her prickly attitude, it would be a real challenge.

Shining the light before him, he made his way over muddy ground before spotting paving stones leading to a pile of logs. He stuffed the flashlight in his pocket and picked up two large logs. Most women wouldn't argue if he offered to get wood. But Sheila wasn't like most women. He wouldn't call her a feminist, exactly. Probably thought she could do anything as good as a man. So far, she'd shown no vulnerability except when he'd accused her of being a rookie.

Juggling the logs and the flashlight, he carefully picked his way to the door and shoved it open. Bright lights made him blink as he made his way to the living room. He dumped his burden on the hearth.

She'd already laid kindling in the fireplace. Above the fireplace hung a picture of a lake surrounded by mountains. A braided rug lay rolled up on polished hardwood floors. "It would be cozier with the couch near the fire. I'll help you spread the rug and move the couch."

Frowning, she looked up from arranging the wood. "I like the couch where it is."

"Just for tonight. We can move it back later."

"Let me light the fire first. This place will be even cozier after Rod installs the furnace."

Brent yawned. "Do we have to sleep in here tonight?"

She nodded, her teeth clamped against her lower lip. "You can have the couch. I'll sleep on the rug in front of the fire."

He shook his head. "No way. You sleep on the couch. I'll take the rug. Just bring some blankets."

"I won't hear of it. Like it or not, you're my guest until I can make other arrangements."

"We'll see." He grasped one end of the couch. "Come on. Give me a hand."

She walked over to the other end. Together they moved it closer to the fire. He helped her spread the braided rug out between the fire and the couch. He might let her start out on the rug, but once she was asleep, he'd pick her up and lay her on the couch. Holding her in his arms, he could at least see if she had any softness. "Got anything to eat? I fix a mean omelet."

She looked at him, a surprised expression molding her face. "Didn't you stuff yourself at my folk's house?"

He nodded. "Yeah, but I'm hungry again. Got any eggs?"

"I'm not letting you cook supper. I'll fix something."

He strode into the kitchen and opened the refrigerator. "Hmmm. Cheese, green pepper, tomato — that should work. Got any mushrooms?"

She grabbed his arm and shut the refrigerator door. "I said I'd fix something, now get out of my way."

He grinned. "What will you fix? Crabmeat hors d'oeuvres?"

She scowled. "No. I have bologna and cheese. I'll make sandwiches."

He put on his most engaging smile. "Wouldn't you rather have a nice hot omelet?" He glanced at a box on the counter. "And some hot chocolate?"

He could tell by the look in her eyes she was tempted.

After a moment's hesitation, she said, "Okay. You fix that, and I'll get out some blankets."

Ten minutes later, he called her. She took a bite of the fluffy, cheese-topped omelet, stuffed with green pepper and tomato. She met his gaze. "It's delicious, and you didn't even burn the toast."

"What did you expect? I told you I could cook, didn't I? My mother saw to that."

Sheila set her fork down. "You've met my family, what's yours like?"

"Why do you ask? You've probably read my whole life history."

"I know you have a mother and father, and a younger sister, but I don't really know much about them."

"Dad blusters a lot. Mom rules the roost. I think she taught me how to cook so I'd bring her breakfast in bed. With just a frown or tears she gets anything she wants. I remember the Christmas I wanted a bike. Dad said money was tight, but she got diamond earrings. All I got was a skateboard. And my sister grabbed that from me and took the first ride."

"Bet that made you mad."

"Damn right." He took the dishes off the table. "It was mine, after all. Mom said to let her ride it a while. I gave her ten minutes, then wrestled it from her."

"Did your sister resist?"

He shook his head. "She scowled, then said she was tired of playing with it and liked her new doll better."

"So, has she matured since then?"

"She's more subtle now. She doesn't lust after my shotguns, just my car, when I had one. She always pestered me to let her drive it, but I never gave in. She tells me I should be nicer to women or I'll never get a wife. What she doesn't understand is that I like my life the way it is."

"You mean playing the field?"

He nodded. "I never lack for feminine companionship." Her lips formed a tight line. Did she believe that?

He'd had to work on developing charm, but now it came easy. He'd dated plenty of attractive women, but none ever inspired a wish to spend a lifetime with her except his ex. Falling for her had been a mistake. Perhaps he wasn't cut out for marriage. If that meant being cajoled into granting a woman's every wish, he wanted no part of it.

Sheila frowned. Time to change the subject. "Can I jog out here? Don't want to get soft."

"Stay off the road. You can run through the woods for a

short way, but don't get lost. I suppose I could borrow my nearest neighbor's bloodhound." She laughed. "I'd feel really stupid if he asked me how I managed to lose my guest."

He scowled. "What makes you think I'm dumb enough to get lost?"

"Most anyone could get lost in those woods. They're pretty thick."

"I have a damn good sense of direction, and I watch where I'm going."

"Okay, okay. Just be careful, and don't run in the dark."

"You're as bad as my mother, always assuming I won't use my head."

"I won't say anything more." She rose from the table. "I'll put some towels out for you and spread out the bedding."

He stacked the plates in the dishwasher. He hoped it was installed. Walking into the living room, he watched her smoothing sheets and tucking in blankets on the couch. Inhaling the smoke reminded him of all the fires he'd sat by as a Boy Scout on campouts. "I'll wait until you've finished in the bathroom. Then I'll take a shower, okay?"

"Fine." She turned and left the room. Holding his hands out to the blazing fire, he studied the framed picture of Sheila's parents and one of a young ascetic looking man on the mantel. Must be a younger picture of Rodney. She didn't have pictures of a boyfriend here. He didn't know why that pleased him, but it did.

Sheila's footsteps caught his attention. "Your turn," she said.

He headed toward the hall, then stopped to face her. "Hope your bathroom has good soundproofing. I sing in the shower."

She cocked an eyebrow. "If it's too loud, I can plug my ears."

He hurried into the bathroom and shut the door. This room wasn't finished either, but the shower looked complete. She must have taken one too, for the mirror was fogged. He closed the frosted glass door and luxuriated in the hot water sluicing over his shoulders.

Now if only she'd agree to share the shower — she wouldn't, but if she ever did, that would be awesome. He broke into song. "The Street Where You Live" seemed appropriate. He followed with "I've Grown Accustomed to Your Face." Probably wouldn't stay here that long. He'd like to become accustomed to her body, but it wasn't likely to happen.

By the time he'd finished and was drying himself, he hoped he wouldn't have long to wait until she slept. After all, she was putting herself out to keep him here. She'd be more comfortable on the couch. And he could keep an eye on the fire and keep them both warm all night.

He'd sleep in his clothes. Maybe tomorrow it would be safe to pick up stuff from his apartment. Too bad he'd spent time neatly arranging everything. Carrying his shoes, he tiptoed into the living room, lit only by the crackling flames and redolent with a warm, smoky smell. He inhaled deeply. Some of that wood must be cedar.

After setting his shoes beside the couch, he slid beneath the silky sheets. She didn't skimp on comfort. He found himself wondering if she wore silk nightgowns. Stealing a glance, his gaze encountered her arm, partially covered by soft looking cotton printed with roses and violets. Her soft, even breathing made him hope she was asleep. Just to test that, he whispered, "Goodnight."

Drowsily, she murmured, "Night," and snuggled into a fluffy pillow.

Somewhere outside an owl hooted. Flames crackled. He checked his watch. He could spend the time until she slept figuring out what kind of job he could get — anything to get his mind off the way her breasts rose and fell with each breath. He'd told the bank president he had a family emergency and needed to take some vacation time. Maybe if he could get the D.A. to agree to a deposition, they would have enough evidence on Dirk Dobson to lock him up. Then Brent could return to his position.

Before moving here from Detroit, he'd worked himself up from a fledgling CPA to loan officer in only one year. Now at a branch bank, he enjoyed being the chief loan officer and helping people get loans. It wasn't as exciting as working the streets of Detroit, but unless he got his name cleared, he'd have a hard time getting a job as a cop. He sighed. Nowadays they always checked your background. He wondered what he could have done differently to save the situation and his partner's life. It had been almost like they'd been set up to take the fall.

He hadn't been so much injured as sick at heart. They'd only managed to arrest one man, but the chief distributor had eluded them.

At any rate, he couldn't work at either job until his stint as a protected witness was over. Too bad, no one else qualified had been available to audit the books when the district attorney asked for the bank's help. But then, he'd been leery of letting anyone else at the bank know what was going on for fear of a leak.

As a loan officer, he had smelled something suspicious when Bart Sheldon had applied for a loan. When he'd called the D.A.'s office to ask if there'd been any complaints, the D.A. had suggested he make auditing the books a requirement for granting the loan.

He'd had to call on all his acting ability to convince Bart Sheldon that was part of their normal procedure for a business with a sketchy credit record. If he'd known what that would lead to, he wondered if he'd have refused. He was glad he'd done his duty as a citizen, but he damn well hated the price he had to pay.

He could testify that the secretary had shown him two sets of books, accidentally of course. She'd probably been placed in the Witness Security Program also.

He yawned. The couch was fairly comfortable. Maybe he'd

let Sheila stay where she was. After all, she had insisted he take the couch.

Her breathing deepened. She must be asleep by now, but she seemed restless. She rolled over, pulling the blanket higher over her neck. She looked damn uncomfortable. His conscience bugged him.

Unable to stand it any longer, he tiptoed to her still form. She looked so peaceful, as if he could kiss her and she'd turn to him with a smile.

He knew better. Bending down, he picked her up. She smelled good, like wildflowers. And her body was soft against him, her breasts so cushiony he wanted to run his hand over them and feel her lush flesh. Though tall, she didn't seem heavy.

He laid her down gently on the couch. He had to move her feet to tuck them under the blanket. She snuggled against the pillow, but didn't open her eyes.

So far, so good. He pulled the covers around her shoulders. Then he knelt to push the edges under the couch cushions.

Why did he have a crazy urge to kiss her forehead, or brush a kiss on the hair atop her head? Instead of waking with a smile like Sleeping Beauty, Sergeant Sheila would probably snarl at him.

He stood and took one last look at her face, then lay down facing the hearth. The floor was hard. The pillow smelled like her, but it barely softened the hardness of the floor. He rolled over to face her.

Her eyes opened, and she smiled.

Chapter 6

Warm and cozy on the couch, Sheila studied Brent, now lying beneath a blanket beside the fireplace. "Thank you," she whispered. Amazed at the lengths he went to make her comfortable — after all, she was no featherweight, she couldn't help smiling. Probably shouldn't let him realize how much she appreciated his gallantry. To keep him safe, she needed to have the upper hand.

She snuggled beneath the warm blankets. Until now, she hadn't realized how nice it was to have someone to talk to who wasn't trying to cut her down to bolster his own position. And it was a welcome treat to eat someone else's cooking for a change.

Sheila glanced at his face. He grinned, rose to a sitting position, then eased from under the blanket, his gaze never leaving hers. Was he only concerned for her comfort or was he planning something more?

She swallowed. Best not to assume anything just yet. Holding her breath, she waited.

He stood, finally pulling his gaze from her face, and turned toward the fire. He bent to pick up a log. In spite of herself she couldn't help noticing his tight buns and powerful legs. He laid the log on the fire, then turned.

She needed to say 'no' to whatever he had in mind, even if it were only a kiss. It was bad enough he was staying in her house. She should forget about that time he kissed her on the landing outside his apartment door, how his lips made her feel, how he'd almost made her forget to care if any neighbors saw them.

Thank goodness she hadn't seen anything amiss after that. If things were different, if she'd met him under other circumstances, she might go for him, but now she had a job to do. Getting involved with Brent was not an option.

He stepped closer and held out his hand. She shrank back against the couch cushions. He withdrew his hand. "Good night and pleasant dreams." Still smiling, he lay down on the rug again, facing her, his chestnut hair burnished by the firelight.

Shutting her eyes, she pulled the covers tightly around her neck. If he had touched her then, and she'd let him, what would he do next? Pull her into his arms for a kiss? Or squeeze in beside her to caress and kiss until she gave in? Annoyed at her runaway thoughts, she tried to think of other things. It was a long time before she slept.

The next morning she was setting out bowls and cold cereal when her cell phone rang.

"Hello," she said. Holding her phone against her ear, she took milk from the refrigerator.

Her friend Darla, the friend she'd entrusted her dearest possession to—the baby her parents insisted she couldn't keep, sounded breathless. "Sheila, I'm sorry to call you when you're trying to get off to work, but I need to talk to you."

A lump formed in Sheila's throat. "Is something wrong with Jason?" Despite the fact that her good friend and her husband had moved back to town and were good parents for Jason, Sheila had avoided visiting her. Her heart pounded as she started the coffee and waited for Darla to explain.

"Jason's fine. It's my husband—" She sounded worried. "He didn't come home last night. I think he's been gambling for high stakes again. I'm afraid something awful happened to him."

Sheila swallowed. She'd hoped Bill would be a good, steady father for Jason. "You must be worried sick. Have you called the police?"

"They won't do anything because he hasn't been missing more than 24 hours."

"How about the hospitals?"

"I called them too, but he wasn't at any of them."

"What about a private detective?"

Darla sniffed. "They're awfully expensive. What more could a private eye do that the police can't?"

Sheila twisted the folds of her robe. "It's your call, but I'm sure he'll turn up okay. Look, I've got to get ready for work. Call me at work after nine."

Frowning, she hung up. Had she made the right decision in giving Jason up four years ago?

What if Darla's husband were involved in something shady, and Jason were threatened?

Right now there was nothing she could do except worry, and that wouldn't help. Hearing Brent's footsteps, she took a deep breath to calm herself.

He paused in the doorway. He looked fresh, and his smile, so warm and appealing, made her feel on top of the world, as if he not only trusted her to keep him safe, but liked her as a person. But that didn't undo the knot inside.

"Morning, sunshine. Heard your phone ring." He slid into a chair, and his gaze met hers. "Something wrong?"

"Nothing I can do anything about."

He opened his mouth, then closed it, perhaps deciding it was better not to ask.

He leaned back in his chair. "Find me a place to live near the commuter rail line so I'll have a better choice of jobs."

"I'll see. How do you like your coffee?"

"Sweet, the way I like a woman." He smiled. "You're going way beyond the call of duty."

She handed him a cup of coffee and set out the sugar bowl.

He was putting on the charm. What would it be like to wake up every morning with him smiling at her?

As for Darla and Jason, she'd have to wait and see what happened. She sighed.

"Got any handyman jobs you need done?"

She stared at him, surprised. "Not unless you know how to put up sheet rock. The kitchen's not finished, but thanks for offering. I'd better call Rodney and tell him you'll be here for a day or two." She dialed his number, but no one answered, so she left a message.

After breakfast she dressed, then returned to the kitchen. Brent was drinking a second cup of coffee. She paused at the door to the garage. "Don't call anyone, and don't let anyone in but Rodney."

He frowned. "Think I'm stupid?"

She shook her head. "No, just reminding you."

"Hey, it's my life on the line. Call when you find me another place to stay."

"I will." She shut the back door and walked around the house, looking for signs of intruders. Seeing none, she went into the garage, pulled the door up, then slid behind the wheel. Her tires crunched on her gravel driveway, then settled into a smooth rhythm as she pulled onto the road heading toward the freeway.

She hadn't gone far when the engine clunked. The car slowed to a stop. She tried to start it again. All she got were a buzz and then a clicking sound. "Damn, that's all I need." She called the office and AAA, and then sat back to wait for a tow.

She called Brent to let him know what happened, but got no answer. Maybe he was taking a shower. She'd get someone at the repair shop to bring her back soon."

Clutching her jacket around her, she shivered as she stood beside her Mustang watching for the tow truck. From there she could keep an eye on her driveway. Only a few cars passed by. Finally, a wrecker, driven by a burly giant of a man, stopped.

He hooked up jumper cables and revved his engine. Hers stayed silent.

The giant came around to her window, fingering his scruffy beard. "Sorry, ma'am. I'll have to take it to a repair place. Get in my truck where it's warm, an' I'll hook 'er up."

On the ride to the repair shop, she pondered her options. Surely, they could fix it in a few hours. If they had a newspaper there, she could survey the classified ads for apartments. She wondered if Carson, the Deputy U. S. Marshal originally assigned to Brent, had something to do with Brent's place being trashed. After being fired in disgrace, he might be just spiteful enough to arrange something like that.

As they neared the repair place, she wondered what it was about Brent that attracted her? It wasn't as if she didn't know any good-looking guys. Neither the handsome Marshal at the office or the new guy she'd seen at the archery range stirred her like Brent did. She'd never felt the urge to walk up to any of them and act friendly. What was the point if she didn't intend to get married? As soon as she got Brent settled, she could stop spending time in his disturbing company.

She might be a modern woman, but for her it wasn't only wrong, but stupid to live with a guy. If she liked someone enough to share her bed, she was sure to get emotionally involved, and then what? Even if she changed her mind about marriage, the man wasn't likely to. Why should he, when he had sex for the asking? Then, when he got tired of her, she'd have nothing but grief.

The truck jerked to a stop. "We're here," the driver said, pulling her from her thoughts.

After he unhooked her Mustang, she arranged to have it fixed. When she asked how long it would take, the mechanic shrugged. "Can't tell until I've looked at it. I'll call you."

The driver of the tow truck took her back home. "Thank you so much," she said, stepping down. As soon as she got out, she grabbed her copy of the newspaper and unlocked the front door.

"Brent," she called. Her heirloom Seth Thomas clock ticked on the fireplace mantel. Outside a crow cawed and then was silent.

"Brent," she called again. No answer. Maybe he'd crawled into her bed and gone back to sleep. If he were her boyfriend here for a weekend, she'd wake him with a kiss. She banished her wayward thoughts and headed for the bedroom. He wasn't there either.

Surely, no one had followed them here. She'd checked her car for tracking devices. So where was he?

Jogging in the woods? She went out back and called. No one answered. She shouted louder. Still no answer.

Clouds hung low, graying the sky. She wished it were spring instead of November. The wind brought flurries of snow. Probably wouldn't stick, but it chilled her face.

Terrible scenes flashed before her eyes. Brent, beaten and bloody, being dragged off. Brent's body lying in the woods for wild animals to ravage. She squeezed her eyes shut. She wouldn't think about that, but where could he be? Why didn't he return?

She shivered. Snow flurries churned the air. It was crazy to stand out here waiting. After shouting his name once more, she went inside and called work to explain she'd be later than she'd thought. She grabbed the classified section and tried to read the apartment ads. The print blurred before her eyes. She looked out the window. A cardinal pecked at the bird feeder, apparently not bothered by the wind or the snow swirling about. She hoped Brent's jacket was warm enough to keep out the cold.

She tried to focus on the paper again. The opening of the back door startled her. She ran to the kitchen, unreasonably glad to see his cheeks flushed with color and his unsettling grin. "Why did you stay out so long? Can't you see it's snowing?"

He laughed. "I won't melt."

"Weren't you cold?"

He shook his head. "Running kept me warm. Why'd you come back? Forget something?"

"My car broke down. I don't know how long it will take to get it working again."

He grinned. "So you're stuck with me for the day. I don't suppose you have a chess set?"

She frowned. "I don't have time for that." She picked up the paper. "I have work to do."

His eyebrows lifted. "Reading the paper?"

"Finding you a place to live."

"Right."

She circled a few likely ones and called to ask questions. The first two weren't suitable. As she waited for the third one to answer, she kept thinking of Darla and Jason. If her husband turned up dead, what kind of home would that be for Jason? After nine rings, she hung up.

"No luck?" Brent asked.

She shook her head.

Brent rubbed the dark stubble on his chin. "May I borrow a razor?'

"Sure, check the medicine cabinet." She watched him walk out of the room, noting how the tan sports shirt stretched over his well-developed muscles.

The phone rang, startling her and drowning out Brent's footsteps as he headed up the stairs. "Hello," she said.

It was Darla. "Bill hasn't called. I'm sure something terrible has happened."

"Be patient. Don't think the worst until you know something."

Anxiety laced Darla's voice. "I can't help worrying."

Sheila willed her voice to be calm, although she was anxious too. "Call me when you know something, okay?"

"All right." Darla hung up.

Sheila gripped the phone, then picked up the paper and

called the fourth number she'd circled. No answer. She'd try again later.

Tires crunched on her gravel driveway. She ran to the window. Rodney's red pick-up truck pulled to a stop. Easing his lanky frame out the door, her brother jumped to the ground. He ran long fingers through his straw-colored hair, strode to her front door and opened it.

She stood there and frowned, her gaze meeting his blue eyes. "Rodney, don't you ever knock?"

He shrugged and pushed back an errant lock of wind-blown hair. "Didn't know you'd be here."

He shut the door. "Did you get a call from that woman who has your son? She called me and asked where you were. She sounded worried. Jason sick or something?"

Sheila nodded. "Her husband's missing, and she's anxious." She held a finger to her lips. "Shhh. I've got company."

Rodney lowered his voice. "New boyfriend? Don't want him knowing you've had a child? Too bad you didn't marry the kid's father. He must have had other fish to fry."

Sheila glared at him. "I heard enough from Mom. Don't you start in." She wanted to deny Brent was her boyfriend, but she couldn't risk anyone else knowing why he was here. "I need a favor."

"Shoot."

"My car broke down. It's at the repair shop, and I don't know how long it will take to fix. Can I borrow your truck to go to the store?"

"Sure." After reaching in his pocket, he dangled the keys before her. She grabbed them just as Brent came downstairs, shirtless. His biceps looked as if he'd done plenty of workouts. His broad chest was covered with brown, downy hair, and his pants fit snugly over his other attributes. Not since summer had she seen that much of a perfect specimen. She took a deep breath. She was supposed to protect him, not ogle him, and especially not in front of her brother.

Brent held out his hand. "Name's Brent. You're Rodney, right?"

Her brother shook his hand. "Nice to see you again. Guess she told you I'm fixing up her house." He glanced into the kitchen. "Hey, who nailed that sheet rock? Nice job."

"I did," said Brent. "It's the least I could do because—"

Sheila shook her head slightly and held her breath.

Brent met her gaze. "I mean because Sheila's been so nice, fixing breakfast for me and all." He turned toward Sheila. "Heard you say you're going to the store. Let me come with you. I need a better razor." He fingered a scratch on his chin.

She didn't want him going out, but she couldn't leave him here. Who knew what Brent might let slip, or worse what Rodney might tell him. The nearest convenience store probably wouldn't be busy on the morning after Thanksgiving. "Get a shirt and come on."

Later, with Brent seated beside her in her brother's truck, she zoomed out of the driveway, spewing gravel in her wake. "When we get to the store, you'd better stay in the cab."

"I'm not letting you pick out a razor for me. Probably be pink and not shave worth a damn."

She frowned and grabbed a baseball cap from the dashboard. "Well, then, wear this and don't say much to anyone."

He saluted. "Yes, sir, I mean ma'am. I'll toe the line." For the rest of the journey along a road lined with post oaks still hanging on to brown leaves, he didn't speak.

Once inside the convenience store, she looked around, glad there were few customers. She gathered up enough food for lunch and dinner and threw a twenty on the counter to pay for that and his razor. He insisted on carrying the bag. After picking up her change, she tried to hurry him out the door before anyone noticed him.

Mrs. Gaddy, her nearest neighbor, stopped them at the door. A smile lit up her wrinkled face. "Well, hello, dear. You must introduce me to your new boyfriend. My, he sure is tall."

Sheila smothered a groan. "Mrs. Gaddy, this is Brent. She lives down the road from me." Sheila pushed the door open, grabbed Brent's arm and pulled. "Nice to see you, but we've got to run."

The woman grinned. "Got to make hay while the sun shines. Go for it, girl. I wish I was young and full of energy like you."

Her face hot, Sheila climbed into the truck and unlocked the door for him.

Brent said, "She seemed nice enough. Why did you practically yank me out of there?"

"She's a dear, but she loves to talk."

"I see. Wonder if Rodney does. I'd love to hear what you were like growing up."

Sheila cringed, hoping Rod wouldn't say anything about Jason. Wishing she hadn't felt forced to give him up, she realized she was fortunate someone she trusted had him. Her friend Darla and her husband hadn't been able to have children of their own, and without a job Sheila had been in no position to raise a child.

She'd feared she couldn't land the position she'd applied for with the U.S. Marshals if they knew she'd had a child out of wedlock. She'd hoped by staying with an aunt in another town and signing into the hospital under Darla's name that no one would find out. However, she'd had to take a lie detector test for her job with the U.S. Marshals. Surprisingly, when they learned she'd given birth, but arranged for him to be adopted, they still gave her the job.

This was better for her son, but she missed not seeing him grow up. Darla and her husband had thought it was better that way.

Her parents blamed it on her, said she should have been on the pill in case a condom broke.

This shouldn't still cause her pain, but just thinking about it brought back how awful she'd felt when her parents put all the blame on her, practically forcing her to relinquish the baby. Now she wondered if they were more concerned with their reputation than her welfare and that of her son.

When she'd contacted the parents of the baby's father, they'd only said he was listed as missing in action and presumed dead. In the end it had been her decision to make the arrangements that were best for Jason.

A tear rolled down her cheek. She brushed it off with the back of her hand, amazed at how dry and rough her skin was. If Brent touched her hand—she shouldn't be thinking about him touching her. She tried to concentrate on the road, but almost missed the turn onto her private drive.

The sound of tires on gravel grated on her ears. Everything around her was rough, her skin, her house, her emotions. She jammed on the brakes, and the truck jerked to a stop.

Brent stared at her, but didn't say anything.

Her brother met them at the door. "I need more tape to finish your walls. I'll come back later." He held out his hand for the keys.

"Thanks, Rod."

Brent strode past her into the kitchen with the groceries. After Sheila shut the door behind her brother, she sank into an easy chair. She slapped her forehead. Damn. She hadn't asked Rodney if Darla had called again. Her friend had said that her husband had been gambling for high stakes. Maybe some enforcer was trying to beat him up to get the money. Where was the happy home she'd envisioned for her child? Covering her face with her hands, she wished she'd never given Jason up. He shouldn't have to suffer for her mistakes.

Unable to wait any longer for news, she dialed Darla's number. It rang and rang. Knowing her husband had their only car, she wondered where Darla and Jason could be.

She glanced out the window. A half grown cocker spaniel lay curled up beside a bush, shivering. That shrub couldn't be much protection from the wind. Brent walked over to the pup and petted it. He picked it up and walked out of her vision. She grabbed her jacket and stepped out, but Brent was nowhere in sight. She called his name, but got no answer.

Wishing she had her car back, she walked around front and shouted. Glad she'd changed his name from the one Carl Carson had given him, she saw him walking toward Mrs. Gaddy's house with the dog in his arms. She hurried to catch up with him.

Out of breath, she managed to step up next to him just as Mrs. Gaddy opened the door.

"Is this your dog?" Brent asked.

"Goodness, no. He's too little. I have a big German shepherd to protect me."

"How about the people in the next house down the road?" Sheila asked.

"Could be. I saw their grandchildren playing with a dog the last time I drove past."

"Thanks," Brent said and turned toward the next house, barely visible through the trees.

Hearing the door shut behind her, Sheila grabbed Brent's arm. "You don't need to be out here on the street where someone might see you or talking to the neighbors either."

"But this dog could get run over. He's obviously lost."

"Okay, we'll go to the next house, but if he doesn't belong to them, you've got to stop."

He frowned, but kept on walking. She had to hurry to keep up with his longer stride.

Luckily, her neighbors in the next house did indeed own the dog. They thanked her and took the animal inside.

"Come on," Sheila said. "We need to get you back to my place quickly."

Once inside, she called Darla. Again the phone rang and rang.

Chapter 7

After dialing her friend Darla's number again, Sheila gripped the phone. It rang and rang. Finally, a little voice said, "Hello."

"Jason, where's your mommy?"

"Mommy won't talk."

Sheila's heart pounded faster. "Is—is she there?"

"Yes."

Sheila let out the breath she'd been holding. At least he wasn't alone. "Is she awake?" She heard the clunk of the phone and little footsteps. She hoped the four-year-old would return to the phone quickly.

Then Jason came back on the line. "Mommy's not awake."

Was she unconscious or—Sheila shuddered. Had she fainted or was she dead?

"Is she breathing?"

Sheila waited anxiously for him to return.

Finally, he picked up the phone. "Uh huh."

"Jason, try to wake her up."

"Okay." She heard footsteps again, then another clunk as if he dropped the receiver.

"Mommy tells me, 'Don't talk to strangers.'"

Sheila groaned. If he only knew. "My name is Sheila. I'm not a stranger. I'm a friend of your mommy." She hoped he'd believe her. "Tell your mommy to come talk to me."

"Okay." Footsteps pattered. Then he was back. "She won't come."

"Is she asleep again?"

"Uh huh."

If she called the police, and Darla was only asleep, they'd frighten her son, and she'd look stupid. "Jason, I'm coming to your house. Don't open the door to anyone else except your daddy, okay? Now hang up the phone."

"Okay."

She heard some clicking sounds as if he were trying to put the receiver back and then a dial tone. She called Rodney.

"What now, Sis?"

"I need you to take me to Darla's. I called, and Jason answered the phone. He said his mommy wouldn't wake up."

"So, call 9-1-1."

"I don't want to do that. She may just be sleeping soundly."

He groaned. "Then call a taxi."

"Rodney, please. I don't want to wait. I'm afraid something bad's happened. Please, you've got to help me."

"Oh, all right. When's your damn car going to be ready?"

"I don't know. They haven't called to tell me what's wrong yet."

After she hung up, she told Brent she was going to check on Darla and that he'd have to come with her.

"Why?

"I'm not leaving you alone here anymore."

He frowned. "Do I have to go everywhere with you?"

"I don't know how long I'll have to be there. Depends on what I find."

When Rod's tires sounded on the gravel driveway, she grabbed a jacket, stuffing her gun in one pocket and her phone in the other. "Come on and shut the door tightly behind you so it will lock."

On the way to Darla's she clenched her hands so tightly her

nails bit into her palms. She had second thoughts about calling the police and dialed 9-1-1.

"I talked to my friend's toddler at 811 Pinella Street. I think something happened to his mother. Could you folks check it out?"

"Ma'am," the female dispatcher said, "we'll send a patrol car."

Rod careened around a curve, shoving her against Brent's hard body. He grinned and slipped an arm around her shoulders as she grabbed hold of the dashboard to steady herself. She should shrug away, but his arm felt so comforting. Rodney picked up speed again.

"You better watch out for cops," Sheila said.

"You said you want to get there quickly."

She nodded. A shiver of anticipation ran through her. She'd wanted to see Jason again, but not under these circumstances. She'd wanted to watch her tiny baby grow, but she'd thought it better to stay away so he could bond with Darla and Bill. She'd missed seeing him learning to walk, missed hearing his first word.

Now she dreaded what she might find.

Jason had seemed unharmed, and apparently Darla wasn't dead. At least she hadn't been when she'd talked to Jason. What if she died before they got there? Her heart pounded. "Drive faster," she said. Rodney shot her a look, but stepped on the gas.

Surely, no one else was there or Jason wouldn't have been able to talk on the phone—unless an attacker let him do it to draw someone there. She swallowed, hoping that wasn't the case.

What might Jason look like now? Would he have dark curly hair like his father or blonde hair like hers? His eyes had been blue as a tiny baby. Had they turned brown or stayed blue like hers?

It didn't matter what he looked like. She'd be overjoyed to

see him if only she weren't so worried. Jason hadn't seemed scared or upset. Could he have been asleep when something happened to Darla?

Rod's truck screeched to a stop in front of Darla's red brick house. Sheila scanned the quiet neighborhood, graced by stately oaks and huge sycamores. The only vehicle she saw was a dusty black pickup parked in a driveway two houses down.

In a no nonsense voice she told Brent to stay in the truck and watch for the police. Ignoring the curving sidewalk, she raced across the grass to the door and banged the brass knocker.

At first no one answered. She remembered she'd told Jason not to let anyone in. "Jason, it's Mommy's friend, Sheila. Please open the door."

She heard nothing. Was there an intruder in the house? Her pulse raced.

She pulled out her gun and waved to Rod, who stood beside his truck. "Come on. I may need help."

Her brother strode across the lawn to stand next to her and stared at her gun. "Expecting burglars?"

"I don't know." She grasped the doorknob and turned it. At her slight push, the door opened. Sturdy and tow-headed, Jason stood there, a grubby blanket clutched to his chest.

She'd wanted to see him so many times. Now she just wanted to gather him up in her arms, hold him close and smell his little boy freshness. Bad idea. She might frighten him. He looked unharmed, but large couch cushions lay on the rug. A desk drawer hung open, and papers littered the tan carpet.

"Darla," she called. No answer. She took a deep breath. "Where's your mommy?"

He hesitated, his blue eyes studying her face. "In kitchen," he said finally.

Her gun ready, Sheila yanked open the nearby coat closet. Nothing but coats met her eye. The leather couch stood tight against the wall with no room to hide behind it. The thin gold draperies couldn't conceal an intruder either. Standing at the foot of the stairs, she listened but heard nothing. She'd look upstairs in a moment, but first she'd check on Darla. She rushed to the kitchen. Her brother's footsteps sounded behind her, as did the patter of Jason's feet.

Darla sat slumped in a chair, her head resting on the table. Stuffing her gun in her pocket, Sheila lifted long blonde curls from her friends' face, saw a lump on her forehead. The house was quiet. Hoping the attacker was far away by now, Sheila glanced out the windows, then looked in the pantry and behind the door.

Sheila touched her friend's slender arm, relieved to find it warm.

The four-year-old tugged on her skirt. "Make mommy wake up."

"In a moment, honey." She bent down, holding her ear close to listen for the sound of breathing. Faint breaths fanned her face, reassuring her.

She shook Darla's shoulder.

Darla's blue eyes blinked, then stared at her. "Sheila, what are you doing here?"

Sheila put a hand on Darla's shoulder. "You wouldn't answer the phone. My brother drove me here. Are you all right? What happened?"

Darla raised up, but she looked confused. "Where's Jason— is he all right?"

"He's fine, and he's standing right beside me. You need to see a doctor."

Darla twisted to see Jason and stuck out her hand to touch him. He laid his head in her lap. She took a deep breath. "I should be all right in a minute."

"Tell me what happened," Sheila said.

"Some guy wearing a ski mask came looking for Bill. Forced his way in. Shouted at me. Claimed Bill owes him plenty. I told him I didn't know where Bill was. He asked for money. I gave him a twenty and all the change in my purse. He wanted more."

"Did he hit you?"

Darla touched the lump on her forehead and flinched. "When I said that was all I had, he hit me. That's all I remember. I guess he left then."

"Have you heard from Bill?"

A pained look changed Darla's face. "No," she whispered.

A soft moan escaped her lips. "Maybe now the police will take me seriously about Bill missing."

"You think something's happened to him?" Rodney asked.

Darla nodded, then groaned, as if it hurt to move her head. "He's been gambling for high stakes, I'm afraid his disappearance has something to do with that."

Sheila groaned. "I didn't know he was into that." She'd never have given Jason to them if she'd known. "Didn't you warn Bill it was dangerous?"

"At first he was just playing with friends, neighbors of ours, but then he said he was moving on because they always squabbled about losing a few lousy bucks. I met one of his new card playing buddies once and didn't like his looks. And now, we never seem to have any money to pay the bills."

"Did you ask him to give it up?"

"He promised he would, but he's seemed anxious lately."

"Did he mention any names?"

"No, but I saw him reading all the articles on Bart Sheldon's upcoming trial. He was busted for keeping two sets of books and running a bookmaking operation. Bill never reads anything but the sports section. When I asked him about it, he claimed he just wanted to find out about it, but he looked worried."

A noise came from upstairs. It sounded like glass breaking. Sheila gasped.

Rod said, "That guy may still be here."

"We have a safe in the bedroom," said Darla.

Sheila yanked her cell phone from her pocket. Thrust it in Rod's hand. "Call 9-1-1 again. Take Darla and Jason outside. I'll check upstairs."

She waited a few seconds to watch them leave. Jason shrunk away from Rodney and clung tightly to Darla's hand.

Gun in hand, she grabbed a large frying pan from the stove top. Tiptoeing up the steps, her pulse racing, she hoped she could best the attacker without killing him.

She flattened herself against the wall. Inched upward. The door of the second bedroom from the stairway stood open. She moved toward it. Hoped whoever was in there wouldn't see her. She needed to get closer.

The frying pan clanked against the wall. She froze. She held her breath. Heard nothing. Gun ready, she moved up.

As her head cleared the top step, a large man wearing a black ski mask stood in the open doorway. He held a gun pointed at her.

"Don't move, or I'll shoot," he growled.

Sheila froze. If he shot first, he might kill her. Then he'd go after Darla, Rod, and Jason. Was that a siren she heard in the distance? If only she could hold him off until the cops came.

"I called 9-1-1. I hear them coming. You want to be nailed for murder?" She scrunched down, trying to be less of a target.

"Hold it right there," the attacker shouted, his voice rough and menacing. His gun was aimed right at her chest.

He could blast her, be gone in seconds before the cops came. She couldn't let him get to Darla and Jason. She couldn't bear the thought of him hurting Jason.

She shoved the iron pan over her chest and took aim. A flash shot from his gun. The bullet struck the edge of her shield, jolting her arm. The iron frying pan shattered. Her ears rang.

She fired, heard his yelp of pain. He ducked behind the door. Nothing showed but his gun, a black-covered nose and one dark eye. Flattening herself against the wall, she crept higher.

The door shut. Sounded like he was barricading the door. She rushed past it. Crouched beside the railing on the landing. Now she had a direct line to the bedroom door. Couldn't miss. The door flew open. A figure scrambled down the stairs. She got off another shot, but missed. The gunman dashed into the living room, yanked open the front door and raced out.

Hoping Darla, Rod, Jason and Brent were safe, Sheila ran after the man. He headed for the back yard. If there were bushes there, he might hide instead of run. And she'd be an easy target.

In the backyard she ducked behind a large tree. She touched her face. Her hand came away bloody. Peeking out, she scanned the yard. No sign of her attacker.

In her mad dash, she hadn't noticed if Rod's truck were still parked out front. If so, the prowler could shoot them. She'd never forgive herself if he shot Jason. Sirens sounded, but didn't seem close. If only Rod had phoned for help.

A shot rang out. She couldn't tell exactly where it came from, nor could she see her attacker. Then it was silent. Her throat grew dry. Had that guy killed her brother? She and Rod had their differences, but she didn't want him to die.

Her breaths came in short pants. Surely the intruder wouldn't kill a child in cold blood. If Jason watched his mother die, he'd be traumatized.

She eyed the wooden fence. Could she get over it before that man could shoot her? If Darla were dead and her husband missing, she'd have to live to take care of Jason. Sirens wailed, closer now, thank goodness. Would they get here in time?

Running footsteps sounded. Her heart lurched. She edged back behind the tree, sucked in her stomach.

The intruder tore through the yard from the other side of the house. Grabbing the wooden fence, he vaulted over. She shot, aiming for his leg. He cursed, but dropped out of sight. She heard him hit the ground. Pounding footsteps followed.

A lean, rangy policeman ran into the yard. "Over the

fence," she shouted. The cop's long legs swung over the fence, and he disappeared. His footsteps echoed, accompanied by the sound of twigs being crunched underfoot.

She stepped out from behind the tree as another policeman, darker skinned and pudgy, ran into the yard. "Who are you?" he asked.

Brent was right behind him. "She's Sheila Talbot, a Deputy U.S. Marshal."

Sheila pointed to the fence. "The perp climbed over the fence. Your partner went after him."

The cop strode to the fence. "Sam will bring him back in cuffs."

"My brother, a woman, and a child—" She took a deep breath. "They were in a truck out front. Are they okay?"

"No one was shot. The woman looks a bit worse for wear."

"The intruder beat her up. Is Jason...is the child all right?" Taking a deep breath, she clenched her fingers into her palms, waiting for his answer.

"The kid's crying," Brent said, "but he's okay."

Sheila glared at Brent. "Why didn't you stay in the car?"

"Saw that guy run around the house. Thought you might be in danger."

The taller cop clambered back over the fence. "Perp got away, damn it." Speaking into his radio, he issued an APB, reminding patrol cars in the area to be on the lookout. He described the man, then signed off and refastened the radio to his belt.

"We'll get him, Sam," the other cop said.

Sheila raced to the front of the house. Shaken but okay, Darla held Jason in her arms. His face was tear-streaked, and his lower lip quivered.

The lanky cop said, "We'll check the house. You'd better take the kid to a hotel until you can get a security system installed."

Darla looked frightened. "You didn't catch him, did you?"

"I broadcast a description. Someone will pick him up."

The cop called Sam stepped closer to Sheila, eyeing her gun. "You have a license to carry that piece, don't you?"

"Certainly. I'm a U.S. Marshal." She showed him her badge. "When I called my friend, things didn't sound right, so I hurried over." She didn't volunteer anything more. This had nothing to do with Brent. The less anyone knew about what she did, the better. For now she was thankful that Jason was all right, and that no one had been seriously hurt.

Sam came out the front door. "Upstairs is a mess. Know what he was looking for?"

"Money," Darla said, "but he wouldn't find any. We—we don't keep much in the house." She sounded shaken.

Sheila touched Darla's arm. "You need to see a doctor and take Jason to a hotel."

Darla shook her head. "I've got to stay here. Bill might call. I'll get a security system installed right away."

Rod touched Sheila's shoulder and looked her in the eye. "You okay, Sis?"

She nodded. "I just wish they'd caught him."

"Can I take you and Brent home now?" Rod asked. "I promised to do a job for someone today."

Darla said, "Go ahead. I don't think that guy will have the nerve to return for a while at least."

"We can have a patrol car cruise by regularly if you like, ma'am," said the pudgy cop.

"Thanks," Darla said.

"We're leaving now," Sheila said, "but call me if you need me or dial 9-1-1."

Ten minutes later, Rod pulled up in front of her place, but didn't get out. She stared at him. "Aren't you going to come in and install the furnace?"

"I'm waiting for a part. Maybe it will come tomorrow."

Sheila shivered as she opened the car door. Back to another night in the living room near the fire—and temptation. She unlocked her front door and stepped inside. Brent followed.

He plopped down on the couch, one tanned arm resting on the back as if ready to wrap around her shoulder if she sat beside him. He looked concerned as she paced the living room and grumbled about not stopping the guy upstairs. "Were you scared?" he asked.

She nodded. "I was afraid he'd hurt Darla or her son, Jason."

His brown-eyed gaze met hers. "Weren't you scared for yourself? You could have been badly wounded or killed."

"I didn't want anything to happen to my friend or...her son." She needed to keep Jason's parentage a secret from him as well as from her coworkers. Again, she blessed her aunt for telling the investigators she'd stayed with her to take classes in Spanish and Mexican culture at the university. It was the truth, after all, but not her main reason for being there.

Brent studied her face. "Looks like you got cut. Did that guy take a knife to you?"

"No. I was holding a frying pan when he shot at me, and it broke. If something happens to Darla and Bill, I'll have to take care of Jason. They put it in their wills."

"Why you? Why not let him be adopted by some nice couple with some brothers and sisters for him? Single mothers have a rough time of it."

"Doesn't matter. I care what happens to him." She swallowed, imagining the row that would have ensued with her parents if she'd kept Jason. She'd given up the baby, but she'd gone for the job she wanted. Her father hadn't really wanted her in his construction business. According to him, that was a son's place, not a daughter's.

Brent took her hand, making her feel warm and comforted. "Maybe you'll meet some nice guy who'd like a ready-made family, one who won't object to a wife with a career."

She frowned. "You say that as if you don't approve of wives having one."

"It's a free country. Who am I to say what women should do?" His smile made her feel as if he'd accept her as a single mother, whether or not she were caught up in a demanding career. Of course, that didn't mean he'd want a wife who was.

Disturbed at where her thoughts were leading, she pulled her hand from his and immediately missed the warmth. Would she regret not seeing him and talking with him after this case was settled? It didn't matter. She had a job to do. And she needed to put some distance between them.

Brent rose and grasped her hand. "Let me take care of those cuts on your face. Come on upstairs."

Unable to summon the strength to pull her hand loose, she let him lead her. In the bathroom, he bathed her face gently with warm water. With his face so close to hers, she could see the concern in his eyes. The tender touch of his fingers on her skin set her heartstrings thrumming. She felt so safe and comforted, sure he'd be gentle. And he was. Looking into those mesmerizing brown eyes, she hardly felt the brush of the washcloth or the sting of the alcohol.

He pulled out some Band-Aids. "What's this, Mickey Mouse?"

She laughed. "The last time my cousin visited with three kids, one of the boys skinned his knee, and I had to buy some fun bandages."

"Bet they stir up comments at the office."

She looked in the mirror. "Maybe I'll go without."

He smiled. "Want me to kiss it and make it well?" His brown eyes twinkled.

Her gaze drawn to his sensuous mouth, she clamped her lips tight. Admitting she wanted him to kiss her lips instead would approach the zenith of madness or catapult her into ecstasy.

Chapter 8

"Want me to kiss it and make it well?" Brent had asked. His gaze met hers. Was that an invitation in his brown eyes? He faced her in the blue tiled bathroom, his sexy mouth only inches away. His hand rested on hers, sending a jolt of awareness through her. She wasn't sure what else might follow, but she should back away.

She forced a laugh. "I'm too big for that now, but thanks for the offer." Slowly, she pulled her hand away and stepped back. "I'm sure my arm will get better without a kiss."

He grinned. "But I bet it would heal faster with one."

She grasped the doorjamb for support. "I need to go downstairs and find you a place to live." He was cramping her style—how long could she resist her attraction to him? Turning away, she hurried down the stairs. If she'd let him kiss her, she wouldn't have noticed the sting from the alcohol.

After this assignment was over, she'd miss that infectious grin. She hoped he couldn't see through her resistance. If he did, goodness knew how he'd take advantage of it. She'd trusted him to treat her wounds, but she didn't dare trust him with her heart. For all she knew, he might still be hung up on his ex-wife or have a girlfriend.

Today's mail lay on the table beside the front door. He must have brought it in. She picked up an envelope with her grandmother's flowery script. Opening it, she found a card and a twenty-dollar bill with a note. It said, "Indulge yourself with something foolish. You're invited for a birthday dinner on Sunday. If you're still seeing that nice young man, bring him along. If not, take a look at the newspaper clipping." Sheila had almost forgotten it was her birthday. How like her grandmother to send money and invite not only her but a date for dinner. The clipped advertisement said, "Meet the mate of your dreams." She didn't have time for that. After pocketing the money, she laid the card down, crumpled the piece of newspaper, and threw it and the envelope in a nearby wastebasket.

She called the car repair shop. "Is my car ready yet?"

"Sorry, Ma'am, we're waiting for a part. Maybe tomorrow."

She groaned. "Okay, call me as soon as it's ready."

Brent stood near the table where she'd left the mail. "Today your birthday?"

She nodded.

"Happy birthday."

"Thanks."

He looked concerned. "Don't let me stand in the way of any plans you might have."

She sighed. "There aren't any. In fact, I'd almost forgotten what day it was."

He grinned. "Then let me take care of dinner. You can dress up special or be casual, whatever you like."

"You mean go to a restaurant?"

"I wasn't planning on that. Do you have candles?"

She nodded. "There are some in a drawer in the kitchen — in case the electricity goes out."

"Good. We can eat by candlelight. Why don't you take a nice long bath to relax? I'll call you when supper, I mean dinner, is ready."

Hmmm. A nice long soak would feel good. "Don't go to any trouble. There's ground beef in the refrigerator and several packages of Hamburger Helper in the cupboard."

"Don't worry. I'll manage."

Upstairs in the tub, she smiled at his thoughtfulness. The last guy she'd dated took her out to dinner on her birthday, but wouldn't dream of cooking for her. In the tub, she inhaled the fragrance of rose bath oil and rubbed herself all over with sweet-smelling soap. A fleeting image of being lathered in soapsuds by a naked Brent made her sit up straight. She had to stop thinking about him that way — but it would be nice. Best to be like Nelly Forbush in "South Pacific" and "Wash that man right out of my hair."

She poured shampoo on her hair and scrubbed vigorously. Wondering what Brent was doing, she sniffed the air, but couldn't smell anything burning.

After hearing the doorbell, she jumped out of the tub and rubbed briskly with a towel. "Don't answer the door," she yelled as she wrapped her head turban style with the towel and struggled into her robe.

She raced downstairs only to see Brent handing money to a young man at the door. Several Styrofoam boxes lay on the table beside a bottle of wine.

He closed the door. "Thought it was a shame you couldn't celebrate your birthday in style. I didn't want to go out or order you a present over the Internet, but having food delivered seemed safe."

Water from her wet hair dripped down her neck. Suddenly conscious of how she must look, she swallowed. "That's very thoughtful. Let me get dressed. I'll be down in a few minutes."

She turned to head up the stairs. His words stopped her.

"Kind of like you better this way. Looks like we'd just made love on a lazy afternoon." He stepped closer. "Not a bad idea at that." His broad smile set her heart fluttering.

She gasped. "We can't—my position—we can't get involved, even if I wanted to, which I don't. 'Liar, liar,' chanted a little voice inside.

He grinned. "Bet it would be terrific."

Sure he was right, she turned and grabbed the banister.

"Maybe you'd better get dressed." He grinned. "Otherwise I might find it hard to keep my hands off."

Racing up the steps, she couldn't stop imagining him touching her, sliding warm fingers beneath the neckline of her robe. Her face burned as she hurried to dress.

Smiling, Brent sauntered into the kitchen. Glad he could do this little thing to make her day special, he set the table with the nicest dishes and silverware he could find. After carefully spooning the food into casserole dishes, he set some coffee to brewing and searched for candlestick holders. After finally finding some, he lit the candles and set them beside the meal from the fanciest restaurant he'd found that delivered.

Remembering how her face looked before she turned and ran upstairs, he could tell she wasn't immune to him. Bet he could tempt a rough and tough U.S. Marshal to drop her heavy-handed manner for a few hours.

He'd pushed her to find him a place to live quickly, but now he wasn't in such a hurry. What harm could a mild flirtation do? No one would have to know, and she could go on with her career without being tied to him. He guessed that was all she'd want. But he'd sure enjoy her company until he was safely settled.

Hearing her step, he watched her descend. Her blue dress hugged her body and swirled about her shapely legs. Her long blond hair swung, and the sweet curve of her hips undulated as she approached. Standing at the bottom of the stairs, he resisted the urge to take her in his arms and kiss her. Maybe later. Instead, he took her hand and led her to the kitchen.

She stood transfixed, her eyes wide as golf balls. "Oh. How fabulous. I can't believe you did all this."

He smiled. "I didn't. The food's from Chez Parisienne. Hope you like lobster." He pulled a chair out for her. "Be seated, madam, and I will serve you." He ladled a creamy mixture with fettuccine and bite-size pieces of lobster onto her plate, passed her a basket of rolls, and poured ruby liquid into her glass.

"Not too much wine," she said. She took a sip, and her eyes lit up. "It's sweet. What kind is it?"

"Lambrusco. I hope you like it."

"I do. She tasted the lobster dish. "It's delicious. What's this called?"

"It's Creme de la Lobster a la Vin. Made with wine and cream sauce I'd guess."

Later, as Sheila licked a dab of frosting left from the last pink petit-four, he walked around the table. Taking her hand, he pulled her to her feet. "Don't I deserve a nice thank you hug for arranging your birthday dinner?"

"You certainly do. It was wonderful." She threw her arms around him and started to kiss his cheek.

He moved quickly to meet her lips with his, warm and oh so sensuous. He nibbled her lower lip. Unable to help himself, he let his mouth rove over hers. After smoothing a lock of hair from her forehead, he kissed her again, then deepened the kiss. Her mouth was sweet and hot.

Sheila joined him, kiss for kiss. He seemed hungry for her kisses. His tongue licked her lips, then pushed its way inside to roam and thrust. He pulled her against him until her breasts were flattened against his hard chest and tingling from the contact.

He held her tightly. In a few seconds she'd have to talk with him, but now she couldn't bring herself to stop. Sliding her fingers into his wavy hair, she kissed him back, abandoning any thoughts of pulling away—for the moment at least. She'd imagined how it might feel to really kiss him, but her imagination had been only a black and white snapshot compared to the real thing.

His kiss went on and on until he broke the kiss and met her gaze. A broad smile blazed on his face. Triumphant or pleased—she couldn't tell which. As his mouth came closer for another kiss, she decided she didn't care. His warm lips moved over hers, as his fingers slid between them to fondle one breast through the thin fabric of her dress. She leaned briefly into his tantalizing caress, then broke away.

"Brent—uh, that's enough."

"But you seemed to enjoy—"

She swallowed. "Well, yes, but we shouldn't. I mean, I can't get involved. It's unprofessional and could endanger you."

He let her move away, but kept hold of her hand. "Don't see how."

"Just think about it. We should never be seen in public together."

"Why not?"

"Because I don't want anyone to connect me to you. They might follow me to get to you. And once I get you settled, I shouldn't visit you any more than necessary to recheck the security."

"How about two-thirty a.m. every Friday and Saturday evening?"

"What could we do at that hour?" Her glance met his wide grin. "Oh."

"This isn't the last century when such affairs were thought shameful. We could be discreet."

"I don't want to sneak around as if I'm ashamed of you."

"What if we kept it above board, if you told your supervisors?"

"I'd probably be fired or at least suspended and told to sever all contact with you. Then you'd be assigned to another Marshal."

"Oh." He took hold of her hand and squeezed it. "I wouldn't want to do that to you. You probably went through a lot to get your job."

She nodded. "It was a long process, and I wasn't sure I'd get it until I got the call saying to report the following Monday. Then I had to go through a long, tough training."

He drew both her hands to his lips and brushed kisses on

her knuckles. "I won't jeopardize your position. What if we just spent one night together? It would be wonderful —"

She pulled her hands away. "Is that all it is to you, a wonderful time?"

"Oh, I'd have fond memories."

She frowned. "I don't believe in recreational sex. I want to feel close to a man before I —"

He grinned. "We'd definitely be close."

"That's not what I mean. I'd want to feel a bond between us before I shared myself with anyone."

"Guess I'll never be able to make you mine."

She backed away. "You're a typical male, always wanting to possess a woman."

He shrugged. "It's just an expression."

"Men...you're all cut from the same pattern, with only minor differences." She turned and left the kitchen.

She strode into her bedroom, slammed the door, and peeled off her dress. Would she ever wear it without remembering how she'd felt in his arms — and how he'd spoiled it when he revealed his true nature? Mastering women must be second nature to him.

The next morning, dressed in jeans and a warm sweater, she marched outside, slammed the back door behind her, and gathered firewood. She didn't need a man. She could manage by herself, including keeping Brent safe.

Rising up, she shifted the logs to get a better grip. Something was slithering across her toe. Holding her breath she glanced down. A snake lay across her foot. She screamed.

Brent hurried out, the door slamming behind him.

"A snake," she shouted.

He grabbed a forked stick from the ground and pinned the creature just behind its head.

She backed away, shaking the snake's body from her shoe.

"It's harmless. I can tell from the shape of its head. Now can I let it go?"

Feeling stupid, she tried to still her quivering arms. "Y-yes."

He lifted the stick. The snake slithered away, undulating into the undergrowth. He held out his arms. "Give me the wood. I'll carry it inside."

Without a word, she let him take the logs, then followed him into the living room. Bending over, he set the logs down. She knelt in front of the fireplace and waved him off. "I can't tell one snake from another, but I can lay a fire. We might need one tonight."

It wasn't really chilly inside, but she needed something to do—anything to keep her mind from the tempting male standing so close she could hear him breathing. "Sit down. I'll handle this," she said.

She heard him walking to the front window and the rasp of the draperies being pulled shut. The room darkened. "What did you do that for?"

"There was a car turning around in the driveway."

"So, that's not unusual."

"But I think I recognize the car. It's a dark gray Viper, the same make and model as the one that Dirk Dobson, the bookkeeper whose books I audited, drove. At the time I thought it was a bit pretentious for a bookkeeper, but he was probably being paid plenty to keep two sets of books."

She ran to the window and pulled back the draperies to see the car Brent had described. Reciting the license number, she hunted for pencil and paper. She'd better get Brent away from here and fast.

Chapter 9

The charcoal gray Viper kept pulling into her driveway instead of turning around. Her pulse raced. She reached for her gun. "Brent, get back." The sound of his footsteps reassured her.

Finally, the car backed out. She jotted down the license number. Time to get Brent away from here. She left a voicemail message for Joe, her partner, to check out the Viper's license number. Then she called the repair shop. They said her car was ready, and she told them to bring it out.

Turning to Brent, she said, "Get your things together. I'm taking you to another place."

Brent stared at her. "What things? We left them all in that apartment."

"I'll get another Deputy Marshal to pick up your belongings. Right now we're going somewhere for coffee. I'll take the classifieds so I can check them out from there."

"Can't we just drive to my place and pick up my stuff?"

"I don't want you anywhere near there. Dobson may be hanging around."

"Good point. Tell your Marshal not to forget my laptop and my running shoes."

"They may not still be there, but I'll tell him."

Fifteen minutes later, she was pacing the floor. "Why isn't my car here yet?"

She reached for her cell phone, but saw her blue Mustang pulling up. Once outside, she directed Brent to sit in the back.

After dropping off the mechanic, she drove to a small donut shop and led Brent to a table in the back. "Wait here," she said and bought a couple of glazed apple fritters and two cups of coffee.

"You didn't ask what I wanted." He sipped his coffee, then took a bite. "But this is good."

Remembering dates who'd tried to order for her, she felt a twinge of guilt for assuming he'd like her favorite treat. She tried again to call Joe. The receptionist said he'd gone out of town. She called Scott Thompson, another Deputy Marshal, and asked him to pick up Brent's belongings.

"No problem," Scott said. I need to interview a possible witness in Dallas. I'll meet you at Denny's on Stemmons at eleven. Maybe even get you to buy me lunch."

"Look, Scott, I'm busy today, but I'll give you a rain check if you do me another favor. Can you check out a license plate for me?"

"Sure. I was kidding about lunch, but I just got a whopping property tax bill, and I'm feeling strapped. What's the number?"

She gave it to him.

"I'll get back to you on that," he said and hung up.

She read some ads for apartments. None of the locations looked good. She frowned. Would she have to wait for tomorrow's paper?

Her cell phone rang. Scott told her the license plate was registered to a Donald Wilson who lived in Rockwall. Breathing easier, she told Brent they could return to her house after she met Scott.

Twenty minutes later, Denny's parking lot was full, so she parked on the street and left Brent in the car. Inside, she found tall, redheaded Scott, sitting at the counter. She followed him to his car and picked up Brent's laptop, his running shoes, and a bag of clothes.

Outside while Brent waited for her, he heard a car honking. A little girl, who looked about three, was pushing a stroller down the middle of the road just ahead of the car.

In seconds he was out of the car and running toward her. Scooping her up in one arm, he reached for the stroller. She struggled in his arms. He let go of the stroller and ran to the sidewalk. The car moved around the stroller and kept on going.

"What's your name?"

"Paula. Let me go." She looked scared and tried to pull her hand from his. "Don't hurt me."

He set her down but kept a tight grip on her hand. "I won't hurt you. Where's your house?"

She rubbed a tear from her cheek and pointed down the street.

"Let's take you there, okay?"

"'kay."

He held her hand, retrieved the stroller and set it on the sidewalk. She didn't seem to mind running to keep up with his long strides as he headed for her house.

Her mother met him at the door of her house with a baby in her arms.

He handed Paula over. "I found her pushing a stroller down the middle of the street. Might be a good idea to watch her more carefully."

"Oh, no. Thank you for rescuing her. I was getting ready to take her and the baby out in the stroller, and had to change a diaper. Paula, why did you take the stroller outside before I was ready?"

"Don't know."

"Look," Brent said, "if you'll keep her inside, I'll get the stroller for you."

"Thank you. I'll watch her more carefully from now on."

Brent pushed the stroller to the house and left it outside the door. He headed back toward Sheila's car.

Sheila walked to her Mustang and opened the rear car door, but Brent wasn't in the car. She scanned the parking lot. "Brent," she called. No answer. Setting down his laptop and an armful of clothes on the back seat, she surveyed the area again, but didn't see him.

Damn, where could he be? She walked back to the restaurant and yanked the door open. He wasn't inside either. Had someone gotten to him already?

Back outside, she saw him walking down the sidewalk and drew a sigh of relief. She hurried back outside.

"Why the hell did you leave the car?" she said, careful to keep her voice low.

"If you must know I had to grab a little girl out of the street so she wouldn't get run over. I took her back home."

"I admire your heroism, but I was worried about you."

He touched her arm, sending a frisson of awareness through her. "Thanks."

Diners stared at them through the window. "We need to leave now." The sooner she could get him settled, the better she'd feel. "Get in, and let's go."

Brent plopped down on the passenger seat and slammed the door. He didn't speak all the way back to her place.

Inside her house he faced her. His eyes seemed to bore through her. "My mother and my older sister always try to boss me around as if I were still a child." His frown said she was trying to do the same.

He stripped off his shirt. "I'm taking a shower."

With that muscular chest and powerful arms—there was no way she'd mistake him for a child or even a teenager. "I'm not trying to tie you to my apron strings. I just want to keep you in one piece."

After yanking off her blazer, she tossed it on the couch. "The guy that's after you might have followed Scott from your apartment to Denny's. He could have been waiting to catch you alone."

Brent stood there, legs planted firmly apart. "Not likely someone's stupid enough to try to kill me in a public place."

"What if he beat you up and—"

Brent stepped closer. He towered over her. "I can take care of myself in a fight."

His self-assured grin reminded her of a lion on the prowl. His amber-brown eyes seemed to mesmerize her. She took a step back. She needed to get some distance between them. "Stop crowding me."

He shrugged as if to say she wasn't worth bothering with, then turned and strode upstairs. The bathroom door slammed behind him.

Well, she wasn't going to lose any sleep thinking about him. She took the folded sheets, blankets, and a pillow from the chair, made a bed on the sofa, and marched upstairs. Good thing the temperature had risen enough to do without a fire. Tonight she could sleep in her bedroom...away from his disturbing presence, but for now, she needed to get to the office and catch up on her work.

When she returned from work at six—thirty, Brent had made a skillet dish with the Hamburger Helper. However, they ate in silence, making her hope he'd given up on the effort to get her in bed.

After supper, she undressed quickly and put on her robe. She'd stay in her room and read. He might be good-looking and even help out at her house, but his attitude put a damper on any attraction she'd felt. Thank goodness for that.

She put on P.J.s instead of a nightgown. She probably wouldn't tempt him if she were naked. And if just any naked woman would, he wasn't the kind of man she'd want.

Besides, she didn't trust instant attraction. Long ago she and her fiancé had grown close over several months, only to be separated by circumstances beyond their control. She sighed. No use dwelling on what might have been.

Now she regretted choosing the name, Brent, for this

witness. It brought back too many memories — of another time and another Brent.

After they declared her fiancé missing in the MiddleEast, she'd known she'd never see him again. She'd given her baby to her friend, Darla and her husband, Bill. They had welcomed him into their childless home with open arms.

Now that Bill had disappeared, she couldn't help worrying. She reminded herself her son, Jason, was safe with Darla for now. She needed to concentrate on her job, the one she'd worked hard to get.

She tried not to think that maybe getting a job with the government was the real reason she'd given him up instead of her parents' total opposition. Unemployed and still in college, she hadn't been in a position to raise a child, but the guilt still lingered.

The sound of running water ceased. Brent hadn't sung in the shower this time. Was he still mad?

From her bedroom door, she watched him step out, a towel wrapped around his hips. Light from the bathroom revealed his chest hair, damp and curly. He marched down the steps. She moved to the landing.

With one smooth motion, Brent slid beneath the covers and tossed the towel on the braided rug in front of the fireplace. He turned his back to her, his tanned broad shoulders contrasting with the white sheet.

She caught herself wondering how it would feel to run her hands over his shoulders. They'd feel firm, smooth, and muscular, she was sure. She imagined tousling his hair and seeing his amused grin. She wouldn't give in to those impulses. But she'd keep him safe, whatever it took.

She was opening her bedroom door when something rustled in the living room, followed by a click. She turned to look.

Brent sat upright on the makeshift bed. He'd wrapped the sheet around his waist. His tanned shoulders and back glistened in the lamplight. He turned from his laptop, shot her a self-assured look. "I'll write a note to my mom—she'll worry about me, and check my e-mail. Only be a few minutes. Then you can turn out the light."

Seconds later, he gasped. "You'd better see this e-mail." He turned the laptop toward her.

She marched downstairs to see it better. She read, "YOU'RE DEAD SCHMIDT, AND SO'S YOUR BITCH."

Sheila drew in a deep breath. How had someone gotten his name and his e-mail address? His former protector had been fired in disgrace. Had he leaked information? She'd raise her vigilance a notch. No one would get to her witness. "Better change your e-mail address."

His Adam's apple moved convulsively. Looking shaken, he scrolled the screen to the end of the message. "That's all there is."

She pointed at his chest. "Now maybe you'll listen to me. I'm the only one standing between you and six feet under."

"Hey. I know I'm in danger. I'm not clueless." Irritation shaped his face.

"Sometimes you can be too reckless. Where's your copy of the rules?"

"With the rest of my stuff you brought."

"Read it one more time."

He saluted. "Yes, sir, Sergeant Sheila."

"Don't call me that." Frowning, she asked, "Anything you haven't told me that could lead Dobson to you?

He shook his head. "How could he find me? You keep moving me."

"I'm going to take a shower." She walked upstairs, went into the bathroom, and slammed the door.

Hearing the water run, Brent imagined her naked, water cascading over her shoulders and her breasts—they'd be perfect, he was sure. He'd caught an occasional look in her eyes that said she wasn't immune to him. Bet she'd be a tiger in bed—it could be exciting to tame her.

Oh, he could take care of himself, but he hated depending on a woman. He wanted his life back again—the way it had been before. He'd told his boss at the bank why he had to take time off, hoping the man would keep his mouth shut, and hold the job open until the damn trial was over.

A few minutes later he heard the sound of the bathroom door opening. Sheila stood at the top of the stairs. Even in that unbelted terry bathrobe, she looked great. Long blond hair hung loose around her shoulders. Droplets of water, glistening in the light, slowly slid from her neck down the open vee of her pajamas to disappear between her breasts. He'd love to lick them off and follow their path down her soft skin. Fat chance. She'd either shove him away or deck him.

Her loose pajamas revealed little of her shape, but he could picture her soft breasts, a slim waist broadening to rounded hips, and curvaceous legs. It was a long time before he slept.

During breakfast the next morning, Sheila marked several ads in the paper.

Brent sipped his coffee. "Why don't you narrow that list down to three, and take me with you. I'm not going to live somewhere without seeing it first. Before we go, check your car for tracking devices and watch for tails."

"I will, but you'd better not come with me this time."

He paced the room while she dialed.

After she called seven places, she crossed off four. "I'll check these three out before I take you to see them." She headed for the office.

The next morning, Brent set down his empty coffee cup and glanced at her black pants and matching blazer. "You look very professional."

"Thanks," she said, surprised he'd noticed.

He touched her arm. "Maybe I'm paranoid, but I'm hesitant to leave the house even to jog in the woods. But if I'm cooped up here for days, I'll go stir crazy."

She pointed to the newspaper. "Read that. Do the

crossword puzzle, watch television, and stay put. If you don't testify, we can't put Dirk Dobson away for good."

"But at the trial Dobson and all his associates will get a good look." He jabbed a thumb at his chest. "It will be open season on me." He shook his head. "It's not worth it. Set me up with another name and social security number. I'll fade into the woodwork."

"No way." She grabbed his wrist, saw him scowl and let go. "You're assigned to me, and I need you where I can check up on you."

For a long moment he just stared at her. "Okay, okay, but what if it's a long wait until the trial? Do you suppose we could go somewhere far from here, just for the day, without being tailed? My uncle told me about Enchanted Rock State Park where we could climb to the top of a granite hill."

"I've never done serious cliff climbing, not the kind where you need equipment."

"They say it's mostly hiking and that you don't need any equipment," he said.

"Forget it. Someone could pick you off and fade into a group of hikers without anyone being the wiser. Maybe you can go there after we've got Dirk Dobson and his associates locked up, that is if you stay with the program—"

He sighed. "I'm not looking forward to the long wait."

She poured them both another cup of coffee. "Must be something you enjoy doing. What activities did you like in college?"

He grinned. "Women."

"Be serious. What else do you like?"

"Theatre. Got a minor part in a play once, and that led to a bigger one in another."

"So you do have some experience in acting."

He nodded. "It was fun being someone else for a while. Not sure I want to be someone else permanently."

"You can always tinker with your personality if you wish."

He grinned. "I can live with the name change, but I like being me. Took twenty-nine years to develop who I am."

"No bad habits you want to get rid of?"

"I already quit smoking. That's enough."

"I admire your determination. Must have been hard."

He nodded. "I still crave them, but it's healthier not to have them. Besides, smoking reminds me of my ex-wife. We'd smoke together after supper. It was the only time we didn't argue. She was a manipulating witch."

Brent glanced out the window. "I miss the good times, not the fights. Maybe she'll find someone who can get along with her."

Sheila bit her lip. She had to admire him for wishing the best for his ex-wife. Best not to mention it could be months before the trial. If he had the strength to quit smoking, surely he could manage to stay with the program.

"You want to keep that crooked Dobson from ruining someone else's legitimate business, don't you?"

He was silent for a moment. "Sure, but how much good can one witness do? I don't know what he was charged with, but Dobson's probably small potatoes."

"Dobson's connected to a whole crime ring. The prosecutor can't put anyone else in jail without evidence. But if your testimony can make Dobson sweat enough to make him accept a plea bargain and give information on the other guys, we could nail the rest of them."

"I'm beginning to I wonder how effective this Witness Security Program is. We've been followed. You've been shot at. My apartment's been ransacked, and now, someone's messed with my e-mail."

"We can fix that."

"What about your friend Darla's missing husband? Could that be connected?"

"I don't think so. Darla said Bill's got some gambling debts. Maybe some enforcer got to him." She shut her eyes for a few seconds, hoping he wouldn't turn up dead in some alley. Best not to worry until she heard something. "If you don't testify so we can round up some of them, you won't be safe. Suppose some woman plays up to you and leads you into a trap?"

He frowned. "I'd see through anyone like that. I can't stand being manipulated. I know the signs. If my mom can't get her way with honey, she pulls the guilt trip."

She gritted her teeth. "What if some woman with a gorgeous body fell all over you?"

He grinned. "It would be hard, but I could resist."

"But what if she seemed really interested in you?" Sheila sidled up to him, tousled his hair, and then ran a finger over his lip.

He blinked, obviously taken aback, then leaned forward, his lips full and inviting. Good heavens. He wasn't going to kiss her, was he?

His amused grin taunted her. Then he backed away several inches. She tried to ignore the sudden disappointment.

"She wouldn't last long. Models with nothing but a great body bore me. I prefer someone intelligent with a mind of her own."

Was he actually referring to her? Couldn't be. He obviously had a problem with strong-minded women. "I'm not out to win Miss Congeniality. Follow my orders, and you'll keep your skin."

"Hey, I'm not stupid. You don't need to remind me."

Seeing how late it was, Sheila dialed work and left a message saying she'd be in later, then went upstairs.

She grabbed her shoulder bag from the bedroom and stepped out into the hall. She hurried across the narrow landing to the first step.

Her purse strap caught on the knob on top of the railing. She tripped. "Owww." She grabbed the railing to stop her fall.

Brent raced up the stairs. "You all right?"

She collapsed onto the step. "I wrenched my ankle. I'll be all right in a moment."

He moved down a few steps and took hold of her ankle. With gentle hands he probed her flesh. "Don't think you broke anything. Let's get you comfortable." He picked her up.

"Put me down. You can't carry me."

"I lift weights, or at least I did until…."

She put her arm around his neck. His wavy hair brushed her arm, springy but soft. She squelched an urge to let her head slip until her cheek touched his. He was only carrying her because she was hurt. But how thrilling it would be if…don't go there, she reminded herself.

Her neck soon ached from the effort to hold her face away, and she rested her head against his chest. His face felt smoother than she'd expected, and warm. How nice it felt being close. She shoved the thought away. She had more important things to think of.

After he laid her on her bed, she leaned her head away. Had he noticed how she'd snuggled close for a moment? How could he not? Her neck and face grew hot.

He turned to face her, an intent look on his face—as if he meant to kiss her.

Her pulse quickened, but she couldn't let that happen, not again. The memory of that time he'd kissed her on the porch of his apartment…his lips, warm, full, and teasing…she stared at him, trying hard not to look like she expected anything.

He stepped back. "Does it hurt much?"

He sounded like he really cared. Her throbbing ankle made her wince. "I'll be okay in a few minutes. Then we'll go look at places for you."

"I'll drive."

"I don't know if that's wise." If anyone at the office knew what happened, they'd insist she turn over anything that wasn't deskwork to her partner. She didn't want that. "I'll put ice on my ankle. By tomorrow it should be better."

"I'll be careful," Brent said, "and you can watch for a tail. That way you only have to visit each apartment once."

"Makes sense, but I have to stop by the office first to get some papers."

Thirty minutes later Brent pulled her Mustang in front of the Earle Cabell Federal Building. Sheila rubbed her neck. "I feel as if my neck has been through a workout after constant turning to look for tails, but I didn't see any." She looked exhausted. Her foot and ankle must hurt more than she let on.

She pointed across the street. "Pull into that parking garage over there. We can park in the handicapped area in the federal garage."

"Don't you have to get a permit for that?"

"I'll ask the attendant if we can do that for a short time."

Later, he held the passenger door open and breathed in the scent of her perfume, something floral, but nice. Gingerly, she lifted her foot out.

"You ought to see a doctor."

She shook her head. "It's probably only a sprain. It will feel better tomorrow, I'm sure."

"I'll wait here in the car for you."

Sheila shook her head. "You're coming up with me."

"Why? You didn't see a tail."

"I'd feel better having you with me. I'll check my messages and pick up what I need."

After getting out of the elevator, Brent felt strange being introduced to the receptionist as Sheila's brother, Rodney.

The skinny blonde looked at him kind of funny. "You don't sound the same in person as you do on the phone."

As they left the reception area, he whispered, "Why'd you do that? She must wonder why I sound different."

"Shhhh. If there's a leak inside, I don't want anyone knowing what my assignment looks like, but I didn't dare leave you outside. Sit beside my desk while I see if Joe's back."

At her desk she introduced him to Scott. Tall and rangy, the guy had probably played basketball in college. Minutes later she clicked her phone off. "Joe's still out of town. I'll connect with him later."

Fifteen minutes later, as they drove away from the parking garage, a dark gray Viper eased into the lane in front of them.

Chapter 10

"Get closer to that Viper," Sheila ordered.

Brent gripped the steering wheel. "Why should I? What if it's Dobson? Jeez. Nothing like having a back seat driver right beside me."

Sheila frowned. "Must you always give me a hard time? I need to check the license number." As soon as she could focus on the plate, she scribbled down the number. "Okay, back off now." She pushed a button on her cell phone. "Scott, can you check another number for me?"

He put her on hold. Minutes later, he advised her this wasn't likely to be Dobson's car either.

Relieved, Sheila looked at Brent. "My ankle's not that bad. I still think you'd be better off staying at my place while I check out the apartments I've chosen."

He shifted into a forward gear. "If I'm going to live somewhere, I want to see it first."

"But I have to decide whether it's a safe place for you to live."

"Okay, but I won't live in some flea-bitten dump."

She glared at him. "Give me credit for a little common sense. A dump is hardly the safest place to hide out."

Thirty minutes later, he pulled up in front of the first place on her list, an upstairs apartment like the last one. "Doesn't look like much from here."

"That's good. You don't want to attract attention."

He gestured to the steps. "I'll look it over while you wait in the car. Then if I like it, you can check it out."

"You won't look for the same things I will."

"You're probably right," he admitted. "I just want someplace comfortable."

She limped toward the outside stairs.

He followed. "I could carry you."

She shook her head. The stubborn set of her chin and a shake of her head told him he'd wasted his breath.

The place was clean, with a window that looked out on the street. The alley was visible from the kitchen window. Only the rug had any color to speak of. Everything else looked plain but serviceable.

Brent frowned. "Not much to look at, is it? That trial better be over soon."

Sheila winced as she made her way back down the stairs.

The next one looked more attractive, but Sheila crossed it off the list.

"What's wrong with this one?"

"The door isn't sturdy enough, and it's on the ground floor. Drive to the next one." She gave him directions.

The next place looked even nicer, but she said, "Go back to the first place."

He headed back the way they'd come. "What's wrong with this one?"

"No separate entrance, and it's on the corner."

Back at the first place, he waited in the downstairs living room of his new landlady, a Mrs. Wilson, as Sheila wrote a check and handed it to the older woman. Sure felt weird having a woman pay his rent, as if he were her lover. Time to get a job. Next time he'd pay.

The landlady handed him a key. He insisted Sheila wait by the car while he carried up his belongings.

The couch looked comfortable enough, more so than the

wooden chair standing against the wall. With gray draperies and no pictures, the place didn't look very homelike. It was only temporary, he reminded himself.

Back in the car, he asked, "How's your ankle?"

"Better, but I'm glad you drove. Even at this hour, you had to hit the brake often with all the stop and go traffic. Thanks for driving. Now I need to stop at my office." She looked around. "I haven't seen any tail. Should be safe to go there now."

When they reached the building where she worked, she stepped out, still limping a bit. "Come on in. I don't know how long it will take to research any records on Bart Sheldon, Dirk Dobson, and other former employees we know about. It may take least three hours' work."

"Can't you ask the police to do that?"

"You don't understand. I'm the rookie. That would make me look bad. And besides we don't usually call in the local police unless it's urgent."

"Isn't my life important?"

"Of course, but we don't want to alert Sheldon's associates that we're looking into more than a bookkeeping sham."

"Didn't you say you thought there might be a leak at your office?"

She nodded.

"Isn't it dangerous for me to be seen with you at your office?"

"They think you're my brother. And he's never been there."

"That's all I need — three hours twiddling my thumbs."

She frowned. "If you don't like it, you can drive straight back to your new apartment. Keep your cell phone on, and call if you see anything suspicious. I'll take a taxi there and get out in the next block."

"That will put a lot of strain on your ankle."

"I'm sure it will feel better by the end of the day. You should be okay if you drive straight home. If you see a tail, go straight to the police station. Garland's is on Fifth Street. We passed it on the way here."

He waved good-bye and drove back to his new place. He hoped he wouldn't have any trouble. It would be hard for her to rescue him.

It didn't take long to put away the few things he'd brought into hiding. He eyed his jogging shoes. Better not. After flipping on the TV he settled into the brown overstuffed chair.

At five o'clock he called Sheila. "I'm coming after you."

When she objected, he hung up. Surely, he could watch for a tail himself. After scanning the area, he walked down the steps and slid behind the wheel.

Traffic crawled on the highway to downtown Dallas. City streets teemed with cars honking horns, people lining up for the DART railway express, and others walking to their cars. Green leaves on the live oak trees contrasted with bare branches of trees that had lost their leaves. He passed a building with a mural of a little girl pulling a wagon, and then parked in front of the building where he'd left Sheila.

She was standing beside a pot of yellow pansies, their faces bobbing in the wind. She waved and headed along the sidewalk toward the car.

Somewhere behind him a car backfired. Sheila ducked behind a lamppost, her brown blazer and slacks blending with the dark metal. Her gun stuck out.

Maybe that was a shot he'd heard. His heart leaped. He stepped on the gas. The Mustang jerked forward. He leaned over to unlock the door for her. Another shot crumpled the window on the driver's side. He shuddered. What if he'd been sitting up? A third shot zinged past.

She raised up and got off one shot before she stepped up to her car. A shouted curse told him she'd probably hit the guy. Brent shoved the door open. "Get in."

She hesitated. He'd never seen her scared before.

Crouching, Sheila scrambled inside. He pulled her in, then slid behind the wheel. "Shut the door!" he yelled.

He gunned the engine. A uniformed security guard stood at the building door, gun in hand. "Which way?" the guy shouted.

"Never mind him. Go that way," Sheila barked. "Turn left...at the next corner." Her breath came in gasps. "Head for...the freeway."

Burning rubber, he careened along the street, scanning the area for someone with a gun. People were running. Sheila was bent over.

"You okay?" he asked.

"Need...my phone. Her fingers jabbed the numbers. "Joe, someone shot at me...on the sidewalk out in front. Think I hit him...got my witness with me. Have to get him out of here. Call the police. Didn't get a good look at the guy. If they insist, give them my cell phone number."

The sound of rustling cloth came next, and then a gasp.

"What's wrong?" Brent asked.

"Must have taken a bullet. Leg's bleeding. I'm...putting pressure...on it."

"Good lord, where's the nearest hospital?"

"It's not serious. Just get out of here. There, turn on that street."

He zoomed through a yellow light and turned left onto the freeway ramp.

"Exit to 35 north, and take the tollway at the next entrance."

"That's not the way to my place."

"I know. If somebody's following, we'll lead them in another direction." She leaned back against the seat.

He swallowed. Even hurt, she was still on the job, looking out for his safety. Sirens wailed in the background.

"Hope the cops get him...need to question him...find out who he works for." She sounded weak. Not good.

The toll plaza loomed ahead. He zoomed through and stepped on the gas. With no attendants, he figured a camera would record her license plate, and she'd get a bill.

He glanced at her face, so pale in the waning light. "You need to see a doctor."

She shook her head. "I'll be okay. Just watch for a tail."

"I'm taking you to a hospital."

"No. I'll be okay until...until we're far enough away. Don't exit until I tell you." Her voice sounded softer, but that damn commanding tone came through, strong and clear.

She'd been shot because of him. He gritted his teeth. He wanted to get her to a doctor as soon as possible, but he'd better let her call the shots.

He glanced in the rearview mirror. Every time he'd decided a car was following, it would pass or turn off. Was he paranoid?

She slumped in the passenger seat.

"You still conscious?"

She nodded. Her phone rang. She fumbled with it, then said, "Hello."

She listened for a few seconds, then said, "I'm a U.S. Marshal transporting a prisoner. Can't talk long." She listened again. "The guy that shot me—big, about six-three, sturdy build, dark hair, dark clothes—think I hit his arm. Got to go." She snapped the phone shut.

He frowned. "So, I'm a prisoner now?"

"We don't need any publicity about a witness."

He maneuvered around some slow cars and glanced her way again. She was leaning against the door, her eyes closed. Bloody tissues littered the floor.

Had she fainted from loss of blood? Her hand was cool. Wasn't that a sign of going into shock?

That did it. "Okay, where's the nearest hospital or emergency clinic?"

"Never mind...just drive to your place."

"You could have a bullet inside your leg."

"I felt a sharp pain, that's all. Not sure it's a bullet... I don't want a doctor to...turn in my name. Police reports are...public records."

He glared at her. "Forget the records. You need attention now."

She looked around. "Take the next exit...then go right. Think there's some emergency place there."

He yanked the wheel, pulled onto an exit and zipped past the tollbooth.

He pulled into the parking lot of an emergency care clinic, stopped the car, and bent over to examine her leg. "If a bullet just grazed your leg, you wouldn't bleed like that."

"Think I'm...getting dizzy."

Her hand felt cool and clammy. "Put your foot on my lap." When she hesitated, he grabbed her leg and lifted it over the console.

She grimaced at each movement, then gave him a puzzled look.

He explained, "Saw this on ER once—something about getting the blood to the vital organs."

"Take deep breaths." He had no idea if that would help, but he didn't know what else to do. The blood had changed the brown of her pants to maroon beside her ankle.

If he hadn't believed those small-time criminals meant business before, he did now. He swallowed. He got out and ran around to the passenger door. After picking her up, he carried her inside.

At the check-in counter she could barely stand to sign in. When the receptionist asked why she was here, Sheila said, "My leg's hurt."

"Forget the questions," Brent said. "My wife's been shot and needs help now."

Sheila glared at him, but said nothing.

The woman at the desk pointed. "First room on the right."

Taking hold of her arm, Brent led her to the examining room. Seeing how pale she looked, he picked her up and set her on the examining table.

Sheila shot him a dark look. "Why did you tell her... I was your wife?"

"Thought she might react quicker if I did." He went to the door and looked out. "Where's the damn doctor?"

She shot him a dark look, then lay down on the table." Be patient... I'll be okay...after he treats my wound. And you can forget about...playing nursemaid."

He frowned. "Haven't offered yet, but you'll need help."

"Been on my own for...years now... I'll manage."

Her chin had that determined look, but her voice sounded weak. "You need to have someone take care of you." Seeing her frown, he added, "Just until you're better."

Brent pulled her purse from her trembling fingers and set it in a chair. He grabbed some paper towels and pressed them against the wound. Blood invaded the towels, turning pristine whiteness to scarlet in seconds.

The doctor hurried in. "Sorry, I had another urgent patient to take care of." He glanced at the bloody towels. "What happened to you?"

Sheila's breaths seemed labored, and her face looked even paler. "I was shot."

The doctor washed his hands at the sink, then lifted the pad of towels soaked with blood and rolled up her pants leg. He frowned. "It's still bleeding, but not profusely, thank goodness." He patted the skin around the wound. "Looks like the bullet's still inside. Can you make it across the hall to the surgery room?"

Sheila nodded.

Brent put an arm around her shoulders to steady her as she limped across the hall to a gray-walled room, its counter lined with instruments.

Once there the doctor said, "Lie down." He looked at Brent. "Why don't you wait out front?"

Brent took her hand in his. "I'm not leaving her. We just got married last month. I'll stay out of your way." He ignored Sheila's scowl.

The doctor frowned, and pointed to a wooden chair in the corner of the small room. "Okay, but sit over there." He studied Sheila's leg.

Sheila grabbed the doctor's sleeve. "I have a favor to ask."

The doctor shook her hand off. "First we need to get that bullet out." He stepped to a stainless steel sink and began scrubbing his hands. He dried his hands and stepped back to her side.

Sheila said, "It's important. If you remove a bullet—" She winced as the doctor turned her leg to examine the wound. "You mustn't report it."

The doctor rubbed the back of his neck. "You want me to disobey the law?"

"I'm a U.S. Marshal... In charge of—protecting this witness." She nodded toward Brent. "He's an innocent bystander in a federal case."

The doctor looked puzzled. "So he's not your husband? Or maybe he is and you're trying to shield him."

"That's not true. Brent, hand me my purse." Sheila rummaged through her purse, finally pulling out her wallet. She flipped it open to show her badge.

"Okay, so you are a U.S. Marshal. The law still requires me to report it."

"Don't need publicity... might draw the criminals to us."

"I understand," said the doctor, "But if anyone finds out, I'll get in trouble."

"Just say it was an order from a government agency."

The doctor frowned. "We can discuss that later. Delaying treatment will endanger your health."

The doctor left and returned with the nurse, who scrubbed her hands at the sink. "Miss Johnson, hand me that hypodermic." The nurse complied.

Sheila touched his arm. "Wait. Couldn't you write it up and maybe mislay the report for a couple of months?"

The doctor frowned. "Do you want me to operate or not?"

"Yes," she whispered.

Brent leaned close to hear. She sounded weaker now.

"Be still and let me work," the doctor barked. "I've delayed too long as it is."

Sheila gasped and raised up on her elbow. "I'm not in danger of dying, am I?"

Brent drew a deep breath. Should have insisted on getting help sooner.

The doctor shook his head. "Of course not, but I need to get started. Lie down."

The shot took effect quickly. She lay so still Brent found himself listening for the sound of her breathing. Sitting in a chair in the corner, he crossed and recrossed his legs. He found it hard to watch.

He'd never put much stock in people who worked for the government, but she'd gone through a lot to protect him. He didn't want to see her crippled because of him.

When Dr. Denton finished and the nurse taped a dressing on her leg, he handed Brent a packet of pills. "Be sure she takes these antibiotics." He held out a prescription slip. "This is for pain. There's a drugstore next door."

The doctor added. "I gave her a shot of Toradol. She'll be groggy for a while. No more walking than necessary—and no driving. Bring her back in a week. Call immediately if she has a temperature or if you see any pus."

Sheila tried to sit up, then lay back down. "Call 214-555-8535," she mumbled… "talk to Joe. He'll tell you we need…secrecy."

The doctor turned to the nurse. "Write that down."

Sheila touched his arm. "Can you ask…ask your nurse…not to say anything?"

Dr. Denton scowled. "That's not necessary. My staff keeps patient information confidential."

As Brent helped Sheila down from the table, Dr. Denton met her gaze. "You just worry about getting well. We'll call your office in the morning."

Brent put an arm around her shoulders to steady her. Her skin didn't seem as cool as before, thank goodness. Still, he'd be relieved when he got her into bed. She walked slowly toward the door to the hall, then stopped suddenly.

"Bullet…need the bullet…" she muttered.

Brent faced the doctor. "Could you put it in a plastic bag?"

"She wants a souvenir?" asked the nurse.

Brent shook his head. "There might be fingerprints. Just slip it in a bag and give it to me."

Using a pair of tongs, the doctor picked it up and dropped it in a plastic bag the nurse held out, then handed it to Brent, who slipped it in his pocket.

Brent led her to the car, helped her ease into the seat, and then gingerly lifted her injured leg inside.

"Does it hurt much?" he asked.

"Don't feel anything yet…probably will later."

"Wait here while I get that prescription filled." A few minutes later he returned with a small bottle and handed it to Sheila.

Sitting behind the wheel, he asked, "Why are you so paranoid about anyone knowing you got shot? You called the police."

"Don't need newspapers getting my name or yours…not while I'm…watching you."

He started the engine and grinned. "Guess it's turnabout time. You'll be my guest now."

"I can't stay…at your apartment."

"Yes, you can. You need someone to take care of you. It's not safe for me at your place, so that leaves mine."

"Just drive me home… I'll be okay."

"What if someone's lurking there with a gun waiting for you?"

"Damn, you're right… must be woozier than I thought."

"Call in, and tell them you've been shot in the line of duty. Get those other Marshals to help catch the ones behind this."

"After the leaks…I'm not sure who to trust."

"Isn't there someone you can?"

"Only Joe. He's my partner and my mentor… joined the program three years before me."

"If you can't trust a mentor, you're in big trouble."

"Okay, I'll ask him. Get back on the tollway, go north to LBJ Freeway, and follow it east to Garland Road."

Brent drove as directed, then glanced her way. She'd fallen asleep, thank goodness. He hoped he could find his new apartment without waking her. After pulling onto Garland road, he turned into a gas station and slammed on the brakes.

The sudden stopping of the car jolted Sheila awake. She opened her eyes. "Where are we?"

"I took LBJ Freeway to Garland Road, and now I need directions."

She looked around. "Turn right on the next street. Have you…been watching for a tail?"

He frowned. "Of course."

After she directed him through several more turns, he asked, "You sure this is the best way to go?"

She looked behind. "Just want to be sure no one's following… okay, turn down that street."

He did. "This looks familiar." Minutes later he stopped in the driveway.

She shook her head. "Park behind the house."

He pulled beside the steps. "I will later." He walked around to her side and opened the door. He supported her elbow as she got out. She took one step, and her leg buckled. Before she realized what he was doing, he'd picked her up.

"Put me down. I can walk."

"Stop struggling. You shouldn't put any pressure on your leg. It might bleed again."

He held her so tightly it would take more effort than she could muster right now to fight him.

"But I'm too heavy…to carry all the way upstairs."

He frowned. "Are you saying I'm not strong enough?"

Giving in, she leaned her head against his shoulder. He smelled of soap and aftershave. His hair was springy against her forehead, his shoulder firm and sturdy. He strode up the outside stairs as if she were no heavier than a bouquet of flowers and set her down in front of his door.

A breeze ruffled his hair as unlocked the door, then turned to grin at her. "I'm pretty lucky."

She met his gaze. "How can you say that? You're hiding out."

"Not every man has a warrior princess in his castle."

She patted her leg. "I'm not much of one right now."

"You've done great so far."

"Thanks." A warm glow spread inside. It had been a while since someone told her she'd done well at something."

Holding the door open, he said, "You can walk to the chair and the bathroom, but that's all."

"Now who's being bossy? I'm not an invalid. Just need to rest a day or two."

He frowned. "More like a week or two, I'd say."

She limped to the couchidehid. He pulled a footstool close for her foot and gently lifted her leg onto it. A minute later she heard him opening cabinet doors in the kitchen.

"Chicken soup—that's what you need."

The savory aroma teased her nose as he set it on a TV tray in front of her.

She took a couple of spoonfuls. It was good, but now she felt too tired to finish. She pushed the tray back, spilling some of the soup, and lay down. "Too tired to eat any more. Just let me sleep."

"I'll feed you."

She frowned. "I can do it. Give me that spoon."

He shook his head. "You did a great job of nailing that gunman, but even the bravest of warrior princesses needs help sometimes."

He held a spoonful of soup to her mouth. Inhaling the

heavenly smell of the broth, she opened her mouth. As soon as she swallowed, he was ready with another spoonful. It tasted so good she let him continue. And continue he did until the bowl was empty.

"Thank you," she said. "No one else has been so attentive for a long time—except one."

"And who was that?" he asked.

"I was engaged once."

"Tell me about it."

"I don't want to bore you."

He took her hand. "You wouldn't."

"Matt and I worked together. Our boss never noticed how hard we worked. One of our co-workers was engaged to the boss's daughter, and he got the promotion we felt one of us should have gotten. After that was announced, I'd left the meeting and retreated to my office. I was trying to hold back the tears when my coworker—"

Brent squeezed her hand. "I find it hard to imagine a warrior princess giving way to tears. What happened then?"

"Well, Matt came into my office and talked me into going for a drink. We spent hours talking. After that we started going together. The day he told me he'd been called up by the National Guard to go to Afghanistan, he proposed."

She'd said, "Yes," melted into his arms, and let him spend the night. "Two days later I kissed him good-bye before he boarded a plane. That was the last time I saw him alive." She brushed a tear from her eye.

"Sorry to hear that. Must have been rough."

She nodded, unable to speak. As Brent took her dish and stepped to the sink, she leaned back and shut her eyes, remembering. She'd lost her job, and after learning she was pregnant, she'd agonized about her child's future. She decided to give him to her married friend, Darla, who had tried so hard to have a baby. Darla and her husband had moved away and only recently moved back.

It had been a shock to see Jason at four with Matthew Brent's brown eyes so wide and trusting in her son's face. She'd had to tear herself away, comforted only by knowing that Darla and her husband could give him a good home. However, Sheila wished she'd known about Darla's husband's tendency to gamble.

She had to stop thinking about Jason. She needed all her wits to keep Brent Broussard safe—and resist his magnetic pull. He needed a new life—one that didn't include her. Eventually, he'd have a girlfriend—she didn't want to imagine him making mad, passionate love to another woman. She bit her lip. She wouldn't think about that.

She'd stay here a day or two, just until her leg was well enough to manage by herself. Surely, she could ignore his rakish charm that long. She drew a deep breath and watched him walk toward her, his smile bright for her alone. She shut her eyes, trying to resist his attentive look.

She felt him lifting her injured leg and opened her eyes as he eased a cushion beneath. "Is that more comfortable?"

She nodded.

"Does your job take up all your time? Don't you have any hobbies?" he asked.

"I took karate up while I was in college and found I was good at it. I also joined an archery club. I'm not too shabby at that either."

"Modest, aren't you?" he said with a grin.

"I try not to boast."

"You should do it more when you're at your grandparents' house. I don't think they realize how much you've accomplished."

"I'm the only woman in the Witness Security Program in the Dallas office so far. The training's tough. I'm sure they make it that way to discourage anyone who isn't really motivated." She picked up her cell phone. "I'm calling Joe, my coworker, to see if they caught that guy who shot me."

After a disappointing conversation, she hung up. "The gunman got away. I can only hope he doesn't know where we are."

Brent walked to the window and pulled the drapery aside. "Don't see anything unusual. If anyone's found me here, he hasn't shown up." Brent stood before her, his gaze meeting hers. "You need to move to the chair so I can make up the bed for us."

Chapter 11

"What do you mean, make up the bed for *us*?" Sheila asked.

His slow grin held her gaze. "Do you see any other beds here?"

She shook her head.

"You need your rest, and I'm not sleeping in that chair. I'd ache all over by morning."

"What about the floor?"

"It was okay when I was a kid, but my back can't take it anymore."

"I'll go to a hotel." She grabbed her purse and tried to stand. Her leg buckled, and Brent grasped her arm to steady her. "Sit down. You shouldn't be driving."

"Then I'll sleep on the floor," Sheila insisted.

"There's only one blanket."

"Do you have a coat?"

"Only a short jacket."

She rose and hobbled toward the hard wooden chair. Brent held her arm for support. "There must be something else we can do."

He walked to the linen closet and took out sheets and a blanket. He changed the couch to a bed, his muscles rippling beneath his shirt. Even if he didn't make a move, just lying next to him, inhaling his masculine smell, feeling his breath caress her....

He'd been helpful when she needed it. He'd driven her here without catching a tail. He'd fed her soup, and even complimented her. But when she got better, he'd probably be difficult again.

She watched him make up the bed with swift, sure movements. He didn't speak, but his damn seductive glances kept pulling at her.

"Let's get one thing straight," she said. "Just because you insist on us sleeping in the same bed doesn't mean—"

"I won't do anything you don't want me to."

After studying his serious brown eyes and hearing his quiet voice, she felt as if she could trust him. But could she trust herself? She wanted to touch him, to explore the hard planes of his broad chest and ruffle his wavy hair. She shoved her hands underneath her. She couldn't and wouldn't give in to asinine cravings.

After losing her heart to Matthew Brent, she hadn't dated much. The pain of losing him had faded, but why were her emotions kicking in now, when she needed to be in firm control? To keep Brent Broussard safe, she needed to be rational and alert constantly.

He touched her arm, startling her. "Do you want to take a shower first?"

She blinked. "No. I'll just wash up. I don't want to disturb the dressing."

As she stood before the mirror washing her face, her leg ached. Gingerly, she touched the area around the dressing and found it tender.

Should have noticed that man aiming a gun at her sooner. Sure she'd hit or at least grazed his arm, she regretted not getting a good look at his face. The baseball cap he'd worn cast too much shadow.

Her co-workers joshed her a lot, but surely none would shoot her. However, if that were a hit man, why hadn't he shot to kill?

She gritted her teeth. She'd keep Brent safe, no matter what.

After washing up, she passed him on his way to the bathroom and limped to the bed. Sitting on the side nearest the window and glad for her long shirt, she pulled off her bloodstained pants and yanked the blanket over her bare legs.

Her Glock, she placed beneath her pillow. She lay with her back to the center of the bed as close to the edge as she dared.

Could she sleep lightly enough to keep her back turned? She'd better. She couldn't let on she was interested in anything more than sleep, but her imagination was fired up. Lying with his arms around her would be wonderful, and so would anything else he'd dare.

When he came out, she pretended to be asleep. The bed shook as he got in and wiggled around — to get comfortable she supposed. The smell of soap and cologne teased her senses. Cologne? Hadn't he taken her seriously?

"Sheila?" His enticing whisper begged her to answer.

She kept silent.

"I know you're not asleep."

Still, she didn't answer.

"Your breathing isn't slow or deep enough."

Sheila shut her eyes tighter and remained still.

"Do you have a problem being close to a man? Is that why you don't have a boyfriend?"

"That's none of your business, "she sputtered, turning to face him.

He lay on his side, supporting himself with one elbow. His seductive grin tempted her to mention some imaginary boyfriend, but unnecessary lies weren't her style.

"Look, the last guy I dated...I broke off because of his gambling. I can't respect a guy who lets an obsession take over his life."

He stared at her. "So I gamble occasionally, but I don't let it rule my life," he said firmly. His serious expression hinted he cared what she thought.

"I read in your file that you blew a whole week's salary once."

"I had my reasons."

"You thought it was a sure thing, right? That's what my brother, Rodney, always says."

"I was in Vegas, and my sister's college tuition and fees were due for her sophomore year. I thought I could win enough to pay them so she could concentrate on her studies and not have to work."

"Why not just give her what you had?"

"That wouldn't have been enough."

"And you lost it all instead."

"So I made a mistake. Does one screw-up ruin me in your book?"

"I don't know you well enough to decide. I haven't seen how you treat your family, or your ex-wife, or your enemy for that matter."

"So, you're withholding judgment?"

"That's right," she said and turned her back. "I'm tired. I need to sleep now."

⟋

Sometime in the night Sheila awoke, immediately aware of his arm around her waist. He held her snugly against his toasty warm body. At least he wasn't trying to caress her or touch her breasts, but she couldn't forget his seductive glances as he made the bed. Was he only waiting for some sign of encouragement? That teased her senses, making her wish for things best left alone.

A noise sent a jolt down her spine. Grasping his wrist, she pulled to loosen his arm. He held tight. She strained to see in the darkness, listening for an intruder.

There it was again. A sort of brushing sound. Hairs rose on her arm. Was someone inside?

Quietly easing back the covers, she pulled on his arm again. This time he let go. She grabbed her gun and struggled to her feet.

A swath of moonlight fell across the myriad display of flowers on the rug, the colors garish and unreal. A cat's silhouette stalked across the outside window ledge and was gone.

A tall, dark form loomed in the corner. Gun in position, she stepped closer so as to see better. Grimacing at the pain in her leg, she saw...a coat rack with Brent's jacket. Breathing easier, she headed back toward the bed, her leg aching with every step.

Outside, metal scraped against metal. Her pulse picked up. Someone was out there.

Edging toward the window, she peered out. Nothing looked unusual. Her heart pounded with a sense of unease. She limped into the kitchen and looked out that window. Streetlights illuminated the alley and most of the back yard.

The clanking noise came again. She laid her gun on the counter. With difficulty she climbed up on the kitchen counter, putting the knee of her good leg up first, then pulling her injured leg up.

Shadows marked the concrete pavement below in shades of gray. The small back yard looked brown. Dark shadows lurked close to the house. They could be bushes, or....

She cranked the casement window open a crack. Cringing at the creaking noise, she held her breath. Over by the fence something bumped against the garbage cans. She watched and waited.

Then she saw him.

Average height, dark hair, dark clothes. No glasses. Was it Dobson, the bookkeeper Brent would testify against—if she could keep him alive long enough? Like the man who'd shot her, this guy wore a baseball cap and held a large plastic bag.

Her pulse raced. She'd been so careful to watch for a tail

while they hurtled along the tollway. Had she missed one? Would he use that bag to strangle or suffocate someone?

Her heart pounded. Was he after Brent or her, or both of them? The man stuffed the bag into his back pocket. The flimsy plastic film sticking out flapped in the breeze. Moonlight revealed his scruffy beard and a determined chin. He stepped closer to the house.

He couldn't see her, could he? Would he come up the stairs after them? Her pulse stepped up its pace. She shrank back. Neither the light from the moon or the lone street lamp in the alley reached this far, but why was he looking her way?

Should she wake Brent? No, better wait to see if the man came near the stairs. He lifted the cover of the garbage can, the clang of metal jarring in the still night. Was he planning to stuff a body in there? She shivered and gripped her gun tighter.

Now he uncovered the other garbage can. It too, was big enough to hold a body stuffed inside with the knees drawn up. Her legs felt cramped just thinking about it.

With both hands, he hefted the can a foot off the ground as easily as if it were empty. He'd be strong enough to heft a body over the top, too.

She clenched her teeth. She wouldn't let it come to that.

Quiet footsteps behind made the hairs on the back of her neck rise. Were there two of them? Tensed for action, she turned her head, swung her gun around.

A figured loomed in the shadows. Her pulse beat erratically. She tried to focus, prepared to fight to the death for herself and Brent.

"It's me," Brent said.

She let out her breath. "Don't sneak up on me like that. I could have shot you."

"Sorry, didn't mean to scare you."

He scared her all right, in more ways than one. Brent's husky whisper had vanquished her apprehension, but smelling his cologne and feeling his touch on her arm awakened a whole new set of sensations, ones she'd tried to ignore.

"What are you doing?" he asked.

"Shhhhh. There's someone out back."

"Why didn't you wake me?" He climbed on the counter beside her, his arm heating hers. His warm breath fanned her neck. How could she concentrate with him so close?

She swallowed and pointed. "See him over there by the alley?" she whispered. She wouldn't mention her gruesome suppositions.

"What's he's doing?" Brent asked, his chin brushing her shoulder. The man bent over and reached inside the trashcan. "Probably looking for something to salvage," said Brent.

She drew a deep breath. "A homeless person. I thought maybe...."

"Someone coming after me?"

She nodded, her eyes glued to the back yard. The man below snatched something from the can, stuffed it in his plastic bag, and scurried off. She let out her breath. "I guess it's safe to go back to bed now."

Brent backed off and landed with a thud on the linoleum. "Even wounded, you're looking out for me. I appreciate that."

"It's my job." Still shaken from having him so close, she leaned toward the window to be sure the man had left. Shivering from the cool night breeze, she cranked the window closed and then sat on the counter facing him.

He grasped her hand. "You're cold. Come back to bed, and I'll keep you warm." He smiled rakishly, his grin pulling at her.

"I'll be all right."

His brown eyes held her gaze. "Like I said, I won't do anything you don't want me to, but I can hold you until you're warm. If you're going to work tomorrow, you need your sleep. Cramped muscles will keep you awake."

"Thanks, but I'll manage." She stared at the floor, trying to figure out how to slide down without putting pressure on her injured leg. Suddenly she felt his strong grip on her waist. He lifted her toward him, then lowered her, letting her slide down, pressing her breasts against his firm body. Somehow, she felt safer now, even though she was the one supposed to be doing the protecting.

But that wasn't all she felt. As her breasts flattened against his broad chest and tingled from the close contact, she needed a different kind of protection, protection from that marvelous grin, that come hither look in his eyes, and her traitorous yearnings.

Her feet, now flat on the floor, should give her some semblance of stability. Time to move away. Though his hands held her lightly, he didn't let go. She needed to pull away, but something in his dark eyes wouldn't let her. Tightening his hold, he kissed her, his mouth roving over hers, nibbling, tasting, teasing. His hands rough, his touch gentle, he cradled her face as his lips traced a path down her neck as far as the neckline of her shirt allowed.

His voice husky, he asked, "Sure you don't want me to do more than keep you warm?"

Breaking his hold, she leaned back against the sharp edge of the counter and wished she'd left the window open. She needed a jolt of cold air to cool her blood. "I...no...we can't."

"Can't what?" His smug grin dared her to spell it out.

"Can't get involved."

He grabbed her hands, urged her toward the bed. "We're already involved. We have to stay close—for my safety. That's your job, isn't it?"

She frowned. "Yes, but you know what I mean."

His grin grew broader. "Tell me."

"Have you thought what might happen if they ask me to testify and the defense lawyer asks me if I've had sex with you?"

"So?"

"Don't you think they might be less inclined to believe my testimony and yours?"

"If we don't act like lovers in court, no one will ask those questions."

"I'm not giving them anything to talk about. If they ask if you spent the night here, I'll tell them I was guarding you."

"Can't blame a guy for trying." He kissed her again, setting her senses on sizzle. She couldn't seem to stem the growing rush of excitement.

She'd loved once. After losing Matt, she'd been so sure she'd never feel this way again about any other man. Now it was all she could do to fight the magnetic force impelling her toward this man, like Niagara rushing headlong toward the falls and a joyous joining with waters below, churning and surging in a tumultuous coming together.

Sheila took a deep breath. Somehow she'd get through this without letting him know how he made her pulse pound and her blood run hot, or worse, how close she was to surrendering. Summoning all her strength, she pulled her hands from his.

He stepped back, a question in his eyes.

She willed her face to appear impassive, though her insides still quivered, and her pulse raced so fast she had to concentrate on breathing normally.

Backing away, she spoke in firm tones. "Even if I wanted to, I can't. I need a clear head to keep you safe."

"If that's the way you want it, fine. I won't mention it again."

His face was stony, but disappointment lurked in his eyes. She should be glad he hadn't guessed how every fiber of her soul pulled her toward him, like a parched panther to water. How could his ex-wife have pushed this marvelous man away?

He headed toward the bed. "I'm going to try to get some sleep. You'd better too."

Surprised he hadn't tried harder to persuade her, she told

herself it was better this way. She should thank him for making it easy to back off. Or was he just biding his time? She sighed and hobbled back to the living area. She crawled onto her side of the bed, and lay close to the edge.

However, her body kept sliding toward the center and Brent. She moved back toward the edge, wincing as she slid her leg across the bottom sheet. It was going to be a long night.

Cozy and warm, she awoke to a faint dawn. His arm was around her waist again, and one leg lay next to hers. No wonder she felt so warm. She managed to wriggle out from under his arm and slide out of bed. In the bathroom, cold tile chilled her bare feet. She drew her ruined pants over her injured leg and winced from the pain. Dressing in the cool morning air, she was glad she'd shut the window. It was chilly enough in the bathroom as it was. She'd have to speak to the landlady about turning on the heat.

Leaving the bathroom, she was greeted by a sleep-ruffled Brent. He smiled. "Morning, Warrior Princess."

She grinned in spite of herself. "Morning yourself."

After a leisurely breakfast of coffee and donuts, which she'd picked up, she limped to the phone and picked it up. "I'd better call work."

"No," her supervisor told her. "The police haven't caught him yet." She didn't mention she'd taken a bullet. They'd insist she let Joe take over. She spent the day on the phone, making arrangements for her next witness to protect.

By the next morning, she could walk without excruciating pain. If she took the elevator and walked slowly, they might not notice how bad her leg was. After all, as long as Brent was safe, she could handle anything connected with him from her desk. Joe had plenty to do, and she didn't want another marshal taking Brent over.

She'd washed her pants and let them dry overnight. When she called to say she was coming in, but would be late, her supervisor told her, "Alert us with your cell phone as you approach the building. Park in front of the door. Stay in your car until a security guard meets you out front of the building. He can park your car after escorting you to the door."

Brent grabbed her car keys from the end table. "Surely, you're not going to work today."

"Yes, I am. The security guard will park my car, and I only have to walk to the elevator. My desk isn't far from the entrance to our department. My leg's injured, not my brain."

"You're a fool to go, but if you insist, I'm driving you in. You don't need to put pressure on that leg."

She turned to Brent. "You're not going near that place again. If I leave after rush hour, I won't have to jam on the brake much. I'll be okay."

He frowned. "That guy would be stupid to venture near your office, but let me drive you there—just in case."

She saw the determined look on his face. "Stay here. I'll take a taxi."

After arranging for a taxi, she said, "I'll be back by six."

He touched her arm and gave her a warm smile that set her heart quivering. "I'll have dinner ready."

With difficulty, she shook off his arm. His brilliant smile would melt gold. Obviously he hadn't given up on persuading her to share the bed as his lover. She'd better be strong enough to resist him.

The next two days she took taxis and worked short hours. The following day she took a taxi to one of the DART train commuter stops and rode downtown. The next day she had a taxi leave her at a different stop. So far, she'd seen no one following her. If nothing more happened, she could leave Brent there when her leg got better.

Brent had a hot meal ready each night. Aside from an

occasional grumble, he seemed to be adjusting to his new situation.

One day Brent called her at work. It was good to hear his voice. "How are you doing?" she asked.

"I'm doing great. Thought I'd let you know I'm blending in just like you ordered. I landed a part in a play, an amateur production. We open on New Year's Day."

"That's pretty public."

He sounded excited. "The leading lady's a knockout. Can't wait to practice love scenes with her."

Gripping the phone, Sheila bit her lip. She didn't want to think of him kissing another woman, even if it were make believe. He was baiting her. She shouldn't let it bother her, but it did. She frowned. What did she expect after telling him they couldn't be involved? Unbidden, memories of the last kiss they shared stirred her senses.

Never mind that. She needed to be tough. "I told you not to try out for the lead. That could get your name and photo in the paper." She could see it all now—Brent and the leading lady kissing, on the front page of the entertainment section. She squeezed her eyes shut in an effort to banish the image. "You'll have to back out."

"Don't worry. All I have is a walk-on part. Just wanted to see what you'd say if you thought I had the lead. I used the name Jamison Bondell when I auditioned. The crew gets a kick out of calling me Bond. Ciao."

On Friday night when she arrived, all she saw on the table were soup bowls. A can of Campbell's tomato soup sat on the counter.

"Tired of cooking meals?" she asked.

He shook his head. "You go out every day, eat lunch in restaurants. You can't understand how cooped up I feel."

"You don't have to stay in the apartment. Check out the library. Go find a job."

"I did go to the library. They told me the Garland Café on

Main Street has entertainment on Friday nights. Tonight it's a jazz band with a singer. It's right downtown in Garland. I can walk there from here."

"That's six blocks, and you shouldn't go out alone at night."

"But you could come along."

"This may not be a big city like Dallas, but that's too public. There must be something good on TV."

He frowned. "There's not." He stood and did a few jumping jacks, his motions smooth. Dropping to the floor, he did pushups, his tanned biceps reminding her of when he lifted her down from the counter and slid her against his heart-stopping body.

After finishing ten pushups, he sat beside her on the couch. He wasn't even breathing heavy. "I need to get out. Watching TV all week will turn me into a fat sloppy couch potato with mush for brains."

If only he were fat and sloppy, she wouldn't have trouble resisting him.

He took her hand. "If you come with me, and we take the car, I'll be safe with my warrior princess. Even an amateur gunman wouldn't be stupid enough to shoot with a lot of witnesses around. How about it?"

He took her hand, his eyes pleading with her.

She swallowed. "Guess that would be okay."

He grinned. "They start at eight. It's seven now. I'll have soup ready in a snap."

After eating, she adjusted her shoulder holster, shrugged into a blazer to conceal it, and then checked her wallet for her badge. She made him wait inside while she checked the quiet street for suspicious persons, then waved for him to join her. He insisted on driving, but handed her the keys after parking the car on a side street near the corner eatery.

Inside the Garland Cafe they walked across a tiled floor past little tables and chairs with curving iron rim backs. He spoke to the teenage girl at the counter and gave her some money. Waving at a long table covered with a white tablecloth, he said, "The admission price includes coffee and dessert."

She helped herself to coffee and chocolate cake. She tried to ignore the pain as she followed him through a doorway into a large room with polished hardwood floors. Seeing no sign of the promised musicians, she halted.

He grasped her hand pointed to another doorway. "This way."

His hand felt strong, but gentle and warm. Hers were cold—she'd pull away in a moment. He led her inside a room with a stage where a young man with a guitar and another with a base guitar were warming up. An older man with a well-trimmed salt and pepper beard and a slouch type cap ran his fingers over a double-decker keyboard.

Brent pointed to the stage. "From the size and amount of equipment, I'd say they're experienced."

Sitting close to Brent in a folding chair, Sheila wasn't surprised when he put his arm around her shoulders. She was going to shrug away, but then the band leader stood before the mike and the small crowd quieted. For now, she leaned back against his arm, enjoying the warmth and the closeness.

The jazz was good, and the girl singer, Diane they said her name was, sang in sultry tones, her red dress swaying in time with the music. When the show was over, Sheila realized she'd let his arm stay around her shoulders the whole time. Feeling heat rise to her face, she stood quickly and whispered, "We need to walk out with the crowd. It's safer that way."

He grasped her hand. "I'm getting used to this cloak and dagger stuff," he whispered, "but it's murder staying in those four walls all day. This has been the only bright spot in the whole week."

She knew he'd enjoyed the music. Perhaps he'd put his arm around her from force of habit. After all, this was like a date. As the group surged into the part of the cafe with large windows facing the corner, Brent stopped to look at books displayed for sale. "Must be a local author." He picked up one and started reading.

She grabbed his arm, felt the firm muscles beneath his shirt. "Come on. We're exposed here. She pulled at his arm and took a step toward a side door leading to the street.

He yanked it loose and glared at her. "I'm not your prize bull to be led around." He strode toward the side door and held it open for her.

The front door opened, and Sheila turned. Two men, one larger than the other, with black, knitted ski masks marched in. The bigger one held a gun. Exiting concertgoers backed away into the hallway.

Sheila shoved Brent out the side door. "Run to the car." Ignoring the pain in her leg, she raced after him. She slid behind the wheel. Yelled at Brent to shut his door. Gunning the motor, she backed out. She grimaced when her foot hit the brake hard.

She glanced back toward the restaurant. The two men were gesturing at the teenage girl behind the counter and an older stout man, probably the manager. She heard shouting, but couldn't make out the words.

She burned rubber getting away. She shoved her cell phone toward Brent. "Call 9-1-1. Don't give your name."

Speeding down a one-way street, she headed for Garland Road. "Better not be traffic at the next light."

Of course the one at Garland Road was red.

She almost made it. A dark car careened around the corner behind them.

No time to wait for the light. She turned right, zoomed down the next street. The police station was too far away. Better lose them on city streets.

Brent grabbed her cell phone. "I'm calling the police, but the damn line's busy."

She turned another corner. This street was too wide. Another turn brought them to a quieter street. Seeing an open garage, she glanced behind. Not seeing their pursuers, she pulled inside and turned off the lights.

He opened the car door. "Of all the dumb stunts. We'll be trapped here."

"Not if they don't notice us. Shut the door so the light will go out."

The slam reverberated in the quiet neighborhood.

Sheila scowled. "Talk about dumb stunts. I said going out in public tonight was a bad idea. Shouldn't have let you talk me into it."

A light came on in the garage. A man with a German shepherd on a leash burst out the back door. "Who the hell do you think you are, pulling into my garage like that?" The dog growled and bared its teeth.

"There's somebody after us, but I'm sure you don't want a shootout in your neighborhood. Act like you know us, and they'll drive on by."

The man pointed a finger at her. "You running from the cops?"

She shook her head. "Hell, no. I'm a U.S. Marshal, but someone's trying to kill my friend here."

He scowled. "I don't believe you."

Sheila grabbed her purse and whipped out her badge.

The man stared at it. "I don't care who you are, but I don't want any trouble. Get out or I'll call the police."

"Wish you would. We could use some backup."

The man shook his head. "Get your damn car out of my garage. My wife will be home any minute, and I don't want any trouble. Leave. Now."

A black car was barreling down the street.

She pointed to the car. "Just wait until they're gone."

The man watched. Sheila heard Brent's quick intake of breath.

In the glare of the streetlights, patches of white skin showed through the holes of the nearest man's ski mask. He appeared to be scanning the area. Her heart thumped, and then escalated to a staccato beat.

She held her gun ready. Either the car would pass—or they'd be caught. She wasn't ready to die, nor did she want Brent to get shot.

The dog growled.

"Don't let him bark," Sheila commanded.

His owner glared at her, but pulled the leash tighter. "Quiet, Bull."

The car passed. Sheila let out her breath and laid her gun on the dash. She limped to the open doorway of the garage. The car had reached the next intersection—too far to read the license plate. She felt Brent's body behind her as he patted her shoulder. She frowned. "You should have stayed in the car."

"They're moving away. We can leave soon," he said.

"Wait. Let's be sure."

She watched the car slow. "They're going to turn the corner." She let out her breath.

Then the car turned around and headed back toward them.

Pulse racing, Sheila shoved Brent behind her and reached for her gun.

Chapter 12

Shoving Brent behind her, Sheila backed into the shadows of the garage. Outside a rabbit hopped from behind a bush. The dog broke loose from owner of the house and ran after the rabbit, its leash snaking a path through the grass. The man started to go after it.

"Don't go out there," Sheila said. "Those men may be dangerous."

"I won't," the man snapped, then whistled for the dog. It kept chasing the rabbit. "Come back, Bull," the man ordered. The rabbit squeezed under a chain link fence into the next yard and hopped away. The German shepherd halted, barking furiously as its prey disappeared behind a shrub. Finally Bull trotted back into the garage where the man grabbed his collar, then picked up the trailing leash. The dog growled at Brent, but the man pulled him back.

Sheila watched the car, now seeing it was a Viper, creep back down the street. She tried to read the license plate, but it was too dark to see it clearly. Finally, the car made a U-turn and moved on down the street. She let out her breath, and thanked the man for shielding them. Brent insisted on driving so she could rest her leg before making the hard climb up the stairs to his apartment.

All that weekend Sheila insisted they stay inside. They ordered groceries online. Even though he didn't try to put his arm around her while she slept, she knew when his body touched hers in the night, imparting a welcome warmth.

She couldn't stand spending one more night next to him, so Saturday morning she went to the nearest Wal-Mart and bought a sleeping bag.

That afternoon and most of Sunday she played endless games of chess with Brent. He waited patiently as she pondered her moves. Though he was an able player and seemed to enjoy beating her more than half the time, he seemed restless.

Pleased he didn't let her win, she did manage to win a few times even though it was hard to concentrate when he smiled at her. And his suggestion they bet a kiss on the outcome of a game didn't help either. She caught herself licking her lips and shook her head. "Look, I'm only here to keep an eye on you and until my foot gets better. We have to keep this on a professional basis."

After losing another game, she said, "I'm glad my leg's getting better. Sorry you've had to put up with a lousy chess player for so long."

"No problem. I've enjoyed your company and playing chess with you."

"After I get back to my place, I don't want to see another chess piece for months."

By Monday her leg had improved considerably. She was glad to go back to working full days and relieved she wouldn't have to resist his inviting smiles all day.

As she combed her hair, ready to walk out the door, Brent asked, "You aren't going to drive yourself today are you?"

She nodded. "I'm tired of depending on taxis, and I don't want you wandering all over town while I'm gone."

He shrugged. "How can I if you take the car?"

She shook a finger at him. "You can't, and don't jog either unless you join a gym."

He scowled. "You're treating me like a child again."

"Look, we've had one close call. You can watch television or play solitaire, but stay here. If nothing more happens next week, it may be safe to look for a job. And I want to screen any offers you get."

"I'll stay here, but I won't like it."

&

He kept thinking about his brother's charcoal Viper as he walked to his own pickup. Ever since riding in Dirk's pride and joy, he'd ached to get his hands on the wheel of one of these. Man, would he like to get his hands on all that power, feel the car charge forth at his command, like a racehorse at the sound of the starting gun.

Still, even with all those horses beneath the hood, they'd lost that Marshal bitch and her witness Friday night. He wished he dared drive it again, but with his record, it was too risky. Besides if he hit Sheldon up for more dough for this job, he could afford to buy one. Sheldon hadn't been sure how much that troublesome witness knew and had offered to pay him to take care of both the stupid blonde Marshal and her witness.

He'd negotiated twenty for each and five thousand in advance in case there were expenses before the job was finished. As soon as he collected, he'd put a down payment on a Viper. He couldn't wait until he could grip the steering wheel with all that horsepower at his command. First he had to take care of business. He had to surprise his prey for his plan to work.

He patted the receiver for the tracking device lying on the dash of his truck. Hadn't been so easy to hide the device, but he wanted to be sure they didn't find it this time. He'd barely been able to get his big frame under her car this morning to place it behind the muffler. Some security guard at the federal parking garage had asked him what he was doing, but seemed to accept his excuse that about looking for a hole in the muffler.

He'd barely finished when he saw her walk into the parking garage. He stepped over to another car and stood on the driver's side as if he were about to unlock the door, but he kept his eyes on her.

She was frowning as she zipped past him on the way out of the parking lot. He raced for his black pickup truck parked on the street. He'd gotten that tracking device installed just in time.

He slid behind the wheel and stepped on the gas, wishing he had a bunch of horses at his command like Dirk's Viper. If he had one of those babies, then his quarry would only notice a great car behind her. But since she'd moved the witness, he had to follow her and let her lead him to the witness.

Catching up with her blue Mustang, he stayed a discreet distance behind. If luck were with him, she'd head for the place where she'd stashed her witness. He followed her onto the freeway. With little traffic, it was tougher to be less noticeable. He passed her once, just to throw her off track, then moved to another lane and let her get ahead of him.

Tuesday morning, when she reached her desk, she realized she'd accidentally left Brent's file at his apartment. She called him to see if she'd left it on an end table, but no one answered. Maybe he had gone back to bed or was taking a shower. Half an hour later he didn't answer either. She told Alice, the receptionist that she had an errand to run. She didn't want Brent reading some unflattering notes she'd made on him.

Glad the rush hour traffic had subsided, Sheila got out of the car and climbed the steps to his apartment. On the landing she rubbed her aching leg. Inserting the key in the door, she almost wished he'd greet her at the door with a kiss. But they'd settled that. She was only his protector and only until the trial. She wished it were otherwise.

After unlocking the door, she opened it to an empty room. Looking longingly at the couch, she wished she could just plop down and rest. Her tote bag with his file lay on an end table. She snatched it up. "Brent," she called, her heart in her throat. Had Sheldon's goons found him and carried him off? Worse yet, would she find a body in the bathroom or the alley?

It took only minutes to search. She saw no signs of a struggle. What had happened?

She sank into a chair, debating her next step. She needed coffee. A Post-it note hung on the jar of instant coffee. He must have remembered she usually made a cup as soon as she got back at night.

The handwriting didn't look hurried or forced. She read it twice to be sure she didn't miss anything.

It said, "I'm tired of being bored and tired of being dependent on you. I'm leaving. Call my cell phone if you want to know more."

"Damn," she muttered. "Why couldn't he wait 'til I got back and tell me in person."

Holding her breath, she dialed his number, hoping the note didn't mean he was being held by Sheldon's men.

It rang and rang. Finally, a recorded message came on. "Wanted to fix a nice dinner for you, but there was no food in the cupboard. Took a taxi to the nearest supermarket. Standing at the checkout counter, I saw Dirk Dobson through the window. Could have handled him but not the big bruiser beside him. Dropped the groceries on the counter, headed for the back of the store, and ran into the alley and down the next block. Won't take long for them to find this place. I'm not putting you or myself in danger anymore.

The message continued. "When it's time for the trial, call me, and I'll fly back. Until then, I'll enjoy good surf."

She listened to it again, but that's all there was. She had only his promise that he'd return. After checking the bureau and the closet, she saw he'd taken most of his clothes with him, but left his winter jacket.

She pounded the table. It hurt that he didn't trust her to keep him safe. It was small comfort to know he was concerned for her safety, but why hadn't he said where he was going?

The answer was clear. Sheldon's men might have found the note before she had. 'Good surf,' he'd said. Probably not Galveston, but that could mean Florida or California or Hawaii. She checked the yellow pages, found ten cab companies with offices nearby. With the ninth one she struck paydirt. A man of Brent's description had been taken to DFW Airport. She frowned. For a short flight, he'd have gone to Love Field in Dallas.

Didn't he think she could find him? She had to before Dirk Dobson and his "persuader" did. Her stomach knotted at the thought of them torturing Brent. Calling the airlines didn't net much luck. She'd have to go and ask questions of each airline. Glad she'd taken his file, she copied down the address of his timeshare and hurried down the steps as best she could with her aching leg.

About to get in her car, she remembered she'd invited Rodney over for supper. On the way to the airport, she called, offered him a rain check, and told him she was heading for the airport because she had to leave town in a hurry. Raising a teenage boy to maturity had been hard, but she'd tried to give him all the love and guidance she could to make up for his losing their parents.

He'd been hitting Rodney up for another payment when the phone call came from Sheila. Rodney had looked at him kind of funny, so he'd pretended not to be paying attention to the conversation, but it sounded as if she was in a hurry to go somewhere. He wondered if that had to do with the witness he wanted to take care of. After Rodney hung up, he'd managed to wrangle the witness's new name from Rodney in exchange for waiting another week for the money Rodney owed.

Now he pounded the dash of his truck. After waiting just past the tollway exit to LBJ Freeway for her to pass, he picked up her trail despite the heavy traffic. Since he knew where she was headed, if she got too far ahead, he'd catch up with her again.

He stayed far enough from her Mustang so she wouldn't notice him. She must have settled her witness somewhere in Garland or Mesquite, judging from where she'd gone before now. The turn-off for the airport was next. Dang if she didn't take it, but he couldn't see a passenger in the car. Was she picking up a new witness, or was she going to meet her current one? Somehow, he'd have to find out before making any moves.

After parking his truck, he followed her on foot at a safe distance. Carrying a briefcase with his equipment inside between the folds of a newspaper, he entered the concourse, glad his wallet held enough to buy a ticket to wherever she was going.

⚘

By the time Sheila parked at DFW Airport and made her way to one of the American Airlines terminals, she was breathing heavily. Her leg hurt so much she could hardly think. After popping a painkiller, she showed the attendant at the counter her badge and held out Brent's picture.

The first one with a cute button nose and hair cut short in a pixie style shook her head. "He's a hunk. I'd remember him in a heartbeat."

At the next desk the attendant, a rather plain looking dishwater blonde with hair skinned back into a pony tail, sighed and tugged down her snug vest. "He might not notice me, but I'd sure remember him."

She questioned attendants at other airline desks with similar results. Stuffing his picture back in her tote bag, Sheila turned and flagged down a passenger cart. When the driver looked at her with a frown on his face, she said, "My leg's injured. I need to ride to the escalator so I can take the little tram to the next terminal."

"Okay," he said and waited until she'd climbed on. He drove on, beeping his horn to warn travelers to stay out of his way.

At Continental's terminal, she showed Brent's picture again and scored a hit. Tall and slender, the smiling attendant brushed back a lock of dark hair. "I remember him. He seemed uptight, but he had the nicest smile. Should be passing over Salt Lake City by now."

"The plane—is it going to L.A. or—"

"Hawaii. Wish I were going with him."

Sheila groaned. "Damn him," she muttered and stuffed his picture back in her purse. "When's the next flight?"

"There's one leaving in two hours. Want me to put you on standby?"

Sheila nodded and whipped out her agency credit card. After a few strokes on the keyboard, the attendant said, "We'll call you."

No time to drive back for her things. She could buy what she needed in Hawaii.

Standing near the window, she called the office to say she wouldn't be in tomorrow. A plane took off outside. She had to ask Alice to repeat what she'd said.

"Are you sick?" asked Alice.

"No. My witness lost his head and bolted. May take me a few days to catch up with him."

A voice announcing her flight sounded over the loud speaker. Sheila clapped her hand over the mouthpiece.

"Are you at the airport?" Alice asked.

"This connection's bad. I'll have to call you back and tell you how many days I'll be out of contact." She hung up.

There'd be hell to pay when she returned, but if she didn't hear anyone tell her not to go, she wouldn't be disobeying orders. She'd be damned if she let Brent get away without making an effort to bring him back. She wanted him where she could keep an eye on him—to see him and touch him, said a little voice in her head—one she ignored. His safety was important now.

When her phone jingled, she ignored the ringing and waited until the caller left a message. It was Alice, asking again where she was going. She shut her phone off.

She stepped over to the ticket counter and showed her badge, explaining she was on official business and taking a gun on board. They hassled her about her gun but let her take it after she filled out some forms. A ticket agent led her to the crew lounge and introduced her to the pilot. She had to tell who she was, show him her badge and the Glock, and then explain why she was taking a gun to Hawaii.

෴

Glad he'd picked up her trail without much trouble, he'd followed her from one airline ticket counter to another, careful to stay in the background. At the last place he overheard her say, "I want the next flight out to Honolulu."

The ticket attendant had told her, "The next one leaves in two hours. Buy your ticket now, and check back in half an hour."

That must have been a picture of the witness she'd showed at the ticket counter. The attendant had pointed to it and nodded. Sheila wouldn't just abandon her witness. He must have taken off, and she was going after him. That was the only explanation that made sense.

Sheila fidgeted as the attendant worked at the computer. She wasn't bad looking. What if he walked up to her and started a conversation? He'd ask if this were a vacation or business and where she was going. Not smart—she could identify him later, and for all he knew, she'd seen a picture of Dirk. His half-brother was more slightly built, but that wouldn't be obvious in a mug shot.

He needed to get on that flight. Keeping his back toward her, he argued with the Continental ticket attendant for several minutes. She finally took his money for a standby ticket, but insisted his chances of getting on the flight he wanted were slim.

Sitting where he could keep an eye on Sheila Talbot and the ticket attendant, he pulled a form from his pocket. That should let him take his equipment onto the plane. However, they hadn't required him to show the paper. He thanked his lucky stars his equipment had only a tiny piece of metal, which hadn't registered on the metal detector he'd gone through.

When he finally got a boarding pass, it was for a seat far in the back. She wouldn't be likely to notice him even though he resembled his half-brother. Careful to turn his face away when they called his group, he boarded the plane and quickly took his seat in the back.

❧

After finally boarding the plane, Sheila fastened her seat belt and leaned back. One of the passengers seated farther back reminded her of the picture she'd seen of Dirk Dobson. A second look convinced her he wasn't.

Why had Brent left in such a hurry? Sure, he'd complained about being cooped up, but that shouldn't be enough make him leave town. He hadn't seemed paranoid when they'd been chased Friday night.

And just seeing Dirk Dobson at the Supermart shouldn't be enough either. After all, Brent had gotten away. And he wasn't trying to get her to follow him. He'd promised to be back for the trial, but she couldn't be sure he would. And what if Dirk

Dobson or Sheldon's men found Brent before then? She had to find him first.

Then it struck her. Grandma would worry if she couldn't get in touch with her for several days. Thank goodness, they hadn't said to turn off cell phones yet. She dialed the number.

After talking to her grandmother, Sheila leaned back in the seat and glanced out the window. Hoping Rodney would stay out of trouble while she was gone, she watched as the plane took off. Sunsets looked different from the air.

She'd always wanted to visit Hawaii, but in her wildest dreams she hadn't imagined it like this. Instead of lying on a romantic beach with a husband or a boyfriend and sipping something cool, she'd be sweating while she hunted for her witness. Lying on the sand with Brent's smile hinting he liked the way she looked in a bathing suit would be nice, but....

It rankled that he hadn't trusted her to protect him. The hours dragged on the long flight, but by the time she rushed through the Honolulu airport, felt the warm breeze wafting over the pink hibiscus and palm fronds visible through the wide glassless windows, she was glad to be here. If only it were on vacation, not hunting down a witness—one she enjoyed being with more than she should.

She wouldn't tell him that. His ego was big enough. Instead she'd give him an earful about endangering his life and wasting government money—except they probably wouldn't reimburse her. Thank goodness her next paycheck would cover the credit card bill when it came due.

In the crowded airport, colorful shirts and tote bags vied with thong sandals with flowers painted on the bottom, begging her to stop and shop. She didn't have time. She marched outside, hailed a taxi, and gave the driver the address for Brent's ex-wife's condo.

The driver of the taxi Sheila hailed wore a yellow shirt, emblazoned with palms and a sandy beach. A tall, hefty prospective passenger shook a fist in their direction. The cab driver zoomed off, making her wonder if the driver were a frustrated race car driver. Thanking her good fortune she'd nabbed the last cab available, she felt relieved to see no one followed them.

❦

Seeing others staring at him, Nate let his arm drop to his side. Why the hell weren't there more cabs hanging around? He'd like to call the chamber of commerce and give them a piece of his mind. He looked down the street to see if another were coming. Nothing. He felt like slamming his briefcase against the light post, but that would only damage his equipment.

Keeping a watch for another cab, he pulled a notebook from his pocket, wrote down the name of the cab company, and then found the name for the contact he'd gotten from Sheldon.

He dialed the number on his cell phone. When the guy said, "Hello," Nate explained what he needed. A bus labeled Hilo Hattie's stopped by, and several passengers got on, suitcases and all. He paced back and forth. Finally a cab came. Scowling, he muscled his way past others waiting and commandeered it. Of course by now, the cab Sheila had taken was long gone. He barked out the address of his contact and dialed directory assistance for the number of the other cab company. It might take a few days, but before he left the islands, that miserable Marshal and her weasel witness would be history.

❦

Sheila's cab driver slowed while passing a stately two-story building, its entrance guarded by thick square pillars with stone balls on top. "That's the governor's palace where the legislature meets." He drove by a larger than life statue adorned with a stone cape and gilded with gold. "That's a statue of King Kamehameha the first." He slowed as they passed a park and pointed toward the undulating blue-green ocean, waves crested with surfers and sand dotted with sunbathers. "There's Waikiki beach."

A fragrant scent greeted her, reminding her of magnolia blooms, no doubt coming from the white flowers on a nearby tree. Spread out, they resembled dogwood blossoms, but they were much larger. "What kind of tree is that?"

"It's plumeria. They use it a lot for fresh leis." He drove past hanging baskets of orange and pink flowers, and then stopped in front of a high-rise building. "Here's where you wanted to go."

After paying him, she stepped out and craned her neck. She could barely see past the trees and hibiscus bushes to the ocean, but she bet any condo above the second floor had a great view. Inside the building she strode through a spacious lobby decorated with tropical greenery and pushed the elevator button.

A tap on her shoulder gave her a start. She turned to see a uniformed security guard. He asked politely who she'd come to visit. She showed him her badge and told him she needed to speak with a resident. The elevator doors opened. Not wanting to answer any more questions, she stepped inside and jabbed the button for the sixth floor.

When she emerged from the elevator, the hallway seemed like any other, except for the bamboo framed mirror and a print of one of Gauguin's flamboyant paintings of native women in grass skirts beneath palm trees.

After checking the number, she knocked on the door. No answer. She'd been so sure this was where he'd go. She knocked again and waited.

Finally she heard a muffled, "Who's there?" It sounded like Brent, but she couldn't be sure. She'd feel like all kinds of fool if she interrupted his ex-wife in a tryst with a lover. Or maybe Brent was here with another woman instead. She swallowed. That thought unsettled her even more.

"Brent, is that you?" she called. No one answered. Hearing footsteps, she rehearsed what to say and finally decided to claim she had the wrong address.

Inside the room, Brent could hardly believe his ears. He'd been lounging on the flowered cushions of a white wicker couch, wearing a Hawaiian shirt. He'd left to avoid Dirk Dobson's relentless pursuit. Brent hated to keep looking over his shoulder, but more important, he'd worried even more about the danger to Sheila. He'd never dreamed she'd come after him.

It was bad enough he had to rely on her to keep himself safe. He hadn't wanted to put her in jeopardy, but here she was.

He yanked the door open. She looked wonderful, but her blue eyes were full of questions and a vulnerability he hadn't expected. "Why did you come?" he asked. Grasping her hand, he pulled her inside and hugged her. "I didn't want you to follow me, but it sure is good to see you again."

If she could find him, so could Dirk or someone else he wouldn't recognize as a threat until too late. He didn't want his brave warrior princess being shot and in pain or worse yet, dying to keep him safe.

She broke away and shut the door. "Why did you leave my protection, and why come here?"

His chin jutted forward. "I thought I'd made it plain. I don't want to cause you any more trouble." He rubbed the back of his neck. "I promised I'd come back for the trial. Didn't you believe me?"

He yanked the door open, then stuck his head out and looked both ways. After shutting the door again, he faced her. "Every time you show up, trouble follows. Some Marshal you are, to let yourself be followed."

She scowled. "What do you are you talking about?"

He held up his hand. "First you got shot at on Thanksgiving."

"How was I to know someone had put a tracer on my car?"

"You should have expected something like that and checked for one. Then you wouldn't have gotten grazed by a bullet. And what about the man who put a bullet in your leg when I came to pick you up at the office?"

"He was shooting at me, not you."

"He shot at me first. He probably would have tried again if you hadn't winged him. And don't forget about my apartment being trashed."

"That could have been a random burglary."

"Maybe, but I don't think so."

"So, no one has found your new apartment, and the time you talked me into going to the music program in Garland — well, we shouldn't have gone to such a public place. This time I checked carefully to be sure no one followed me. I took the last cab available, and nothing came right after me but a tour bus."

Sheila caught her breath and tried not to think about how wonderful he looked. His crisp red shirt, sporting men in an outrigger canoe silhouetted against the sunset, emphasized his golden tan. He might have strolled on the beach in plain sight for some marksman to pick him off. Her heart lurched at the thought. But no one had followed her. They'd be safe here.

She stepped closer and jabbed a finger against his broad chest. "You had no business running off like this. What the hell were you thinking? It's my job to keep you safe. Hasn't anything that's happened convinced you this is serious?"

"I didn't think anyone could find me this fast. Figured it would take Dobson at least a week to discover my whereabouts, and by then I'd have moved on."

"If I can find you this easily, Dirk Dobson or Bart Sheldon's men can too." Realizing her finger was still touching him, Sheila let it drop and squelched an insane urge to run her hands over his chest.

"Pack your things," she said in her most authoritative tones. "I'll call the airline. We can fly out tonight."

"You said you didn't think anyone followed you. This is registered in my ex-wife's name, not mine. They won't find me here without looking for a few days. Stay a day or two." He took her hand. "I could really show you a good time." His grin tugged at her, promised things she dare not think about. "You haven't lived until you've experienced a luau or strolled the beach at sunset. And I bet you look fantastic in a bikini."

The look in his eyes drew her, said he found her desirable. She took a deep breath. It was all she could do to resist his magnetic attraction. Straightening, she shook off his hand and stepped back. "It's only a matter of time until someone finds you here."

His expression sobered. "You knew where to look. It should take at least a couple of days before anyone else does. At least step out on my balcony. He grasped both her hands. Lifting first one and then the other to his lips, he pressed a kiss in each palm, then tugged her toward the glass door.

Pulling at her hands, she shook her head. "A good marksman could pick us off with two shots."

He didn't let go. "All right, then stand in the doorway. You have to see the view to believe it."

She let him lead her to the glass doors. Just as he'd said, the view was fabulous. She could even make out Diamond Head beyond the last luxury hotel to the left. And on the right a sailboat rode the waves. Faint strains of "Sweet Leilani" came from someone playing a ukulele.

The same scent that intrigued her earlier wafted up. "Is there one of those plumeria trees down below?"

He nodded. "They were brought here from South America where they call them frangipani. The women used to rub the petals all over the bodies of brides before the wedding. Bet it drove the new husbands wild. Want to try it? See if that's true?"

She shook her head, trying not to imagine what it would feel like to have his hands rubbing petals on her bare body, his lips kissing her neck and shoulders…and more intimate places. She took a deep breath. Mustn't think of things like that.

He placed his hand over hers. "I'm starved. How about an early dinner? I'll order Chinese. We can sit near the window and watch the sunset together. Then if you insist, you can call the airlines. You probably can't get a flight out for a few days anyway."

"I guess we'd be safe inside for a day or two, but you can't stay here. We can reserve rooms at a hotel for tonight and fly back tomorrow." With two rooms she wouldn't be tempted to melt into his arms, but here….

He caressed her hand. He looked at her as if she were Venus herself, making her feel all goose-bumpily and warm inside.

He led her toward the phone without letting go of her hand. His sensual touch unnerved her so, she could hardly pull away, but she had to. Standing a few steps away, she listened to his deep velvet voice as he ordered food. After hanging up, he said, "That's a café downstairs. They have great food."

When the food arrived, she told him to stay in the bedroom. She opened the door with the chain still on to be sure it was okay. The Asian delivery boy was tapping his foot and holding out a large bag. After undoing the chain, she took the bag, handed him money, and said, "Keep the change."

She shut the door behind him, set the package with its mouth-watering aromas on a table against the wall, and refastened the chain.

Turning back to pick up the food, she bumped into a firm body and inhaled his tantalizing aftershave. He now smelled of sandalwood.

His lips brushed the back of her neck. "That food smells good. I don't know whether I'd rather have that or you." He gently nibbled her ear, leaving no doubt which he'd prefer.

Her stomach rumbled, reminding her that sometimes her body knew what was best. But after this hunger was satisfied, she'd let her head, not her body rule—because if she didn't….

Her throat tightened. "We can move the table near the open door to the balcony. I don't think anyone could see us well enough to shoot from the street."

He moved a small table near the window door, and then got long-stemmed glasses and a bottle of sparkling white grape juice from the tiny kitchenette. Later, as they tried to eat with the chopsticks, Sheila laughed as he reached over to wipe a sliver of bean sprout off her chin.

His face was disturbingly close. His lips met hers, soft and inviting. She should break away, but his mouth felt so good on hers. His hands, warm and comforting, grasped her arms. The look in his brown eyes enthralled her. She couldn't move away if her life depended on it. Thank goodness the table prevented him from moving any closer.

He smiled. "I didn't really think you'd come after me, but it's so good to see you, to touch you. It was so quiet and lonely here. I didn't realize how much I'd miss seeing your face, and hearing you laugh."

His words touched an empty place deep within, filling and warming her. She wanted to shove the table away and melt into his arms. But she couldn't—shouldn't.

He leaned back in the chair and took a deep breath of the salty ocean breeze. "Now this is the life."

"I know you worked in a bank and kept strict hours. Don't you miss the routine?"

Smiling, he shook his head. "You should try being laid back sometime. You might like it."

'Laid back,' he'd said. She searched his expression for a telltale smirk, but saw none. "I don't know. It takes a lot to get ahead in my job. Maybe after I get established there, I could."

But after he testified, and she got him set up in another town, perhaps with a different identity, she wouldn't be seeing him again. He was warm and personable. He'd be okay, probably have a girlfriend in no time.

She squeezed her eyes shut for an instant. Her heart would be empty inside, but she'd handle it, wouldn't she? Besides, now was the time to concentrate on her career. Her next witness would probably be a bum or an informer, someone who didn't appeal to her. And no one else would stir her senses quite the way Brent Broussard did now. Maybe no man ever would again.

Perhaps after a year, when she felt more secure in her job, she could think about having a life. Until then she'd stick with archery and karate.

Brent's hands grasped hers. "You seem awfully quiet. What are you thinking of?"

The look in his eyes challenged her. "I'll miss taking care of you when this is over, but right now you need to get back to the mainland where I can keep an eye on you."

Letting go of her hand, he frowned. "And get us both shot at?"

"Not if we're careful. No one's found your new apartment. It should be safe there if I don't visit you."

He grinned. "You mean you'll only act like my nursemaid over the phone?"

She laughed. "I can see you as a little boy. If you had a nanny, she'd probably have to chase after you all the time."

He grinned. "I didn't need one. My bossy sister wouldn't let me out of her sight. That's when I took up jogging, so I could run away from her. And it got worse when she got older. She pestered me to date her girlfriends."

"And did you?"

He laughed. "The one time I did, it was a disaster. I was so conscious of what I said, for fear of the girl repeating it to her, that I could hardly think of anything to say. My sister never asked me again, thank goodness."

He leaned back in his chair. "Between her and Mom, I had my fill of manipulative and bossy women."

Sheila rose. "I see why you don't take orders well." She

pulled out her cell phone. "Would you bring me a phone book please?"

He plunked one on the table beside her plate. "At least you say please—once in a while."

She thumbed through the yellow pages until she found Airlines. "I can't always say 'please.' By the time I'd say 'would you please duck down so you won't be a target,' you'd be shot and wounded—or dead."

"Right, but a 'please' now and then wouldn't hurt."

"I don't want you thinking you can choose not to do something necessary for your safety. Right now flying back to the mainland is."

He took her hand again, enveloping it in warmth, making her wonder why she felt safe when she was supposed to be protecting him.

After pulling the phone book from her hand, he kissed her fingertips, one by one. "Couldn't we stay a few more days? You said you were sure no one followed you. Haven't you always wanted to see Hawaii?"

She pulled her hand away. "I'd love to, but we need to get back." She reached for the phone book. "I should have called them right away."

"Did the government pay your way here?"

"I used my federal credit card. They'll probably ask me to reimburse them…since I didn't ask permission. I just left. I was afraid Dobson might find you before I did."

He smiled, his face lighting up like morning. "Nice to have someone besides family worry about me, but let me show you a bit of Hawaii first."

She looked longingly out the window at the azure waters. "Not Waikiki Beach. Too easy for someone to shoot you or me."

A shudder rippled over him, then was gone. "I doubt someone would dare with all those people."

She dialed a number and got the reservations desk. "What do you mean we can't get reservations for at least a week?"

"We're all booked up. Would you like to fly the following week?" Sheila hesitated while trying to discourage Brent, who was caressing her shoulder. Finally she said, "I'll call back later."

She hung up the phone. "Brent," she said, annoyed at the breathless way she sounded. "You've got to stop that. I need to think of what to do next."

He grinned. "You mean I actually can make it hard for Miss No Nonsense to concentrate."

She dialed another airline, gently pulling her hand from his while the phone rang and rang. "Do I seem as bad as all that?"

"You must think it's a sin to enjoy yourself."

"That's not true. I enjoy my job. It's full of challenges."

"I hear Six Flags Over Texas Park is near Dallas. Do you ever go there?"

She nodded. Another airline reservationist came on the line. They had no seats available until the following week either. She hung up, and then tried another, finally making reservations for three days later.

"Sheila, when was the last time you went dancing?"

"Think I went with a date once, but he wasn't a good dancer."

"We could dance right here." He rose, put a disc in a CD player, and pushed a button. Strains of something peppy emerged. Taking her hand, he pulled her up. With music like that, it wouldn't hurt to dance with him — just once wouldn't hurt.

She enjoyed meeting his smiling eyes with grins of her own as they kept up with the fast tune. "Blue Tango" was next. He dipped and turned in perfect timing, his hand on her back, guiding her so smoothly she almost forget she was only going to do one dance.

The tempo changed to something lyrical and dreamy. Hearing "Smoke Gets in Your Eyes" she swallowed. If she weren't careful, she'd be overcome by his smoky brown eyes and mesmerizing gaze, to say nothing of the way his hard body felt against hers, the way he made her want to move even closer. He dropped her hand, grasped her waist with both hands and pulled her tight against the length of him, never missing a beat.

His cheek touched hers, warm and slightly rough. Her breasts, squeezed against his firm chest, tingled and swelled. She could feel the tips harden in response. She felt safe and cozy in his arms while they moved as one for the rest of the number.

When the music ended, he beamed with that warm smile of his and just stood there, looking at her expectantly. His slumberous brown eyes held her spellbound. It was time to move away, but she couldn't bring herself to.

His gaze met hers, warm and tender, with a hint of something more. After a long moment, he touched her lips with his. It was a sweet kiss and over too soon. He then raised her hand to his mouth to press a kiss on her palm. "Couldn't we stay here instead of going to a hotel? The place has a good security team. I could alert them to be on the lookout. Do you really think Dobson could find me this soon?"

Chapter 13

Standing on the polished oak floor of the condo, Sheila's gaze met Brent's. "It won't take Dobson or another of Sheldon's men long to find you here. It was pretty reckless to fly under your own name."

"Didn't know what else to do. They check I.D. That's all I had."

"What did you use for money?"

"You said no credit cards. I called my sister. She put my flight on her credit card. I'll have to pay her back later."

Sheila groaned. "Now you really will need to get a job as soon as you get back." She looked around. "We should be safe here for tonight," she said. "Is that door chain sturdy? Can we move the couch out of line from the doorway?"

"You're paranoid. Sheldon's in prison. It should take a while for him to get someone to follow me. Don't see how Dobson and his bodyguard could have followed me. We should be safe for two or three days at least. Why not enjoy the sights?"

He looked at her tote bag. "Is that all you brought?"

"Didn't take time to pack. When I found out which flight you were on, I took the next one. I wanted to bring you back before Dobson or his bodyguard found you. I brought my gun just in case."

He gestured toward the bedroom. "You can have the bed.

I'll take the couch…unless you want to share the bed." Eyes the color of coffee and a captivating smile pounded at her resolve.

Why did he have to look so damn sexy? Despite her resolve, her pulse raced. She'd give anything to be able to say yes, but she needed to stay alert—not risk his life and her job.

She took a deep breath. "Forget it," she said. "I'll sleep on the couch, with my gun. I don't need any distractions."

"Is that all I'd be—a distraction?" He sounded hurt.

"I doubt I'd even hear a scuffle in the hall if…if we…."

He took her hand, his grin wide as the Mississippi. "I'd make sure of that."

His fingers interlocked with hers. Her breath caught in her throat. She wasn't sure which she wanted more, to wipe that smug grin off his face or rush into his arms.

He leaned close, his sensuous mouth near enough to kiss. "You sure?"

Unable to trust her voice, she nodded…and hated herself for being sensible.

He let go of her hand and backed off. "I found a couple of videos here. How about 'Casablanca'?"

"Okay." She took one last look out the balcony door, then closed the glass doors and drew the drapes.

He started the VCR, then sat on the couch and patted the space beside him.

She sat at the opposite end. He scooted over and draped his arm around her shoulders, making her feel warm and comfortable. Any minute now, she expected him to pull her closer or try to kiss her, but he only held her hand.

Finally, she relaxed and became absorbed in the movie, watching Rick's delighted surprise when he saw Ilsa, feeling his frustration when he learned she'd missed their last rendezvous because her missing husband had been found alive.

On the screen Rick urged Ilsa onto the plane with her husband to fly to safety. Brent squeezed her hand. "Don't see how he could have done anything else if he really loved her."

"Would you have let her go?"

"Only if I thought that would be best for her, but it would have torn me in two. I'd remember her for the rest of my life."

So he had a touch of the romantic in him. She wondered what the woman he finally gave his heart to would be like. Did he still love his ex-wife? That shouldn't bother her, but it did. He's a witness to protect, that's all, she reminded herself.

Later, after she'd showered and wrapped up in Brent's robe, Sheila inhaled the faint scent of his aftershave lingering in the fabric. As she entered the living room, he was spreading a blanket on the couch. She put her gun beneath the pillow and wedged a chair under the doorknob. She'd be ready if someone tried to break in.

He was standing on the balcony against a backdrop of sparkling stars. She gasped. "Brent, come back inside." She rushed to the open window door, grabbed his hand and pulled him inside.

He spun around. "Are you worried you'll lose a witness?"

"Of course I am. I don't want you getting hurt."

He grasped her hands, "Can't we just be a man and a woman who find themselves drawn together?"

Here it was—out in the open again, the invitation she needed to refuse, but wanted more than anything to accept. She took a deep breath, digging way down for strength. "We shouldn't... I shouldn't." She shut the window doors and closed the draperies.

Brent took Sheila's hands and turned her to face him. He looked deep into her eyes. Despite all her bluster, she seemed to care about him. His ex-wife hadn't cared about making him happy. He wasn't ready to get in too deep with another woman. He might never be. Much as Sheila tried to deny it, she had the hots for him. That should be enough for now, but he found himself hoping there was more.

He cleared his throat. "Sheila, I'd like to kiss you all over and—" Damn, he sounded like a love-struck teenager. He swallowed. "What I mean is, as long as we're safe here...I'd like to make love to you. I know we'd be good together."

Her blue eyes seemed to melt, but was he seeing apprehension or anticipation in her expression? He pulled her into his arms and nuzzled her neck. "Can't we enjoy ourselves for a little while? Umm, your skin is so soft and kissable."

Action, that's what he needed, not words. He cradled her face in his hands and kissed her, gently at first, but then he couldn't help himself. He kissed her hard, his tongue delving deep. She met it with equal fervor. His hands slid to her shoulders, then touched her lovely soft breasts molding his robe. He kept his touch gentle, hoping she wouldn't push him away.

She leaned into his palms. Hallelujah. He gloried in the feel of them, then pushed the sides of the robe apart and pressed kisses on her bare rounded flesh. He gazed in wonder. Her breasts were as exquisite as they were soft. Her hands pushed at his T-shirt. He let her pull it off. "You're beautiful," he whispered as he took her hand and led her into the bedroom.

Sheila watched, mesmerized as he loosened the sash of the robe she wore. His hands warmed her quivering flesh, sending shivers of delight throughout.

His voice, low and seductive, murmured into her ear. "I want to touch you all over, feel your sweet bare breasts pressed against my chest."

His mouth came down on hers again, obliterating all sensible thought. And when his fingers caressed her breasts, she gave herself up to feeling. Feeling cool air brush over her chest as he slid the robe off. Feeling his warm lips kiss each pouting nipple. Feeling adored as he said, "You're beautiful."

Heart pounding, pulse quickening, Sheila unfastened his belt. With trembling fingers she reached for his zipper. As the zipper rasped, his mouth met hers, staying there while she shoved at his khakis, ruffled his hair, and rained kisses on his face and neck.

He pushed her hands away, letting his clothes drift to the carpet like falling leaves.

Beautifully naked, he stood there, all male and powerful. If she didn't know better, she'd think she'd glimpsed a touch of uncertainty. She met his gaze.

The vulnerability, if it ever was there, had vanished. In his eyes was a welcoming invitation.

She smoothed back a lock of hair from his forehead and pressed a soft kiss on his lips. She put her arms around his waist and pulled his warm, firm body to her. She loved the feel of his hard chest against her breasts. He grasped her buttocks, pulling her tight against his arousal, setting her senses sizzling.

She planted a kiss on his mouth and let her tongue delve into his mouth to twist and tangle with his. Never had she felt so alive, so exhilarated, or so reckless.

When they came up for air, he smiled. "You're as forceful in this as you are in other things." Taking her hand, he pulled her down onto the bed.

He caressed her skin as if it were made of fine velvet. She couldn't help smiling. So much attention, all for her. It felt wonderful.

His lips trailed kisses from her ear to her chin, stopping for a hungry kiss on her mouth, then continuing down to her breasts. His hands squeezed and massaged her breasts, making her catch her breath. His mouth blazed a path from her swollen nipples to her navel and kept on going. Every place he touched grew warm.

He was setting her afire. She tousled his hair and sprinkled kisses on his shoulders, hoping she could please him half as much. She gloried in the look of fascination in his eyes and the way his hands caressed her breasts, her hips, and her bottom.

He suckled one breast, then the other, until she writhed in

delight. His hands moved between her thighs, his fingers teasing and tantalizing until she throbbed with longing.

Boldly she reached for him, thrilling in the size and hardness of him as she ran a finger down his length, and then grasped him firmly. "I want you," she whispered.

He smiled. His eyes sparkled, and his face was wreathed in a seductive smile.

"Never would have guessed," he said with a confident grin as he slid inside.

Nothing wrong with his ego, she decided as he pushed further in, filling her so full she wondered how she managed to hold all of him.

They rocked together, advancing and retreating. Time seemed to stand still and yet flash by with terrifying speed—until they trembled together in a rush of passion. Tingles rippled through her, like the waters of a thundering waterfall undulating downriver, changing calmness to teeming life. As her life would be forever changed after truly knowing him.

She kissed him, and then gazed into the deep brown pools of his eyes, trying to peer beneath the surface. Was he as moved as she?

Tenderly, he brushed a lock of hair from her face and smiled. "Wow," he whispered as he rolled off her. "You're something else, Warrior Princess. I'd like an encore sometime, sometime soon."

Is that all it was to him—some great sex? Good thing she hadn't said something foolish like "I love you."

The next morning, on the other side of Honolulu, Nate forced his eyes open and surveyed his contact's cheap rented apartment. He looked at the clock. Eight. Too early for the cab company's phone to answer with anything but an automated message. His contact wasn't much use except to provide a bed and a beat up old car. If Kazuhiro had any smarts, he would have gotten a list of hotels and motels before Nate arrived. With no Yellow Pages here, he'd have to call the Chamber of Commerce.

His contact's name, Chinese or Japanese, sounded too stupid to pronounce. "Kazoo," Nate called. There was no answer. He must have left.

Nate took a shower and shaved. He didn't want to look slovenly. That might draw attention. Standing in what passed for a living room, he was buttoning a Hawaiian print shirt when Kazuhiro came back with a paper bag.

Kazuhiro set the bag on the bamboo coffee table and ran his fingers through his dark,coarse hair. "Brought us breakfast."

Suddenly ravenous, Nate opened the bag, hoping Kazoo hadn't brought Asian food. Relieved to see McDonald wrappers, he wolfed down the scrambled eggs, sausage and biscuit. Then he picked up the phone and dialed the number for the cab company of the car that had driven away with Sheila. If he found her, he'd find Brent Broussard. Finally getting a live person, he sat there, fidgeting while the dispatcher kept him on hold.

"Sorry, sir, but no one on duty remembers that lady. I still have to get in touch with the two drivers that called in sick, and there's another one that just left on vacation that might be able to tell you something. Call back at six o'clock."

Nate slammed the phone down, and then called the Chamber of Commerce to find out where to get a list of hotels with phone numbers.

❧

Sheila awakened to sunshine, the magnolia-like smell of plumeria blossoms, and coffee. Brent, freshly shaved and smiling in khaki shorts and a T-shirt that showed off his impressive chest, bore a tray with steaming mugs and a plate of doughnuts. "Morning, Warrior Princess. How about breakfast in bed before I take you sightseeing?" He set the tray down beside her.

She took a sip of raspberry flavored coffee. Damn, he looked good. No wonder she hadn't been able to resist. Heaven help her if anyone at headquarters found out.

He looked at expectantly. "I could rent a car."

"They usually want a credit card. You don't have any."

"I've got cash. If they want a credit card, we'll show them yours. Satisfied?"

She nodded. "Uh, look Brent, about last night...."

He grinned broadly. "You were terrific."

She wouldn't tell him how great she'd felt, how he'd set her spirits soaring, made her forget why she was here. He'd push for more. "I-we can't do that again."

His face came closer, his lips full and sexy. "Darn, I was hoping. How about a kiss to thank me for bringing you breakfast?"

"We'd better not."

"Mom always says, 'Faint heart never won fair lady.'" He sat on the bed beside her and took one hand in his.

Pulling it loose, she managed to spill coffee on the front of the robe she wore. "Damn, that's hot."

He jumped up, grabbed a napkin and patted the robe right over her breast, which tingled in spite of her resolve to stay aloof. She leaned over to set the cup and plate with the doughnut on the bedside table and met his lips on the way up, soft, warm, and incredibly tender.

After several long glorious seconds, it took all her willpower to pull away.

He grinned sheepishly, "Couldn't help it. You look so sexy, like you'd been romping and rolling half the night."

Now she felt sheepish and guilty as hell. "Guess we did, but we can't do it again."

"Why not? No one has to know."

"It was unprofessional of me. I'm supposed to be protecting you. I'd never even notice an intruder if...."

His grin grew broader. She hadn't meant to give herself away like that, but he knew, damn him. He hadn't said he loved her, but then neither had she. Until she knew how she stood with him, she'd pretend she hadn't been interested in more than great sex. It had been incredible. Too bad she dare not risk doing it again.

She grabbed the napkin from his warm fingers and rubbed at the damp robe. "Let me take care of this. Sorry about your robe." The damp silk fabric clung, showing every inch of the curve of her breast. Embarrassed, she pulled it loose, and then rose. "I've got to get dressed."

He grinned. "Don't. I like you better this way."

Ignoring him, she went in the bathroom and dressed in the clothes she'd worn yesterday.

Later, she returned to the table and finished her coffee and doughnut. "What have you planned for today?" Since they couldn't get a flight today, she might as well go sightseeing. But she'd insist on staying where there were crowds and watch those around her like a hawk.

He smiled. "We can visit a church built from blocks of coral, tour a four-masted, ocean-going ship, and take in a luau." After riding the elevator down, they walked out into warm sunshine past hibiscus bushes with bright yellow blooms and bird of paradise flowers. He led her to a small boutique. "You'll need a few things."

Before going in, she looked around, but saw no one acting suspicious. Inside she picked up a swimsuit and change of underwear. Brent encouraged her to buy a bright red dress with white flowers to wear to the luau that evening. "That short skirt shows off your great legs." He insisted on paying for everything in cash.

While the clerk rang up the purchases, Sheila asked, "Aren't you going to run out of cash? I didn't give you a lot."

He smiled. "Don't worry. I had my sister wire me money."

After they arranged for a car, he drove to the harbor and parked near a pier where a large cruise ship was docking. He took her hand and led her along the sidewalk to a three-foot stone wall separating the road from the ocean water. "Look down."

She did. "The water's so clear. Look at all those brightly colored fish. That yellow one with big black stripes is shaped like an angelfish, but it's much bigger. What's it called?"

He pointed to an information sign. "A Moorish Idol. The solid yellow one with the same shape is a Yellow Tang."

After entering the Hawaiian Maritime Center Museum to buy tickets, they stepped outside and walked all over the wooden plank deck of the iron ship called the Falls of Clyde.

Brent glanced at the flyer in his hand. "This was built in Scotland in 1878."

Sheila grasped a thick rope attached to the ship's bell and pulled. A resounding clang sounded.

Brent said, "Bet it sounded just like that in 1899 when this ship was the first to fly the Hawaiian flag."

Inside in the museum next to the ship, Sheila craned her neck to study the outrigger canoe hanging from the ceiling. "It's hard to imagine how those outriggers keep from turning over in rough seas." She imagined being rocked from side to side and worrying about falling out. She studied the three layers of teeth from a twelve-foot tiger shark and shuddered.

Brent grasped her hand. She tried to pull it loose gracefully, but he held on. She turned to look at him.

"I'm not going to make a move on you." Then he squeezed it and winked as if to say he didn't mean a word.

His hand felt warm and comfortable, so she let him hold hers as they strolled past exhibits of early Hawaiian life.

Later, back at Waikiki Beach near his condo, after putting on swimsuits, Sheila raced with Brent into the rolling surf. With a grin he splashed her, getting her wet all over.

Laughing, she did the same, but kept an eye out for anyone acting suspiciously.

After they'd played in the waves a while, he tugged at her hand and led her across the sand onto the grass. He backed her against a plumeria tree and kissed her.

She reveled in the feel of his mouth on hers, the strong grip of his fingers on her arms, the way he pulled her tight against him as if he wanted to keep her with him always. Her senses shimmered. Shouldn't be doing this, not with all these people here, not with Sheldon's men possibly arriving in a day or two. The fragrance of the white blossoms enveloped her, casting a spell she didn't want to break.

She couldn't bear to pull away as his sensuous lips captured hers again. Her heart danced in rhythm with the waves as his mouth roved over hers. At last he backed off with a bemused look on his face.

Could the kiss have affected him the way it had her? She swallowed and broke away to dash into the surging waters. He swam beside her until she turned to head back, then he accompanied her back to shore.

For lunch they ate succulent fried shrimp with their fingers. Afterwards sand flowed up between Sheila's toes as they walked along the beach. Warm breezes caressed her skin, bearing a whiff of fragrant plumeria blossoms and the salty tang of the ocean. Agile swimmers rode the waves on surfboards. Pleasure boats, silhouetted against an azure sky, skimmed the blue-green water beyond the swimmers.

Surely, none of Sheldon's men could be lurking about, not yet anyway, but Sheila watched warily just the same. She wouldn't feel completely safe until she had him on that plane back to the mainland.

She was looking forward to the luau tonight. She wouldn't feel as if she had really been to Hawaii unless she went, but she'd take her gun in her purse.

For the luau she wore her new red dress. Brent bought her a

lei. Lifting it to her face, she inhaled the delicate scent as the soft white flowers brushed against her nose. His arm was warm around her waist as guitars played "Blue Hawaii" and "Sweet Leilani." He eyed the dancers in grass skirts, and then said, "I'd like to see you do the hula."

"It wouldn't be the same without a grass skirt."

"You'd look great doing it even in a bathing suit, but a private showing with you wearing only a lei and the grass skirt—now, I'd really enjoy that." He grinned.

Her face grew warm. Imagining what would surely follow made her pulse speed up.

Standing with her back to him and his arms around her, she watched the dancers as the aroma of roast pork blended with the sweet smell of fresh pineapple being set on a long table.

A balding tourist pulled out his handkerchief and gently wiped the chin of his aging wife whose shaking hands betrayed her battle with Parkinson's disease. She swallowed a chunk of pineapple and smiled up at him. When the man tried to push her wheelchair closer to the table, it got stuck in the dirt.

"Let me help," Brent said and lifted the chair and the woman over the rough place.

The woman smiled. The man said, "Mahalo nui."

Brent stepped back beside Sheila. "That's Hawaiian for thanks."

As an intent guitar player rendered the strains of the "Hawaiian Wedding Song," the bald man held his wife's hand. Sheila swallowed the lump in her throat. "Sometimes I wonder if getting ahead in my chosen career will rule out any chance for a relationship like that."

"It would take an exceptional man to live with a strong woman like you."

Sheila studied him. Did that mean he wouldn't want to try?

Stepping behind her, Brent wrapped his arms around her waist. He smoothed her hair to one side and pressed a kiss to the back of her neck, making her want to snuggle even closer.

The balding man glanced at her, his blue eyes twinkling. "Honeymooners, aren't you?"

Brent kissed her bare shoulder. "How'd you guess?"

His arms tightened around her waist, making her wonder how she'd feel if that were true. At the same time, she felt like a hypocrite. Their relationship was intense, but it couldn't last.

He kissed her on the lips, and then whispered. "Be a shame to disappoint them. I can play at adoring a beautiful woman for one night at least."

'For one night at least,' he'd said. Is that all she meant to him—a night or two of pleasure? She's felt they shared something special, but maybe she'd read more into it than he. Then he turned her in his arms, and his mouth joined hers for a long, bittersweet kiss.

Held tight against him, she felt his hard chest crushing her breasts. With his firm thighs and his very evident desire straining against her, it was a good thing they were flying out at the end of the week. If they spent many more nights in his condo….

Later, pleasantly stuffed after eating succulent roast pork, mashed yams sweetened with honey, and tasting poi, which was rather bland, they strolled arm in arm to the car. "It's still warm outside. Let's leave the windows open," he said, rolling his down. She did the same.

Following a short drive through city streets, Brent drove past a fragrant plumeria tree in full bloom and cruised down the driveway into the basement garage of the building. After parking the car, he gave her a heart-stopping kiss before pulling the key from the ignition.

His hands caressed her shoulders, and the look in his eyes captivated her. He cradled her face, his hands gentle as a collector with a priceless vase.

"Sheila," he whispered, "You'd tempt the heart of a saint." He followed a light kiss on her mouth with a trail of kisses to her ear and lower. He cupped her breasts, sending waves of desire coursing through her. He pressed kisses just above the neckline of her dress, warming the tops of her breasts. He kissed her again, harder this time. She found it hard to concentrate on anything except the way he made her heart pound.

His gaze held hers as he pulled her against his broad chest. She laid her head against his chest as his fingers ruffled her hair. So close she could feel his heart beating, she became aware of her own heart throbbing in rhythm with his. She'd never felt so alive, so full of zest for living. Would it be so bad if they gave in to passion again? No one would have to know.

She blinked. She wasn't thinking straight. He was her witness. He couldn't be her lover. As appealing as that sounded, she couldn't let it happen again.

Still reeling from the way he'd kissed her and the possessive way he'd looked at her, she edged away. "Why did you park in the darkest corner? A gunman could be hiding in the shadows."

He frowned. "We haven't seen anyone threatening so far, but let's go upstairs now." He got out, walked around the front of the car. He had to back up beside a square concrete pillar to open her door.

Loving the way he smiled at her through the open car window, she stepped out.

Trying to remember all the reasons she should resist him, she leaned over to get her purse. Something sharp poked into her side.

"Say or do anything," a voice behind her said, "and Nate here will inject your snitch with poison."

She swallowed and glanced at a bigger, dark-haired man standing behind the pillar. He had something in his hand. Brent grabbed the man's wrist, and they struggled. Sheila tried to inch away from the knife.

She felt the knife go in harder. She pivoted and grabbed her attacker's knife arm. He pulled back. She used his movement to swing his arm down until the blade pressed against his leg. He recoiled, cursing. She gave him a karate chop to the neck, followed by a knee to the groin.

He bent at the middle, the knife clattering to the concrete floor. She kicked it under the car and twisted his wrist behind him. Stepping away from the car, she crooked her leg behind his. He fell, writhing in pain.

She turned her back on him and went to help Brent. His attacker wrenched an arm loose and swung. He punched Brent in the nose, and then hit him in the stomach. Brent bent double. The man called Nate held an oversized syringe poised over Brent's shoulder.

Poison, she guessed. For all she knew it might kill on contact. She gasped, shoved Brent aside. She grabbed Nate's arm and struggled to twist it behind him.

He cursed and aimed the needle at her. She pushed Nate against the post. It took all her strength. She struggled, tried to make him drop the syringe. How long could she hold him? What if he stuck the needle in Brent, and he died before she could get help?

In the blink of an eye, Nate transferred the syringe to his other hand.

She grabbed for the death-dealing arm. He swung it out of her reach.

Again she grabbed for the needle and felt a prick.

She screamed, hoping a security guard would hear.

Feeling weak, she gulped in air. Couldn't get enough. She felt as if she'd been working hard all day. It became a struggle to keep her eyes open.

Then everything went black.

Chapter 14

"Hold still," said a commanding voice.

Someone held a cloth over her nose with an irritating smell. Sheila strained her neck away and pushed at an arm. She pried her eyes open. Looked like she was lying on the concrete floor of the parking garage.

The young man leaning over her said, "Stop fighting me. I'm trying to take your pulse." He frowned. "Too fast."

"Is she going to be okay?" asked a familiar voice.

She turned her head. Finally focusing on Brent's face, she gulped in air. "The man with the knife, and the other man... where are they?"

"Over there," said Brent, pointing.

Several feet away, one uniformed cop spoke in low tones to the smaller of their two attackers, who stood there handcuffed.

The one called Nate, although handcuffed, slouched against the wall as if this were only a formality.

"Pay attention," the taller policeman barked. "I'm reading you your rights."

"Skip the frigging drill," Nate spat out. "Heard it all before."

Brent stood beside Sheila. His brown eyes looked anxious. "You all right?" he asked.

"I think so," she said, "but I feel nauseous."

Sheila blinked, tried to focus on the police and their attackers. "What's going on?"

Brent nodded toward a man in uniform. "When you screamed, that security guard rushed here with a gun. I got yours from your purse. We held those bastards at gunpoint. He called the police. When they got here, the one called Nate dashed for the stairs, but one of the cops caught him and dragged him back."

The paramedic was taking her pulse. "Can you tell me what happened to you?"

"That big guy…stuck me with a needle."

"Any idea what he gave you?"

She tried to focus, but the basement garage area seemed to revolve before her eyes. "I'm dizzy."

"Any other symptoms?" the paramedic asked.

"I feel groggy. Am I going to die?"

"No. Let me prick your finger to test your blood."

"Ow," she said.

A minute later, he took hold of her hand again. "Your blood sugar's low. Are you a diabetic?" the paramedic asked.

She shook her head, then wished she hadn't. The nausea worsened, and her hands shook.

"Why — why…. "She took a deep breath. "Why do you ask?"

"Your blood sugar's only 50, but it should be more like 100. When did you eat last?"

"About six o'clock," Brent said, "but we were at a luau, and we ate plenty."

"I have some fruit juice," the paramedic said, reaching in his satchel. The sound of a can being opened echoed in the suddenly quiet parking garage. He lifted her shoulders and held it to her mouth. It tasted sweet and wonderful. She gulped it down, then sat up and tried to focus on his face.

About fifteen minutes later the paramedic took her pulse again. "That's better." He pulled a stethoscope from his breast pocket, placed it over her heart and listened. "Much better." He pulled a packet of pretzels from the bag, tore it open and handed it to her. "Eat these."

She gobbled them down and blinked her eyes. She felt better, but still woozy.

"Whatever was in that hypodermic only knocked you out. You should be okay soon, but I suspect they used insulin—not too hard to get, but too much can be fatal."

Sheila shuddered.

He put a hand on her shoulder. "We're taking you to the hospital immediately. They'll check you out." He motioned toward the gurney.

She shook off his hand. "I can walk."

The paramedic grasped her arm. "You might collapse again."

Sheila frowned. "I won't either." On shaky feet she stumbled to the ambulance with Brent holding her arm on one side and the paramedic supporting her on the other.

Before getting in she looked back. The shorter of the uniformed cops, his Hawaiian heritage evident in his tan skin and dark hair, looked under the rented car and scooped the knife into a plastic bag. "Did he cut anyone with this?"

"He stuck me with it," Sheila said, touching her side. "But I think it only scratched my skin."

The policeman bent down beside the square concrete pillar and rose with the broken hypodermic needle in another bag.

The paramedic rushed over to the officer. "Wait a minute. I was going to take it to the hospital with this young lady. We'll do tests on her, but maybe we can analyze what's left of that fluid."

The cop ran a finger inside his starched collar. "I can't release this. It's evidence." He held the bag between his thumb and fingers.

The other officer, his pudgy chest straining the buttons of his uniform as he questioned the man who'd pulled the knife on Sheila, spoke. "We'll take it to our lab for analysis and fingerprints. We'll let you know in a day or two what it is."

The paramedic said, "It acts like insulin, but I can't be sure until we test our patient."

Brent's arm snaked out, grabbed the bag with the hypodermic. "We'll return it when the hospital is through with it."

The shorter cop grabbed Brent's arm. "Give that back or I'll arrest you. If you take it, we won't have a clear chain of custody."

Sheila's chin jutted out. "There'll be fingerprints on the knife. That should convince a judge to lock them up."

Brent shook his arm free and held the bag out of reach of the cop.

The short cop scowled. "I can add resisting arrest to your charges."

Brent took a step back. "I won't give this up until it's analyzed."

Sheila, supported on one side by a paramedic, grabbed the open door of the emergency vehicle to steady herself. She was beginning to think clearer now. She ignored the ache in her leg. "You want to be charged with endangering the life of a U.S. Marshal?"

The cop turned to Brent. "Okay, show me your badge," he barked.

Sheila bristled. "Get my purse, Brent."

He snatched it from the car and handed it to her.

She pulled out her leather-covered badge.

The cop stared. "Oh, you're the Marshal. I thought he was...."

"You thought wrong. Now let go of him. How long can you hold those men?"

"Twenty-four hours. We have to release them on bond after that. Of course, with all that necessary paperwork, it might take several hours before we can let them make a phone call to arrange bond. And by that time, there won't be any magistrates on duty to sign the release papers until say, about nine o'clock the next day." He grinned. "That good enough for you?"

Brent held on to it. "I'm not letting the syringe go. You can damn well come to the hospital and wait there. And if you try to force it from me, I'll report you to IA. Want to chance a demotion?" He walked back toward Sheila. "You need to go to the hospital now."

"Let him have it," said the older paramedic. "Our tests on the patient will be more conclusive."

The cop turned back to Brent. "Give me that bag. I'll take it to our lab and wait for the report. Then I'll lock it in our evidence room."

Sheila sighed, hoping to hell the paramedic was right about what was in that needle. She still felt awfully weak, but didn't notice any other ill effects. She let Brent and the paramedic help her inside the vehicle, then slumped down on the cot.

She couldn't see much beyond the open doors.

The gruff voice of the bigger perpetrator echoed through the parking garage. "Hell, no. There's nobody else workin' with us. We ain't weenies. We could have taken care of him if she hadn't butted in."

Brent climbed in and took her hand. "Lie down. Let the cops worry about those guys. "You've risked your life for me I don't know how many times. Should have let me disappear on my own."

"I found you," she said, annoyed at the weak way her voice sounded. "But so did Sheldon's men."

"I'm okay. Right now, all I care about is that you'll be all right."

The intense look in his eyes and the iron grip on her arm unnerved her. Maybe he cared about more than a walk in the park and sizzling sex in the sheets. "After a doctor looks you over, we should be able to go on about our lives. At least you can."

Not knowing what else to say, she used the standard bureau line. "We can't guarantee your safety one...one hundred percent, but we'll do the best we can to protect you."

"I trust you to do that, but you could have been killed. I don't want to think about losing you." He squeezed her hand. The look in his eyes was serious as if he really cared for her. It gave her a warm feeling. Did he mean it?

The ambulance lurched forward. Brent grabbed the edge of the cot to steady it as the vehicle angled its way up the incline to ground level. The paramedic bent to wrap a blood pressure cuff around her arm. He stuck a thermometer in her mouth.

She wrapped her lips and tongue around it. She wouldn't stop worrying until they tested her and treated her. Then she could concentrate on his safety.

He'd need to be sent far away immediately after the trial. She'd have a new witness to watch over. If that person were as much trouble as Brent had been, it would keep her busy. Why didn't that sound as challenging as it had before—before Brent?

Feeling suddenly exhausted, she leaned back and closed her eyes. The paramedic poked and prodded her. She felt a prick on her finger. A minute later, she felt a sharper prick in her arm. She wanted to ask what they were giving her, but couldn't get the words out. She felt so sleepy.

Brent knelt on the floor beside her and spoke in low tones to the paramedic. "She looks so pale. Is she unconscious?"

The paramedic shook his head. "I gave her glucose. She should wake up by the time we get to the hospital."

Sheila's hands felt icy cold. He tried to warm them. "Can't we go any faster? She might die before we get there." He tried to swallow the lump in his throat.

The paramedic shot him an annoyed look. "We won't lose her. She's got too much spunk to give up."

After what seemed an eternity, the ambulance pulled to a stop at the emergency entrance. Thank the lord. Brent helped them wheel her still form into the hospital and down a hall to an examining room. There a white-coated doctor said, "Stand back. We'll handle this." He pointed to the hall. "Check in at the desk. They'll want information."

Feeling helpless, Brent trudged down a short hall to the counter in an area bustling with nurses and waiting patients.

Awakened by someone grasping her hand, Sheila opened her eyes to meet Brent's concerned gaze. Standing beside her hospital bed, he pressed his lips to her palm. "Thank goodness you're all right. I'm supposed to wake you every hour to be sure you're not harboring any ill effects. Might be nice if what you got turns out to be sodium pentothal."

"Isn't that truth serum?"

Brent nodded. "Then I could press my advantage — ask you what you really think about me."

Captivated by his endearing smile, she bit her lip. "You want me to tell you I find you sexy and irresistible? Forget it. Might swell your head so big you couldn't see it all at one time in the mirror."

"You mean you don't like my arm around your waist, and you don't like it when I kiss you?" He pressed a kiss on her forehead.

"Your...your ego doesn't need any help." Damn guy — he knew she wasn't immune to him.

"You saying I'm conceited? Moi?"

"You think you're God's gift to women and Superman all rolled up in one. Not only that, but you're bull-headed and stubborn." She couldn't believe she'd said all that.

His look of astonishment was priceless, but didn't quite ring true.

She remembered he liked acting. "Your actions say it all. You think you know what's best when you don't follow my orders — "

"I hate being bossed, and especially — "

"By a woman you mean? You not only have a problem with authority, but you're a bigot."

"I am not. I treat a black man the same as I would a white one."

"But you don't extend the same courtesy to a woman."

"I'm always courteous to women."

"Except you have a hang-up when it comes to women authority figures."

"I always hated it when my mother said, 'you're not a good boy unless you do as I say.'"

"Do you have a problem obeying a policeman?"

"No. Remember, I used to be one."

"But you have a problem with obeying me, right?"

He didn't answer.

"Following instructions doesn't make you less of a man. It just shows you're using your head."

"When you put it like that, it sounds reasonable, but—"

"Remember that the next time I tell you what to do."

His eyes, intent and serious, focused on her face. "That's the problem. You're always ordering me to do something. Couldn't you at least say please sometimes?"

"But if I say 'please,' you might take it as a request you can follow only if you choose to."

"Not if you give me a good reason."

Satisfied that he meant it, she took a deep breath, and then exhaled. "I can do that, but if there's danger, you may have to wait for a reason."

"Okay. I can live with that. For now I just want to see you get well."

"What happened to those guys that attacked us?"

"The cops took them away in handcuffs, said they could hold them for twenty-four hours."

"By then we can be on a flight to the mainland."

"There's something I should tell you."

She raised up in the bed. "What?"

"That big guy was the one with Dobson when I saw him outside the grocery store. Dobson or his boss Sheldon has to be behind these attacks."

"You have good instincts. How come you quit being a cop?"

His face clouded over. "You need to rest now, and that's a long story."

Was he being considerate or did he really not want to tell her?

She laid her head back on the pillow. "I'd like to know, that is, if you want to tell me about it."

He pulled a chair close to her bed. "It started with a drug raid, one we'd been setting up for months. I'd done the investigation and made friends with one of the cookers."

"Cookers?"

"Methamphetamine. It was a family operation—uncles, nephews, even a daughter."

"Where was this, somewhere out from town?"

He shook his head. "In an abandoned warehouse, not far from downtown Detroit."

"What happened?"

"A raid went bad even though we planned it carefully. Had a task force of four plus three we recruited the week before. Maynard was in charge. My partner, Smitty, and I took orders from him."

"So what went wrong?"

"A mistake in judgment. Not mine. Someone else's."

"You want to talk about it?"

"There's not much to tell. I took part in a flawed drug raid. Everything went wrong. Maynard, my supervisor, had transferred two of the four original men to work parade detail. It was the fourth of July."

"They had an arsenal of guns. We didn't have enough manpower. My partner and I both took shots to the chest."

"Oh, no. Were you injured badly?"

"Yes, I finally recovered, but that wasn't the worst. My

partner, Smitty — I loved him like a brother — he died, leaving a grieving widow and two little kids without a father. That wouldn't have happened if Maynard hadn't taken two men off the team."

"I see. Was that why you resigned?"

"Partly. As soon as I got out of the hospital, I stormed into Maynard's office and demanded to know why he'd reassigned those two men. He shouted at me and told me to leave. I didn't until I'd told him it was his fault and called him a bastard."

"And?"

"The chief called me in and told me to resign or I'd be fired, and he'd hold a press conference to explain why."

"But didn't you explain what happened?"

Brent slumped in the chair. "I tried, but he wouldn't listen."

She reached out to touch his arm. "That's a bum rap and so unfair. I'm sorry it happened. Isn't there anything you can do to straighten the record out?"

He shook his head. "No police force will touch me now."

"Is that why you keep resisting my orders?"

He was silent for a long minute. "I suppose that's part of it. I'll try to remember you have my best interests at heart. I know that now."

Suddenly feeling very tired, she sank back into the pillow and closed her eyes.

Brent pressed a kiss on her lips. His mouth, soft and moist against hers, seemed to link with her spirit as if forging an invisible bond between them. He still held her hand, his fingers intertwined with hers. "Sleep now," he said. "I'll be right here and wake you later to be sure you're all right."

❦

Sometime later, she surfaced from a dream that she was Cinderella, dancing with Prince Charming who kissed her shoulders and her neck. He pressed a kiss just above the neckline of her strapless gown, and then raised his lips to hers. Lost in the wonder of his kiss, she opened her eyes to see Brent's warm brown ones gazing at her with an adoring look and his mouth descending for a kiss—a second one she guessed.

"Wake up, Sleeping Beauty," he said and kissed her.

She should discourage him, but she hadn't the strength to resist. His kisses bred an insatiable desire for more. Hoping he didn't consider her just another conquest, she raised one arm to encircle his neck.

His mouth felt so right and yet unlike any others. She'd thought she'd loved Matthew Brent, but this Brent drew her into an irresistible tango, one she couldn't stop even if she wanted to. But she had better tear herself away, and soon, for his safety and to keep her job.

His mouth roved. His fingers smoothed her hair from her forehead. She lay there, meeting his lips with fervor and drinking in the heady feeling. Running her fingers through the crisp waves of his hair, she realized she'd feel empty without him. When this assignment was over, she'd feel as if part of her heart had been wrenched away.

He probably could have any woman he chose to charm. She squeezed her eyes shut. She hadn't meant to care about him, other than to keep him safe. She hadn't meant to fall in love. Being emotionally involved could slow her reactions to danger. She wanted him alive and well, even if a future together wasn't likely.

His other hand clasped hers tightly against his heart. "You can't realize how worried I was that you wouldn't make it. That's what's important now, except I still have to face Dobson in trial. I won't let them get away with hurting you. You've risked your life and put up with my...my little mistakes, to keep me in one piece."

"Little mistakes that could have cost your life."

"Okay, some things I did weren't too smart." Gently, he released her hand. "Sleep now. I've alerted hospital security to watch for intruders, and I'll be right here with the call button just inches away."

She awoke to sunlight and a gentle breeze from the window.

Brent sat in the chair beside her bed. "Morning, Warrior Princess."

She smiled. "I like that better than Sergeant Sheila."

"I won't call you that again, but I will listen to your instructions if you explain why I should follow them."

She let out a breath. Thank goodness for that. "But if we're in danger, there won't be time for explanations or 'please.'" She looked around. "Where are my clothes, and when will they let me out of here?"

He pointed to a closet. "Your things are in there. You can leave as soon as the doctor okays it. Your symptoms and your blood tests indicate you were given insulin. They analyzed your blood again. You don't have enough insulin in your blood now to cause any problems." He smiled. "Too bad I didn't ask you more questions when you were vulnerable. Guess I'll have to fill you up with wine to get you to talk freely now."

"I thought you were ready to reform, but you're already planning to take advantage of me."

He patted her arm. "No one can steal a march on you, but if a little wine will help me persuade you to crawl in my bed — "

"Crawl? No way."

"Forgive me. I wasn't thinking. You wouldn't crawl for anyone. I mean share my bed. I can only hope you'd find that appealing...."

If only he knew how little persuasion it would take. "It's not about finding you appealing." That was an understatement. It was all she could do to resist him. "This isn't just about a man and a woman enjoying each other."

"You mean you're like all the other women — you want promises of love and forever after?"

"Is that too much to ask of a man if he really cares for a woman?"

"I promised that once. It didn't work out. I don't know if I can ever make it work."

"But you meant it at the time."

He nodded. "I did, but she was like my mother and my sister all over again, only she at least said, 'please.' She didn't like me being a cop, and later she wanted me to leave the bank and go for a better paying job, one more prestigious."

"And you didn't want to?"

"Actually, no. Suburbia Bank doesn't pay a lot, but the employees are like a big happy family. And even the lowest paid worker is given a loan if his credit is good, and they promote from within. Since I transferred from a higher position in the Fort Worth branch, I should be able to make executive vice-president before too long. Or maybe, if I can get my record cleared, I can go back to being a cop in Detroit, just not undercover."

"I see." So he still hoped to go back to Michigan. No chance of him even considering a future with her. "I'd better warn you. It may be a while before this comes to trial, and sometimes, trials get postponed just because another trial takes too long. However, if you go back to Michigan, how can you get back on the police force?"

His expression fell. "Going back may be wishful thinking on my part."

"But those criminals you helped catch are probably all in jail. Let me guess. You got blamed for everything going wrong."

He nodded. "Not only was my cover blown, but I was a pariah at the station, thanks to my supervisor bad-mouthing me." Anger punctuated the set of his chin. "My record there will stand in the way of my working as a cop anywhere I go."

"I'm sorry."

"Don't be. It's something I have to live with and get over if I can. But I can't help thinking about Dorrie trying to raise those two little kids on her own. I sent her money when I could. That caused arguments with my wife. She accused me of an affair."

"After all you'd been through?"

He nodded. A pained look flashed across his face. "One of the reasons we got a divorce. She didn't trust me to tell the truth."

Sheila sat up in bed and felt a breeze at her back. She'd forgotten hospital gowns opened at the back. She threw off the covers. "I'm going to get dressed. Would you please check to see if they'll release me soon?"

After the door closed behind him, she dressed hurriedly and worked the tangles out of her long blonde hair. She looked in the mirror. Her blue eyes looked alert, but she didn't look like the glamour queens Brent probably dated either. Nevertheless, knowing he was attracted to her filled her with excitement.

Maybe that was all she could count on. She had no qualms about protecting Brent. She could do it, but she'd have to tread carefully to keep her job, especially after chasing him to Hawaii. There'd be a hearing with her supervisors she was sure.

For now she had to remember to act professional in public. However, that would be hard to keep up when they were alone. Unfortunately, that happened a lot.

Just remembering how he'd caressed and kissed her and more set her senses sizzling. She licked her lips and wished she didn't have to be sensible.

She was smoothing on pink lip-gloss when she heard a knock on the door.

"You dressed yet?" asked Brent.

"Come in," she said, trying to smooth down the wrinkles in her dress.

His broad grin said he was glad to see her. "Ready? The nurse said you could leave now."

She took a deep breath. "First let me call the airline and leave my cell phone number in case there's space on an early flight. I'll wait in the lobby until you can bring a car around. Then we can go to a hotel."

Brent shook his head. "Don't think we need to worry about our attackers. Those guys are locked up for at least twenty-four hours. I'd say it was more like thirty-six, reading between the lines of what that cop said. Don't know if you remember, but that one guy claimed no one else on the island was involved, so we should be safe for a while. Besides, the condo is so much more comfortable."

She followed Brent into the elevator. When they reached the lobby, she stopped at the front desk to sign out.

The desk clerk looked up. "You're all over the news this morning. The headline said, 'Couple foils attack in basement condo garage.'"

Sheila groaned. Here she'd been so careful to keep news of Brent out of the paper. "Did the article give my name?"

"Oh, yes. You and your boyfriend are today's heroes. The man you took the knife from claims you injured his arm when you threw him to the floor, but he's in jail."

She called the airline but the line was busy. Then she called the U.S. Marshal's office on Oahu and told them what happened. They promised someone would make sure those guys were held for forty-eight hours. Five minutes later, Brent helped her into the rented car.

Seated behind the wheel, he took her hand. "You were great dealing with those thugs. Taking the poison meant for me — that's beyond the call of duty. If *I'd* gotten the full dose, I might be dead by now. I owe you my life."

Sheila shook her head. "If I'd done my job right, I'd have noticed those guys before they attacked us." She gritted her teeth, wishing she'd been more alert. "They must have tailed us from the luau. I should have seen them."

"I thought you were gawking at the scenery, but you were constantly scanning the roadside all the way to my condo, weren't you?"

"Yes, but I must have missed them."

"Maybe not. They could have been waiting for us at that parking garage."

Brent parked the car at his condo and helped her out.

After scanning the area, Sheila hurried him into the elevator. Inside she said, "You're damn lucky I was with you. Other Marshals would have kicked you out of the program long ago."

He leaned back against the elevator wall. "Guess I gave you a hard time."

"You just don't want to admit you're vulnerable." She sighed. "I should have handed you over to someone who'd make you toe the line."

He grinned. "But not one as pretty as you, I bet."

She smiled as the elevator doors opened. After scanning the hall, she nodded for him to follow her. Her leg ached a bit, but she ignored the twinges. It was getting better now.

Walking down the hall, he grasped her arm, halting her progress. "I don't want another Marshal to guard me. I want you." He straightened and saluted. "Sergeant Sheila, I promise I'll obey orders from now on."

She shook off his hand. "Don't call me that. I can't promise to keep you safe. But I'll do all I can." And, she admonished herself, there'd be no more thoughts about spending another night in bed with him. She'd ignore those irresistible smiles and admiring looks. He didn't want a future with her. That trial had better not be postponed. She didn't know how much more she could take.

She made him stand in the doorway until she checked his place and made sure no one was lurking about. Inside, after locking and bolting the front door, she dialed the airline again and told them to call as soon as there was room on a flight.

As she hung up the phone, Brent said. "You sure were quick to lay that guy on the floor. Would you show me how that's done, if you feel up to it, that is?"

"I feel okay, but I don't want to hurt you."

"The rug's soft, and you can let me down easily."

"That's not how it works." Shoving at his shoulder and hooking her foot behind his leg, she had him flat in seconds.

Brent just lay there.

She gasped and bent over him. "Are you hurt? I didn't mean to be rough."

"Think I'm okay. Would you help me up?" He held out his hand.

Bending down, she took his hand and pulled. He gripped hers and pulled harder. The next thing she knew, she was lying on top of him, her breasts flattened against his broad chest. And he was grinning, damn him.

"Don't I deserve a kiss for all you put me through?"

"What about all I went through?"

His smile broadened. Before she could say anything more, he pulled her face closer. His lips were gentle on hers. He brushed a lock of hair from her forehead, then caressed her cheek and kissed her again.

His mouth roved over hers, awakening a hunger inside, one she'd barely managed to suppress before. She couldn't help responding.

His eyes, deep brown and flecked with amber, seemed to look deep into her soul and say it wasn't fair to hide how she felt.

He smiled. "Never thought I'd fall for a warrior princess."

She took a deep breath. What was he trying to tell her? She gripped his shoulders.

His hands caressed her shoulders, sending waves of awareness down her arms. His look was serious now. "I was so worried you wouldn't make it."

"But I did, and you're okay. I really should get up now." She tried to rise. He gripped her arms, held her down.

She managed to get one arm free to push against his rock hard chest. "This is not a good idea."

His grin met her determined look. "But we're safe now."

"You said you'd obey orders. Now please, let me go."

"I will—after this." His lips met hers. She tried to strain away, but he held her tightly.

His lips ravished her mouth, her face and her forehead, weakening her resolve.

She drew a deep breath, and then met his lips for a fervent kiss. In a minute she'd insist he let her up. If he didn't want a future with her, she'd only be prolonging the agony of letting him go.

She ran her fingers through his hair and trailed her fingers over his face, felt the hard planes of his cheeks and his firm chin. She kissed him thoroughly, longingly, holding nothing back. His mesmerizing kiss only made her want more. She let his tongue inside to roam and explore, then dipped hers into his mouth to do the same.

His hand caressed her breast. His eyes captivated her. Again she tried to rise, but he grasped her arms, pulling her tightly against him for another kiss.

"Brent, stop."

"When I saw you fighting with that guy in the parking garage, I wanted to beat the life out of him. I would have if I could have reached him. But you risked your life for me."

"That's my job."

"But you even took the poison that was meant for me."

"I couldn't let him kill you."

"Is that all it was to you... doing your job?"

A flash of vulnerability showed in his brown eyes. She'd do it again in a heartbeat to keep him safe, not only because it was her job, but because she loved him.

How had this arrogant bachelor stolen her heart despite his attempts to thwart her every command? But she couldn't tell him that. He'd feel obligated and perhaps jeopardize his own safety.

Protecting him from harm was paramount. If she had to, she'd frame her orders like requests. Anything to keep him alive and safe, even if it were only to warm another woman's bed. She didn't want to think about that.

And there would be other women. For all he'd said about liking her independent spirit, he must prefer a less assertive woman, a beauty who'd let him take control.

He was still looking at her, but the vulnerability, if it ever was there, had vanished. In his eyes was an invitation to join him in paradise.

"Let me thank you properly." His hand squeezed her breast, while his thumb roved across the tip, making her catch her breath. "Well, Warrior Princess?"

She should call the airline again, but his kiss took her breath away.

He trailed tiny kisses down her neck and along the neckline of her dress. When he reached the buttons, he undid the top one and kissed the flesh beneath it.

She grasped his wrist. She should stop him now, but she couldn't make herself do it.

His eyes sparkled. His face was wreathed in a seductive smile. He slid his fingers beneath the neckline of her dress. Her flesh quivered at his touch. "This time I want to pleasure you long and leisurely — if you feel up to it, that is." He rolled her over until he was on top, but kept firm hold on her shoulders.

"Don't you mean down to it?" She asked.

He chuckled, then rose to his knees, his gaze locked on hers.

Now what? If she said she didn't feel up to it, after kissing him like that, he'd know it for a blatant lie. And he wouldn't listen to her claim it was unprofessional — not after what they'd already done.

Before she could come up with a clever phrase, he was lifting her in his arms. Grinning, he said, "You have until I lay you on the bed to say no, but I don't think you will." Swiftly, he carried her to the bed.

He was right. She didn't say no — couldn't bring herself to.

After he laid her down, he undid her sandals. They plopped to the floor, one by one. He massaged her feet, and then caressed his way up to her knees. "You have such pretty legs," he said as he undid the last of the buttons on her dress. It parted, followed by cool air.

She smiled as he leaned forward to kiss her. His lips were soft and tender. He slid one arm around her waist to raise her, and then eased her dress off her shoulders. He slid it off, leaving her wearing only a lace bra and panties.

After releasing the front bra clasp, he dropped tiny kisses on each breast, making them tingle, making her breathless, and making her heart beat faster.

"You're so beautiful," he whispered as he slowly brushed the backs of his fingers across her cheeks. His eyes met hers in an adoring look; then his lips descended for a tender kiss.

Her heart swelled. She'd never felt so cherished.

His warm fingers eased her panties off, and then slid up her legs. His hands glided between her thighs, caressing and fondling until all she could do was to wrap her arms around his neck and kiss him back.

One thing she knew for sure. He certainly knew how to pleasure a woman. With his fingers, he worshiped her until she could hardly stand to wait for more.

He eased out of her arms, and then backed off to shed his clothes and shoes. He turned, and she heard a crinkle, foil tearing, she guessed. Seconds later, he settled above her, warm and hard. His fingers caressing her thighs and higher sent her senses careening like a runaway racecar.

He moved over her with maddening slowness, and then slid inside, filling her completely. With long, slow strokes, he stoked her fire, bringing her to a fevered pitch. She grasped his shoulders and kissed him hard, hoping against hope he'd say something about how he felt, or even hint they had a future together.

Her climax, when it came, was even more earth shaking

than last time. She felt him come, his body heaving. He collapsed above her, his weight warm and comforting.

"You're fantastic," he said.

He gave her a soft kiss and rolled to one side, pulling her with him.

She lay there, wrapped in his arms.

Then the phone rang.

He grabbed it, said, "Hello," then listened. Finally, he put it down. "We're on standby for the next flight. Leaves in two hours. We need to get to the airport as soon as we can."

Chapter 15

After a quick shower, Sheila struggled to pull clothes over damp skin. She'd been unprofessional and given in to his charms, not once, but twice. And if that weren't enough, she wasn't really sure how he felt about her.

What if he told someone? He wouldn't. He was a gentleman. Her impromptu trip could get her fired or at least demoted, but at least she'd kept Brent from serious injury.

And what if she were pregnant again? He hadn't used protection the first time. Somehow she knew he'd stand by her if she were, but she didn't want to tie him to her because of that. She swallowed. She wanted his heart, but she wanted it given freely.

❧

On the long flight back Sheila had a lot of time to think. Brent put his arm around her shoulders and even held her hand occasionally. He smiled at her a lot, too. Was he thinking he'd found another playmate?

She reminded herself of all the reasons why she should resist him, but she only had to look at his mesmerizing smile, and she wanted to kiss him again. What was the matter with her? U. S. Marshals in "Wit Sec" were supposed to think only of security for their witnesses. Well, she had screwed up royally…and literally. Brent might call her a warrior princess, but that was as close as she'd get to royalty.

Time to pull herself together and repair the damage. She'd tell Brent what they'd done was strictly forbidden, which was true, and that they should never speak of it again. She hoped that would discourage him from trying to persuade her otherwise, because she wasn't sure she could resist him.

Besides, she had to concentrate on her job. She could explain she didn't have a serious boyfriend because she might have to spend a lot of time with male witnesses in the program, and she didn't figure any boyfriend would accept that.

She couldn't trust herself where Brent was concerned. She'd ask her partner, Joe, to take charge of Brent. She'd offer to take over the most time-consuming witness he was working with. Her decision made, tired and sleepy, she leaned back against the seat. She dreamed they were lying in bed and doing it again. "Ohh, Brent," she murmured.

"Yes," he said in low velvet tones, his arm resting against the back of the seat and his fingers caressing her shoulder.

She opened her eyes. He was looking at her expectantly. "I-I was dreaming."

He smiled. "About me I hope."

"Why would you think that?" Suddenly realizing what she'd uttered, she said, "Okay, maybe I was, but let's drop it."

After the plane landed, they didn't have to wait long to pick up Brent's bag and hail a taxi. "I'll tell the driver to drop you off before he takes me home."

"But your leg."

"It only hurts occasionally."

Brent took her hand. "I was hoping you'd stay a few more days with me."

"I don't think that's wise."

"But you and I, we're great together," he whispered back.

"I—I can't deny that, but—"

His grin faded. "Because of your job, you mean?"

She nodded.

His eyes focused on her, and his smile pulled at her resolve. "What about after the trial? We could live together openly then."

She caught her breath. She couldn't help thinking how wonderful it would be to spend her days and nights with him, but he didn't sound like he wanted a lasting relationship. "I don't think that's a good idea."

"I see," he said and looked out the window at the office buildings with well-landscaped grounds they were passing.

If he'd wanted something more than just living together, he would have said so. Disappointed, she told herself it was better this way. At least he'd be safer with Joe watching him.

When the taxi reached Brent's place, she made the driver wait while she checked out his apartment. Nothing seemed amiss. She strode back to the cab. "Check your e-mail for threatening messages, and call me if there are." She grasped the car door. She didn't dare linger here.

"You didn't have to remind me." Brent grasped her hand, pulled her close and kissed her hard. She kissed him back, trying to memorize the taste and feel of his mouth on hers.

He smiled. "That's to remember me by. Until tomorrow, then."

His adoring look as she pulled away was almost her undoing. They'd have no tomorrow. He might argue, but he'd have to accept a change in protectors.

"Be strong, be strong," she chanted under her breath minutes later as the taxi door snapped shut. His smile and the look in his eyes as he waved, tempted her to spring out of the taxi and run to his arms for one more kiss, but she held firm.

The taxi driver gave her a knowing look as she settled back in the seat. "Ain't love grand?" he said and started the engine.

It didn't matter whether or not she loved him. She'd do what was needed to keep him safe. She couldn't be the best protector for him now.

The next morning her cell phone rang. "Hello," she said.

"Sheila, it's nine o'clock. When are you going to come check on me?"

"Look, I have to go to a meeting. I'll call you later." She broke the connection. Telling him was going to be hard.

Finding Joe Berg at his desk, she said, "How about a coffee break? I'll treat you to a blueberry muffin."

Joe smoothed back blond hair and rose to his full height, a bit taller than her five-feet-eight. "Sounds good. I could use a break."

As they headed toward the hall, her redheaded co-worker, Scott Thompson stood. "I heard that. You going to buy me a muffin, too?"

"Maybe some other time. Thought you were going on a diet."

"Not if someone's buying muffins."

Sheila pointed a finger at him. "So, buy yourself one if that's what you want. I need to talk confidentially with my partner."

In the lunchroom, she led Joe to a gray Formica-topped table in the corner, then went to buy coffee and muffins.

Back at the corner booth, she set down the tray and slid into a chair. Watching him stir sugar into his coffee, she tried to think how to begin.

"Okay, what gives?" he asked.

"You mustn't breathe a word of this to anyone, okay?"

"I won't." He leaned closer, his elbows on the table.

"I want to switch witnesses with you."

Joe shot her an inquisitive look. "Why? Can't you handle yours?"

"It's not that, although he often questions my orders."

"Don't mince words with him. His life is in danger."

"I'm afraid I'm becoming too close."

"Involved you mean?"

Suddenly embarrassed, she nodded.

"It happens. We work hard to keep them safe. You can't let

them become like family. You have to stay objective to keep him out of trouble."

"I wasn't alert enough to avert a near disaster."

"What happened?"

"I made a mistake taking in some of the sights with Broussard."

"And?"

Sheila told him about the attack in the parking garage.

"Where did that happen?"

"Hawaii."

"Why the hell did you take him there?"

"He took off by himself without telling me."

"You should kick him out of the program?"

"I went there to talk him into coming back."

"Did you run that by our supervisor?"

"No time. I had to take the next flight so I wouldn't lose track of him."

"And you knew he wouldn't approve."

"If I didn't ask, he couldn't tell me not to go."

"Why the hell do you think we have rules?"

"Thought this might be the exception—especially if the witness might be killed."

"So the hit man followed you there?"

"I don't know how he found out. Figured no one would follow that soon, but I was wrong."

"And you weren't watching for a tail?"

"I thought I was." She leaned back in the booth. Somehow he and an accomplice found us in the parking garage. The big guy came at me with a knife, but I took care of him."

"Bet you kicked ass."

"Took both of us to fight off the attackers."

"But you got him back in one piece. So why do you want to switch witnesses?"

"I was too involved with enjoying the sights to keep a constant watch."

Joe shot her a quizzical look. "Hope you weren't dumb enough to screw with him."

"Why would I do that?" she asked, hoping he'd believe her.

"You did, didn't you?"

Sheila wanted to wipe that knowing grin off his face, but she couldn't deny it.

"Hey, I couldn't resist Elizabeth either, but we're married now. However, if our supervisor finds out what you did, it could ruin your chances for promotion or maybe cost your job. Face it, Sheila, this business is no piece of cake."

"I know that. I won't have that problem with another witness. Broussard wanted a male Marshal, so he should feel confident with you. Just give me the file for one of your witnesses, and I'll hand over Broussard's."

She rose and hurried out of the cafe before he could say any more. Joe had been a good partner and a mentor, but he might say it was in her best interest to confess to their boss, because if it came out later, it would look worse.

But just because Joe had skated by, didn't mean she could. She twisted the fabric of her pants, and then crossed her fingers.

At eleven-thirty Joe called, said to meet him for lunch and bring the file on her witness.

Ten minutes later, she took a lunch tray to that same corner table and sat across from Joe. She hoped those nearby were too engrossed in their conversation to notice they were exchanging files.

She adopted a poker face. "If you take over the responsibility for Brent Broussard, I can manage one or two of your witnesses. It's time I took on more."

Joe shoved the file toward her. "This one's a white collar type. He's no angel, but he agreed to testify against his former boss."

She touched Joe's arm. "Thanks. I don't know how I would have made it this far without your help."

"Maybe you can help the next recruit."

"If I'm good enough," she said, hoping she'd still be in the program.

"You will be. You're better than most of the men here." He grinned. "But if you quote me, I'll deny it. Have to warn you, though, my guy isn't very cooperative either."

"Let me tell Broussard before you contact him."

Joe nodded. As if by common consent, they said no more while they ate. Later, she shoved her tray aside and flipped open her file to Brent's picture.

She wrote his new address and phone number on a slip of paper and handed it to Joe. "As you once told me, memorize this and then destroy it. I'll tell him about the change tonight after work."

Joe pulled a picture from his file. Proud that Joe had enough confidence in her to trade, she gasped when she saw his picture. Dressed in a white shirt and striped tie and sporting a blond mustache, Dirk Dobson looked harmless. Joe scribbled on a piece of paper, and then tucked it inside. "And you can burn this guy's contact info after you memorize it. His crime doesn't amount to much, but his boss was into gambling, stealing, and selling stolen goods.

"Broussard's okay, just didn't always take me seriously. We had a close call in Hawaii, so I think he'll listen now."

Joe handed her the thick file. "We just signed him up. Keep the guy safe, and don't let him change his mind about testifying."

"Thanks. I'll reassure him about relocating him after he testifies."

After Joe walked out, she picked up the file. She definitely wouldn't tell Brent the name of her new witness.

❦

All afternoon Sheila dreaded telling Brent. On the way to his place she thought about different reasons she could give and finally settled on the truth.

After climbing the stairs to his place, she knocked. There was no answer. She called his name. Still no answer.

Her heart skipped a beat. Had someone gotten to him?

She pulled out her key and unlocked the door, but couldn't open it because the chain guard was hooked. Footsteps told her someone was coming.

"Who's there?" he barked.

"It's me." Brent's eyes met hers as he undid the chain. "I thought you were only going to call me." He had a towel wrapped around his waist. Memories surfaced—how his body had felt against hers, how his strong arms had held her, how his hands caressed her all over—how she'd ignored every reason not to get involved.

"I wanted to see you in person." And she was doing just that—seeing almost all of his gorgeous body. She wasn't sorry she'd traveled to paradise with him—it had been wonderful, but now she had to give him up. She sighed. He couldn't help being irresistible.

He let her in. "Want to dry my back?" His smile tore at her resolve.

Sadly, she shook her head. "We have to talk."

He grasped both her hands. "I'd rather we do something else."

She pulled her hands away. "This is serious. Go get dressed." That would give her time to bolster her courage.

After he walked into the bedroom, she wandered around the living room and noticed an audition notice. Maybe he was planning to try for a part in a local theatre group. At least he was getting on with his life. But her future without him seemed empty.

He came out, fully dressed in brown trousers and a tan shirt that intensified the dark brown of his eyes.

She held up the paper. "If you're going to try out for a part, don't go for the lead. I don't want to see your name in the paper, even a small town one."

He frowned. "You're a spoilsport, but I guess you're right." He sat on the couch and patted a space beside him.

She chose the chair instead. "Look. There's no easy way to say this. I won't be handling your case anymore. My teammate, Joe Berg, will take responsibility for you. I'll manage one of his witnesses instead."

His jaw dropped open. "You can't do that."

"Yes, I can."

Brent stood, then paced. "So, you Marshals just pass your witnesses around, like unwanted puppies."

Facing his frown, Sheila gripped the arms of the chair, her stomach in knots. This was harder than she'd expected. "It's not like that. I can't be objective about you."

"How can you just walk away?"

"We-I've gotten too involved. I can't do my job effectively." She stood. "It's for your own good."

"But you care about me. You'll be more careful than some yahoo who doesn't know me."

"Joe's got your file. He'll know all about you." But not about how Brent made her feel, not about how he caressed her in bed, took her to paradise and back. She bit her lip.

Brent rose from the couch and walked disturbingly close to her. His scowl was unnerving. "Hell, I don't want you to stop protecting me. I'm not sure I can trust someone else."

"I can vouch for Joe Berg. He's been my mentor. I'd trust him with my life." Biting her lip, she hoped she could trust Joe with her secret.

"But," Brent looked longingly at her. "It won't be the same. What if I promise not to entice you?" he grinned.

"That won't cut it. You'd distract me. I'm not jeopardizing your safety"

"I'm flattered — I think." He frowned. "Is there some other reason?"

"No. It's unprofessional, besides it's against the rules."

He stepped to the window and looked out. Then he faced

her. "You found a new boyfriend. That's why you're shoving me onto someone else."

"I haven't had time for that. How could you say that after we —"

"Had sex you mean?"

She closed her eyes to shut out his angry face. Tears welled up and threatened to spill out. She wouldn't cry. He'd think she were weak and looking for sympathy.

He grabbed her wrist, pulled her up to face him. "Look at me, damn it. Tell me there's not another important man in your life."

She brushed the telltale wetness from her cheeks. She wouldn't let him see her cry. "The only other males in my life are my brother and my son."

"You have a son?"

She nodded. She hadn't meant to tell him her deepest secret, but it didn't matter now.

He stared at her. "You mean from the man you were engaged to?"

"My fiancé's dead — missing in action, they said."

"Why didn't you tell me? I thought we had something special going, but you never even mentioned a son."

"It's part of my past that I try not to think of."

"So where is he?"

"I gave him up for adoption to a married friend."

"Darla, right?"

She nodded. "At the time I thought it was best, but I didn't know her husband Bill was into gambling. Now he's disappeared. He may even be dead."

"He's a cute kid. Does Darla let you visit him?"

"I stayed out of their lives until they moved back to the metroplex — thought it was best. If Darla agrees, I may visit occasionally, just to be sure he's all right."

"What's his name?"

"Jason Brent Walker. Darla let me pick his middle name."

He frowned. "You named him after his father, didn't you?"

She nodded, afraid to meet his gaze.

He scowled. "Why the hell did you give me the name of your dead fiancé'?"

"I like the name. Brent Broussard has a nice ring, don't you think?"

"What were you trying to do, resurrect your dead lover? Is that why you fell into my arms? Every time you shut your eyes you pretended I was your lost fiancé'?"

She shook her head. "That's not true."

"The hell it isn't. You played me for a fool."

He wasn't going to believe her, no matter what she said. She rose, so mad she could hardly speak. "I'm leaving. Joe will take good care of you. You won't have to see me or talk to me again." She walked toward the door. "Good-bye and..." she brushed away an angry tear. "take care."

A lump rose in her throat. She had to leave now—before she broke down and cried right in front of him. She rushed out the door and slammed it behind her.

Hurrying down the stairs, her leg ached, reminding her how he'd taken care of her when she'd been shot, waited on her, even fed her. Now, the tears came in earnest. She hated being weak. She ran to the car, limping all the way.

Unlocking the door, she felt Brent pulling at her arm. She hadn't even heard him behind her. Looking at his face pulled on her heartstrings, but she remembered to look around to see if anyone were watching. She wouldn't let her emotions blind her to things she should be aware of. No matter how much it hurt, she couldn't go back on her decision.

Brent gripped her arm. "I won't let you go."

She wrenched away and slid behind the wheel. "That's...that's the way it has to be." She scrubbed at the wetness on her cheeks, hoping he wouldn't notice.

"You're crying. You care, don't you?"

"Yes, I care, but it doesn't matter. Please go back inside before someone notices you."

His warm fingers caressed her arm. "Promise me that when this is over, and I'm safe, you'll look me up."

She shook her head. "I can't. I won't even know where you're living. After the trial Joe will find you another place, probably far away."

He frowned. "That figures."

"Go back inside."

He scowled. "Can't resist one last order, can you?"

"Just do it, please."

He stopped at the bottom of the steps. "That's the last order you'll give me, because after the trial you'll never see me again."

The bitterness in his tones cut deep. She watched him stride up the stairs, and then waited until he stepped inside and shut the door to start the engine.

She pulled away, tears running down her face. Her vision blurred so she could hardly see where she was going. Around the corner she parked the car beside the curb and let the tears fall. His last words, 'you'll never see me again,' sounded over and over like a mantra in her head.

Chapter 16

Brent slammed his fist against the apartment wall. Damn her. She'd made love to him with such abandon. He couldn't help remembering how it felt to sink inside and her soft pleas urging him to go deeper and faster. She was one hell of a woman when it came to making out—he wouldn't call it making love—she wouldn't ditch him like this if she loved him.

He'd been a damn fool to think she felt the same as he did. He'd seen the way she looked at him when she thought he wasn't watching. He'd seen how she'd trembled when he kissed her. That slumberous look in her eyes was a terrific come on. Oh she was attracted to him all right, but was she, like women always accused men of doing, only acting on her attraction. Somehow that wasn't enough now.

She must not want a lasting relationship. Why did that gnaw at his gut like an ulcer?

He'd trusted Sheila, and now she'd left him high and dry and then handed him to some other marshal like an unwanted homework assignment.

He'd miss sparring with her in conversation, but even more he'd miss rocking with her in bed. The last time they almost didn't make it to the bed. He clenched his hands into fists. The next few days might be rough, but from this day on, women were only for sex.

Now he'd have to depend on this Joe character to keep him

safe. Why the hell hadn't she brought the guy over to meet him, or at least had him call? The whole program stank.

What if Joe were behind the leaks? He paced the floor, trying to ignore his uneasy feeling.

His cell phone rang, startling him. He grabbed it. "Hello?"

"Joe Berg here. Sheila asked me to take over your case, so we traded responsibilities."

"Witnesses you mean?"

"Yes. Her new charge will keep her pretty busy. Stay where you are. I'm coming over to check out your place. I may have to move you again."

"So who's she guarding now, a woman?"

"No."

A knife twisted in Brent's gut. That guy better not seduce her. "It isn't anyone connected with my case, is it?"

"That's classified."

"Then he is."

"I didn't say that," Joe answered quickly, too quickly.

Brent gripped the phone. "If that puts me at risk, don't I have a right to know?

"No need for you to worry."

"But what if she gets kidnapped by someone connected with my case?"

"You afraid they might force her to tell where you're staying? Don't be. You'll be moved by then. Pack your things. I'm coming over."

"Dobson must have agreed to testify, and you traded him for me."

"It doesn't concern you. Get your stuff together. I'll be there in twenty minutes."

"But—" The dial tone interrupted him.

"Damn." Brent threw the phone down on the couch.

That slimy bookkeeper could probably deliver more dirt on Sheldon. He'd be in even more danger than Brent. And so would she.

He'd seen Dobson flirting with Bart Sheldon's secretary while Brent studied the books.

Brent imagined the slime ball, fingering his pale mustache and ogling Sheila's breasts.

How could she take on his enemy? He punched the wall. The resounding thwack helped a little. Rubbing his sore hand, he picked up the phone.

℘

At her desk Sheila's cell phone rang. "Hello," she said.

"Damn it, Sheila. How could you do this to me?" Brent's voice was harsh, demanding. Gone was the velvet softness he'd used to whisper sweet nothings when they'd made love in Hawaii.

She gripped the phone. "Hold on. I need to move this conversation into the hall." She strode past other agents busy at their desks. Finally, out of earshot of all but the receptionist, she turned away so Alice couldn't hear. "Brent, I'm sorry. I can't be objective where you're concerned any more. I can't risk your life. I had to let Joe take over."

"That's water under the bridge now. He's already called, and he's coming over. Tell me about your new assignment. Why did you take that creep on?"

"What creep?"

"Don't play games with me. Dobson, that's who!" he barked. His harsh tones made her feel like scum. Gone was all the tenderness he'd shown her in Hawaii. Or had that all been pretense to get her in his bed?

She swallowed. "Joe wouldn't tell you who my assignment is."

"Didn't have to. I guessed."

"Well, I'm not confirming anything."

"Are you crazy? He's probably behind the guy that's been following you."

"Joe checked out the license number of that black pick-up. It wasn't Dobson's. Besides, he has a Viper. Joe wouldn't assign anyone to me if there were a chance he was the one tailing me."

"Carson insisted I get rid of my Corvette. You going to make him sell the Viper?"

"It's none of your business what I do with my witness. What is it with you guys and your muscle cars? They're no good to you if you're dead."

"How can you work with that sleaze-bag day after day? I watched Dobson when I audited the books he kept. He'll try to convince you he's innocent—might even make a play for you."

Frowning, Sheila paced the floor. "So what? I'm a big girl now. And even if I were protecting Dobson, he couldn't convince me he's innocent. You said you saw his two sets of books. I believe you."

"Do you have to stay with him twenty-four hours a day?"

"I don't stay with any witness that much. My witness is in a secure location. I only have to check on him during the day."

"So what will you do while you're there—play chess with him while he tries to seduce you?"

Sheila bristled. "Don't be ridiculous. I won't be spending much time with him. Just because—"

"Because we slept together, you mean?"

Sheila moved outside into the hall. Thank goodness it was deserted. "I don't go around doing that with witnesses."

"That's right, I was your first. You haven't had a chance to do it with someone else."

"I don't need your insults." She disconnected her phone.

She could feel the steam erupting from her ears. She clenched her fists. She couldn't let this bother her now. She had a job to do. A break might help her to cool down. Then she'd get back to work, and not think about Brent.

Back at her desk she read over the facts on Dobson twice. Brent's angry accusations kept getting in the way. She almost wished she'd never met him, never known his kisses or the way he'd made her feel so alive, so special—had it all been an illusion?

Angry tears threatened to break forth. She brushed at the annoying wetness. She had no time for regrets.

She tried once more to concentrate on the file on her desk. She studied Dobson's picture. Blond hair, blue eyes. Even behind glasses they looked shifty. He didn't look like the man who'd shot at her from the parking lot in front of her office building. He wasn't big enough. But she hadn't gotten a good look at the guy who'd shot at her on the highway on Thanksgiving Day. He'd stood behind the open door of his pickup.

She pulled the slip of paper with Dobson's address from her purse. Now was as good a time as any to visit him and check his place out.

She waited to call until she was in her car. Even though the windows were shut, a whiff of smoked meat as she passed a barbecue restaurant, reminded her it had been a long time since lunch.

Dobson didn't answer until the phone had rung six times. "Hello," he grunted.

"This is Deputy Marshal Sheila Talbot."

"Yeah, yeah, Joe told me someone would call, but I'm watching a movie on TV. Can't you call later?"

"No. This is important. Did Joe tell you I'm your new contact?"

"Yeah, he did. Gave me some shit-assed excuse for switching. Must think I'm not in much danger."

Sounds of gunfire gave her a start until she heard music rising to a crescendo and realized what it was. "Turn off the TV."

The background noise ceased. "Shit," he snarled. "Things were getting exciting."

"I'm coming over in the morning to check out security at your place. You're in apartment number twenty-two, right?"

Dobson said, "Yes," then whined about losing his CPA license and going to jail even if he cooperated by testifying. She told him she couldn't promise anything.

She was about to hang up when he said, "Wait. Something I gotta tell you."

"What is it?"

"Heard by the grapevine that Sheldon's gonna lean on me not to testify. Probably send some torture-hungry enforcer. I need muscle, not some puny female watchdog to yap at his heels."

"Brains outwit muscles any day. We'll keep you out of sight."

"But what if there's a showdown and no time to call in backup?"

"That's not likely."

"Joe says you're a good-looking woman, but tell him to get someone with muscle if he's not gonna protect me."

"No way. I've already been assigned to you. However, I have a black belt in karate. I'll see you in the morning." She hung up.

❦

Brent shoved some cash and his new ID card on the counter of Rent a Wreck Today. "Give me a black Jetta for tonight. I'll trade it for that gray Civic tomorrow." He leaned closer to the teenage boy and whispered. "I'm tailing someone, and I don't want to be recognized. Even left my badge at home in case the guy confronts me."

Judging from the awe in the young man's eyes, the guy was too impressed with Brent's supposed assignment to ask any questions.

However, even though he parked down the block from Sheila's house, she never left. At midnight, he yawned and called it a night.

Bright and early next morning, he was there again in the gray Civic. He followed her to work, parked on Commerce Street, and waited.

Inside the building, Sheila told Alice, the receptionist, she was going to check on a witness, then noticed her new tennis bracelet with rubies alternating with sparkling diamonds. "Nice bracelet."

Alice smiled. "Thank you. It was a birthday present."

"New boyfriend?"

Alice beamed. "Think he really likes me. Maybe I'll get a ring for Christmas."

Well, Sheila thought wistfully, no one would give her one any time soon.

As she rode down the elevator, she scanned the address Joe had scribbled on a scrap of paper, and then tucked it in her briefcase. Maybe Joe suspected a leak also.

Outside, unseasonably warm December sun heated her face. She drove to Dobson's place in the west Oak Cliff section of Dallas. She passed a couple of Mexican restaurants. Several Hispanics strolled along the sidewalks. One man snapped his fingers in time with mariachi music from one of the restaurants as she parked across the street.

Dobson lived on the second floor of a six flat apartment building with no elevator. She trudged up worn wooden steps and knocked on his door.

"Yeah?"

"It's Deputy Marshal Sheila Talbot."

A wiry man with glasses fiddled with his blond mustache as he opened the door. A long, thin cigarette dangled from thin fingers. Its distinctive aroma washed over her.

Flashing her badge, she wrinkled her nose and frowned at the lack of a chain for the door. Stepping inside, she closed the door behind her. "As I told you on the phone, I'll be responsible for your safety from now on. You shouldn't open your door without asking who's there."

"What's the big deal? I knew you were coming."

"Bart Sheldon doesn't want you to testify. You can't be too careful."

"Guess you're right. Didn't think anyone else could find me."

"I'll need to check out your place."

He stepped back. "What the hell for? Joe's already done that."

"Look, your life's in danger. You need to put up with our checking and follow our orders to the letter." She walked around checking things. He followed closely on her heels.

He appeared harmless, but his way of looking her up and down made her uncomfortable. He might be a white-collar criminal, but she was glad she wore a gun in the holster hidden under her suit jacket.

Dobson's face, bristly with a day's growth of beard, looked out of place beside his neatly trimmed mustache, clean knit shirt and khaki pants. He wasn't much to look at, but at least he didn't argue with her as much as Brent. His smirk as he looked her over didn't warm her like Brent's smile. Except Brent probably wouldn't smile at her again.

She glanced out the window. "Don't know why Joe set you up here in a Mexican-American neighborhood. With your blond hair and fair skin, you'll stand out."

Dobson took a drag on his cigarette. "Said it was the only place he could find on short notice."

"I'll find you a better place in a day or two."

"Why the hell did they give me a female watchdog?" he said as she checked the latch on a window.

Sheila bristled. Things would have been easier if she'd been assigned to a woman, but she'd show this guy who was in charge. She turned to face him. "Just follow orders and stay out of trouble."

"And if I don't?"

She stepped closer. "Look. You worked for Sheldon. He won't think twice about having you put down."

Dobson scowled. "Don't you think I know that?"

"You've read the rules, haven't you?"

"Yeah, so don't bore me with more instructions."

She handed him a slip of paper. "Here's my cell phone number. Call me everyday. Don't walk farther than the next block to a restaurant or a deli and order most of your food delivered."

"That'll get old in a hurry. The video rental is three blocks away. I'll go stir crazy without some entertainment."

"You have a VCR?"

"Yeah. Joe brought that and the TV from my old place, but I can't get cable here."

"Tell me what you like, and I'll bring you some videos."

"Can't you just drive me to a rental place?"

She shook her head. "Someone might see you there. Must be something you like on regular TV. Look in *TV Guide*."

"Don't have one."

"I'll bring you one after I check out the security." She walked around, checking all the window locks. "Scan the area before you step outside." She pointed toward the door. "Hallway and stairs too."

His laugh sounded bitter. "What do you take me for, an idiot? Sheldon's probably got bullets engraved with my name."

Eyeing Dobson warily, she paused at the doorway. "By the way, where did you spend Thanksgiving?"

"Huh? What's it to you?"

"Just answer the question." She watched his face.

Dobson frowned. "Joe brought me a stinking TV dinner, said I could heat it up in the microwave. Said he had to hurry 'cause his mom was cooking a turkey an' all the fixings. Shit, he could have at least taken me to a cafeteria."

She shut the door behind her. His bitter tones had the ring of truth, but she'd check it out with Joe.

After buying a paper and taking Dobson a *TV Guide*, she

headed back to the office. For a while she thought a gray Civic was following her, but it turned left at the second light, and she didn't see it again.

She wondered how Brent was doing. Biting her lip, she hoped Joe was taking good care of him. Sighing, she tucked the classified section of the paper in her roomy purse and headed out for lunch.

She drove to the West End area and parked, then stepped out and walked into Dick's Last Resort. The food was good, and no one except the waiter would pay attention to her in this noisy restaurant. She felt safer calling about apartments here instead of the office. After calling six and checking each one out, she picked a furnished apartment in the Dallas suburb of Addison near some restaurants and shops and wrote a check for one month's rent. He'd be less noticeable here. She picked up two videos she thought he'd like from a nearby Blockbuster store and drove back to his place.

Not trusting someone else to know where she was taking him, she helped him load his stuff, including the TV and VCR into her car and his Viper, and then had him follow her.

In Addison, she helped him carry his belongings inside. When he finished, she reminded him to only go out when there were plenty of people about and not to do it too often. "Stay away from bars. And call me if you see anyone acting suspiciously."

"Sure." He gave her a long hard stare. "Lot of help you'll be with that bum leg of yours."

She frowned. "It's not a problem. In the meantime, keep a low profile."

He nodded. "That's boring as hell, but I don't want to tangle with Sheldon's men."

She paused at the door. "By the way, where were you last Friday night?"

"Huh? This a murder investigation? I haven't bumped anyone off."

"Just answer the question."

He shrugged. "If it was Friday, I was probably at a bar, can't remember which one though."

"What town?"

"Mesquite. That's where I lived until Berg moved me."

"Did you and someone else drive to Garland that night?"

"What do you want to know for?"

"Two guys in a black Viper like yours stormed a Garland Cafe."

"Shit. Why would I do a crazy thing like that? Maybe I cooked books for Sheldon, but armed robbery? That's major jail time."

Looking at his bland expression, she couldn't tell if he were lying or not. For now she'd act as if she believed him. Keeping her eye on him, she backed out the door and pulled it shut.

She headed back to the office and parked her car in the handicapped spot in the parking garage. Inside she waved at Steven, the tall security guard, as she pushed the button for the elevator.

He ran his hand through dark wavy hair and glanced at her leg. "Can't understand why you came back to work so soon after being shot."

She smiled. "I have too much work to stay away," she said as the elevator door closed in front of her. And besides, she didn't want anyone messing with stuff in her desk. From now on she'd take her file on Dobson home with her each night. His address wasn't in it, but those of his friends and relatives were. She'd have to remind him again not to contact them.

She stopped at Joe's desk. "Have you gotten Brent taken care of?"

He nodded. "Moved him to a safer place, just in case someone found out where you'd put him."

She bristled, but didn't comment on that. "Well, I moved Dobson, too."

Joe looked affronted. "What the hell for? That's an out of the way place."

"He looked too obvious in that Latino neighborhood. We

don't know how many hit men Sheldon can contact from jail. By the way, what happened with Carl Carson, the Marshal Brent was originally assigned to?"

"He's still locked away in a minimum security prison for leaking information to Sheldon and shooting at his former secretary, another witness in the case."

Sheila stepped closer. "Brent told me he saw Dobson and a well-built bodyguard outside a supermarket the day he flew to Hawaii. Brent claims it's the same guy who attacked us in Hawaii. I hope he's still locked up there."

Joe kept his voice low. "According to Dobson, Sheldon's 'enforcer' tried to convince Dobson not to turn himself in. Dobson claims he went straight to the D. A.'s office after giving that big guy the slip. I'd be extra careful if I were you. If that guy's been released from the Honolulu jail, he's probably scouting around for Dobson right now."

"Dobson said you brought him dinner on Thanksgiving, the day someone shot at me. Did you?"

Joe looked surprised. "Yeah, I did. Felt sorry for the bastard—though he's probably guilty as hell of cooking Sheldon's books. Bet he's done it for others, too. He may talk tough, but he's running scared."

She leaned close so no one else could hear. "Thanks again for giving me the chance to take on a bigger fish."

Joe smiled. "I knew you could handle it."

Back at her desk, she busied herself in paperwork until it was time to leave. Driving home, she wondered why she felt as if she were missing something. Okay, so she missed Brent like crazy, but that relationship had nowhere to go. Maybe even now, he was meeting new friends and making a conquest of some attractive woman.

She should be glad for him, shouldn't she? Unbidden, memories of their lovemaking in Hawaii washed over her, his tender touches, his fevered kisses. She sighed. She'd never experience anything that wonderful again.

Chapter 17

Sheila dialed Brent's number, but then canceled the call. She sighed. She'd done the right thing, but it tore at her heart like a bulldozer ripping out saplings. He needed a protector, not a lover. What she needed didn't count, not at the price of risking his life.

Rubbing her neck, she took a deep breath. Joe would keep him safe. That's what mattered, more than anything else. She had to remember that. What if something else went wrong? Was she being paranoid about a leak? She trusted Joe, but it wouldn't hurt to keep an eye on her co-workers, especially those complaining about the high cost of living like Joe's ex-partner, Scott Thompson. At least Brent was getting a life for himself, while her life seemed caught up with work and not much else that was meaningful.

She gritted her teeth. So what if he kissed someone else? The thought of his sexy mouth capturing some pretty woman's lips and heart made her wince. Knowing firsthand how she'd felt like a flower opening up to the sun, she reminded herself she wouldn't see him again until the trial.

At home she tried to lose herself in a movie on TV and not think about Brent. She glanced at her watch. Ten-forty-five and Dobson hadn't called yet. She dialed his number.

"Hello," he mumbled into the phone. "Oh, it's you. Can't you call later? I'm busy now." His voice lowered, took on a softer tone. "Ain't that right, sweet thing?" The unmistakable sound of someone giggling came over the wire. Dobson must have a woman there.

Sheila suppressed a groan.

"Hey, Mom, lay off," he said. "I just met this pretty little gal tonight, so give me a break. I'll call you in the morning." He hung up.

Sheesh. That's all she needed—Dobson pretending she was his mother.

Sheila set down the phone and grabbed some pajamas. He might not be any easier to manage than Brent. She undressed and got into bed, hoping she wouldn't dream of Brent tonight. In the morning the phone rang just as she was about to leave. She'd have to instruct Dobson when to call her.

However, it was Joe instead. "I have to transport a new witness to a safe place. Dallas General Hospital just called, looking for Broussard. His dad's there. Apparently he was on a business trip somewhere south of here and was driving back to Dallas to catch a plane to Detroit when he had a heart attack. Can you take Brent to see his father?"

"I'll take care of it." She hoped the heart attack was a mild one and wondered how Brent would take the news.

The phone rang again. It was Dobson this time.

She looked at her watch. "Can't you call later? I'm just about to leave for work, but about that woman. Where did you find her? Did you go out to a bar?"

"Hell, no. This gal lives across the hall. Real friendly type. Came over to say hello."

"Be careful who you get friendly with. You might let something slip that your enemies could pick up on. Is she still there?"

"Hell, no. She's a real hot pepper, but you spoiled the moment. You really know how to cut off a guy's tailin'."

"Just call me after eight o'clock in the morning tomorrow."

"Yes ma'am."

Sheila hung up and dialed Brent's number. Her pulse sped up. She was going to see him again, but she reminded herself, this was strictly business. Was he still mad at her for switching witnesses?

A sleepy Brent answered. "Hello."

"Brent, Joe's tied up, and I'm sorry to have to tell you this, but your father's in the hospital here in Dallas. They think he had a heart attack."

"Which hospital?" Anxiety colored his voice. "I'll call a taxi."

"You're not going alone. I'll pick you up. What's your address?"

He told her, and she hung up. Twenty minutes later she drove up in front of his new place, an apartment building where you had to buzz someone to get in. At least security was good here. Joe had done a better job in locating Brent than Dobson.

She knocked on the door. Brent opened it. He held a coffee mug in one hand and sock in the other. He looked great in a close fitting T-shirt, but worry lines furrowed his forehead like a freshly plowed field. She wanted to comfort him, but suspected he wouldn't welcome it. She wasn't exactly one of his favorite people. "Sorry about your father," she said. "Maybe it's not as bad as you think."

He frowned. "A heart attack, how can it be anything but bad?" She braced for another tirade about handling him over to Joe and taking on Dobson. However, all he said was, "How is he?"

"I don't know. I'll get you there as fast as I can."

Brent gulped his coffee, pulled on his sock on, then his other shoe. A few minutes later he followed her to her Mustang.

His expression serious, he rested his chin in his hand, but said nothing as she headed for Dallas General. He drummed his fingers on one knee. He must be worried sick. She couldn't help reaching out one hand to comfort him. "It may not be so bad. Your father's probably tougher than you think."

He shoved her hand away as if it were a pesky horsefly.

Sheila frowned. She'd wanted to rebuild the bond they'd shared, wanted to show Brent she cared and help him through this.

"My old man's a tough old bird." His voice sounded strained. "Sure was rough on me while I was growing up. He claimed it was for my own good…but I wouldn't wish this on him. He's got to pull through. Mom will be devastated if he doesn't."

"Has your father mellowed any since you left home?"

"Well, he doesn't whip me anymore if that's what you mean. Didn't dare after I got some muscle built up."

"Bet you were a rebellious teenager."

His harsh laugh echoed in the small space. "One Halloween a buddy and I drove way out in the country and overturned some farmer's outhouse. Turned out it belonged to a man my dad was trying to buy some property from. Don't know how he found out, but he worked me over until it hurt to sit down. Told me he'd throw me out on the streets if I did anything like that again. But that doesn't matter now. I just want to see him and know he'll be okay."

At the hospital, as they approached the information desk, Sheila touched his arm. "Let me handle this."

Brent shook his head and shrugged her hand off, looking as if she were smothering him. She bit her lip. Okay, if that's the way he was going to be, she'd do what she could to get him in to see his dad quickly.

After the clerk gave them the floor and room number and said not to stay long, Brent headed for the elevator.

"Not that way," she said in low tones and reached for his hand.

Instead of the warm clasp she remembered, he grabbed her wrist so hard she let go. His brows knotted, he said, "You never learn, do you? I don't like being pushed around. You're not responsible for me now, so lay off, Sergeant Sheila."

Through clenched teeth, she whispered, "You want to get yourself knocked off in an elevator? You need to take the stairs." She stepped behind him and pushed on his back. "That way."

He glared at her, but headed for the stairway.

All the way up their footsteps echoed against pristine white walls. She kept looking back to make sure they were the only ones in the stairway. He said not a word, but marched beside her. He was careful not to brush against her as if she might contaminate him. Like she had AIDS or something.

At the landing on the fourth floor, she stuck out her arm to bar his way. "Let me check out the floor."

He frowned, but let her step out first.

Seeing only a white-clad nurse assisting an elderly man in pajamas to make his way down the hall, Sheila beckoned to Brent. She walked beside him to room 409.

She paused at the doorway. The face of the man in the bed lit up, but didn't smile. She could see a faint resemblance to Brent, but his father's hair was thinner and streaked with gray. A double chin, fuzzy with a day's growth of beard, and protruding stomach hinted at the cause of his heart attack.

Mr. Schmidt yanked the covers up to his neck. "You came. Wasn't sure you would." His lips curled into a slight smile, but his voice sounded weak. "Didn't want to worry your mother, but it's good to see family."

Brent grasped the older man's hand. "You're my father. I couldn't stay away. How are you feeling? What do the doctors say?"

His father waved a hand at the IV stand and wires attached to him. "Ask the nurses about my damn condition. They won't even tell me if I'm going to live or die." His gaze fastened on Sheila. "Aren't you going to introduce me?"

Sheila waited, wondering what he'd say. She didn't want to

be here with him, but she didn't dare let him visit a big hospital by himself. She straightened her spine, ready to add to whatever explanation he gave to make it plausible.

Brent cleared his throat. "This is Sheila Talbot, a friend who offered to give me a lift."

Well at least he'd called her a friend. She stepped forward. "Nice to meet you. Sorry you're laid up."

He frowned and raised up on his elbows. "Won't be for long. Soon as they let me out of here, I've got to get back and take care of business."

"Dad, don't worry about the business. Your health is what's important. Jody—" he turned toward Sheila "—that's my sister, can look after Mom. And I'm sure your assistant can manage the hardware store for a while. You need to mind the doctor."

Mr. Schmidt's eyebrows drew closer, digging a furrow between them. "You think I'm a damn fool?"

Brent shook his head. "No, just obstinate."

"Like you."

A nurse stepped in. "You've been here long enough. He needs to rest. If you like, you can come back after lunchtime."

Sheila edged toward the door.

"Just get well," Brent said, gripping his dad's hand. Brent hugged his father. "Don't forget, we all love you and want you back home." After giving his father a smile, Brent turned to Sheila. His smile disappeared, and a strained expression took over. "Let's go."

She stepped into the hall and scanned the walkway. A man in hospital scrubs strode down the hall, his face partially covered with a surgical mask. "Get back," she said as Brent bumped into her.

The man shoved her to one side, grabbed Brent's arm and punched his face. "You sorry S.O.B.! You're the one who got me into this mess. I ought to—"

Reacting instinctively, Sheila grabbed the man's arm, stuck her foot behind his ankle and shoved him down. She straddled him, yanked his arms over his head and yelled, "Someone get security."

As the man struggled to sit up, Brent grabbed his wrists with one hand and pressed on the man's shoulder with the other.

The man looked familiar. Sheila tore the surgical mask away. "Dobson!" she exclaimed.

A nurse rushed over. "I called. They'll be here in a minute."

"What the hell is he doing here?" asked Brent.

Dobson squirmed. "I work here. Needed dough. Hospital was shorthanded. They hired me as an orderly."

She scowled at him. "You should have checked with me before you took a job. Why attack Brent? Didn't they give you a deal when you agreed to testify?"

"My lawyer said to hold out. Said they'd come up with something better if I balked." He struggled to get loose.

Brent tightened his hold on Dobson's wrists. "What are you doing on this floor?"

"Saw you two in the lobby." He gasped. "Just wanted to get in a few licks."

"Oww," Dobson wailed. "That hurts. You're supposed to protect me, not let someone attack me."

Sheila put on her sternest look. "I ought to kick you out of the program and have you thrown in jail for assaulting this witness."

He glared at her. "I know too much. That would get me killed." His face turned pale.

At the sound of heavy footsteps, Sheila looked up to see a beefy security guard striding toward them.

"What's going on here?" he asked.

She kept a firm hold on Dobson. "I'm a federal Marshal, and this is my witness who got out of hand."

The well-muscled guard bent over to look at Dobson. "What's he doing in our hospital uniform?"

"He said he has a job here, but I'm not sure you want him for an employee."

The guard rubbed his chin. "Didn't know they had female U.S. Marshals. You got a badge?"

She gestured at her purse, now lying on the floor and looked at Brent. "Take my place while I get out my credentials."

"Be glad to."

"The hell he will," growled Dobson. He struggled, but Brent straddled the guy and held him down.

Dobson let out a stream of profanity. Brent wrenched Dobson's arm behind his back. Sheila held out her badge.

The guard studied it. "Sure you can manage this guy now?"

She nodded, then fished out a set of handcuffs and locked Dobson's wrists together. "Now get up slowly. Try anything stupid, and you'll be charged with assault and kicked out of the program. You going to play ball or not?"

"Man, you're tough. I like women who are soft and clingy."

Sheila glared at him. Only Brent knew how soft she could be. "I'll help you hold onto your skin. That's the kind of woman you need now."

He glowered at her. "Why'd I have to get tangled up with you?"

"Just be quiet," Sheila barked. "Now come with me."

She marched Dobson to her car and opened the back door. "Get in," she barked. She turned to Brent. "Sit back there, and keep an eye on him. Dobson, if you so much as lay a hand on him, I'll kick you out of the program and let Sheldon's men have at you."

She dropped Dobson off first, then took Brent to his new place. After dropping him off, she called Joe on his cell phone.

"Berg here, what's up, Sheila?"

"Joe, where are you? I took Brent to see his dad." She didn't want to let Joe know Dobson had slipped from her control, but figured she'd better tell him what happened.

231

"Dobson got a job at the hospital where I took Brent without telling me."

"So? I did tell him he needed to get a job. I paid the rent, but I didn't give him much cash."

"He saw us come in and assaulted Brent. I had to knock him down and cuff him, then drop him off at his apartment before I took your witness home."

"I'm sure you handled it okay."

"I wouldn't have had to if you'd planned your time better." As soon as she said that, she realized she shouldn't have talked to her mentor that way.

"You take care of your business, and I'll take care of mine," he snapped and broke the connection.

She rubbed the back of her neck. Criticizing her mentor had been a bad move—even though she was right. If he were mad at her, how could she manage with no one else at the agency she dared trust?

❧

On the other side of Dallas, Nate was just waking up when the phone rang. He stretched and grabbed the phone. "Hello," he growled. What idiot called at seven in the morning?

Bart Sheldon was on the line. "You screwed up in Hawaii. This time you'd better do it right. I can drop an anonymous hint to the D.A., and you'll be toast in this town. But if you handle it right, I'll see you get enough for a down payment on a car like your brother's."

"Hey. I can handle it. But Boss, if you're in jail, how am I goin' to get my money?"

"Don't worry. I may be in the slammer, but I have ways. I'll see that thirty-five grand gets deposited to your account in amounts less than ten grand, of course. Don't want the feds chargin' anyone with money laundering."

"What do you want me to do?"

"That female Marshal and her pretty boy witness, Schmidt I think his real name is, see they have a fatal accident, one the cops can't trace."

"Consider it done, boss." His mind raced. This would be the biggest challenge he'd ever had. He needed to plan very carefully.

Chapter 18

It was a bright sunny day — not like the rainy cold day she'd held Darla's hand at her husband's funeral. Bill had been found lying in an alley behind a seedy bar. Sheila didn't know whether to avoid the subject or encourage Darla to talk about it. Sheila pushed a grinning Jason in the back yard swing and smiled at Darla. "I appreciate your letting me spend some time with my — with your son."

Darla brushed tears from her eyes, but didn't mention Bill. "It's the least I could do. He's been a delight ever since you placed him in my arms."

"He seems happy and healthy. You've taken good care of him."

Darla sighed. "I try, but it's been hard taking care of him alone and dealing with Bill's senseless murder. Jason keeps asking where his daddy is. Maybe I should have taken him to the funeral instead of having Mary next door keep him."

Sheila patted her friend's shoulder. "He's too young for that. Tell him Daddy's in Heaven. They still don't have any suspects, do they?"

Darla brushed tears from her eyes and shook her head. "Must have been something to do with his gambling debts. I can't believe he forged my signature on a home equity loan and turned over what little we'd invested in the house to that enforcer. I'll have to go to work to keep up the payments."

"Did you ever meet the man?"

Darla rubbed at her eyes. "I wish I had. I'd have chased him out of the house with a baseball bat for harassing Bill."

"Did Bill ever say anything about the guy or mention his name?"

"No, but he called our house once. I might recognize his voice. It was deep, like Neil Diamond's."

Sheila tried to remember how her attackers had sounded. The one who looked like a native Hawaiian spoke in angry tones, but she didn't seem to remember him having a deep voice. And the other guy, Nate, had frightened her so much she couldn't remember much about him.

"Darla, do you suppose he was the one I chased from your house that day?"

A look of fear shaped her friend's face. "I hope not. If it was, then he knows where we live. Maybe he thinks I have cash hidden in the house. Am I being paranoid?"

Sheila shook her head. "No. I'm glad you got that security system installed. You need to get a dog too. A woman alone with a child can't be too careful."

Darla frowned. "Okay, I'll do it, but the dog will have to stay in the yard. I won't let it be alone with Jason. He might pull his tail, and then the dog might attack him. Let's not think about that this afternoon. I'll go make some coffee and set out some cookies."

"I want a cookie," chanted Jason, as Darla slammed the back door behind her. Minutes later, she was back and handed the boy a cookie. It disappeared in seconds.

Standing in front of him, Sheila pushed Jason higher on the swing, hoping he wouldn't let go of the rope. He chortled, then did exactly what she'd feared. He let go of the ropes and reached for her.

She caught him and stumbled backwards. Hugging him to her, she inhaled his chocolate cookie smell. If only she'd kept him, she could be watching him grow and develop every day.

But at the time, she'd felt so helpless to take care of him. With no job and disapproving parents, who'd never accept her or her baby if she'd kept him, she'd done the best thing she could at the time.

Jason wriggled in her arms. "Put me down," he said in a commanding voice.

She laughed. If only her co-workers could see her now, being ordered about by a four-year old. At least now she could see him sometimes. She set him down.

"Another cookie," Jason said. Sheila hugged him and took his hand to take him inside.

As she opened the screen door, a large man wearing a black ski mask grabbed them both. Even with the ski mask, she knew it was Nate. Behind him she heard moans. She struggled against his rock-hard frame, then kicked him, but he held her arm in a vice-like grip. "Hands off. I'm a U.S. Marshal," she barked.

"I don't care who the hell you are. You're coming with me."

Sheila broke the man's hold. "Go to Mommy," she told Jason.

His uneven footsteps were followed by an anguished cry. "Mommy, Mommy."

Through the open door she glimpsed Darla, lying still on the floor. Blood painted the floor in macabre streaks. Nate grabbed Sheila. Whirling, she punched him in the gut. He recoiled for an instant, then swung at her. Jason screamed, "Mommy's bleeding!"

"Shut the fuck up, kid," Nate barked. He shook cookies from a box onto the table. "Eat those."

Jason kept screaming. Nate backhanded the kid's face.

"You monster!" Sheila shouted. Adrenaline surging, she lit into her attacker. Punched his chest, his face, his stomach, anywhere she could get in a blow. "Call 9-1-1," she shouted to Jason, but the boy just stood there, crying. "Go to Mary next door, quick." Hearing the back door slam, she hoped Jason had obeyed.

"So," he growled in a deep voice, "you want to fight, do you?" He threw a punch toward her.

She ducked. His blow missed her face, caught her shoulder. She ignored the searing pain, turned sideways. Aimed a backwards kick to his groin.

"You bitch!" He doubled over—for an instant. She ran toward the living room for her gun in her purse. His heavy footsteps pounded behind her like thundering hoof beats. Before she could get her gun, he grabbed her arms, pinning them to her sides.

She broke loose, hit his face with her fist. He retaliated with a blow to her nose.

The pain was intense. Blood ran down her chin. She aimed a forward kick at his groin and connected.

This time he took a few seconds longer to recover. Enough for her to see blood spreading out on the floor around Darla.

Nate let up for an instant. Then he grabbed her arm. She struggled, saw a hypodermic needle. "No!" she screamed. Frantic now, she yanked her arm. His grip proved stronger. She tried to kick him. No good—he was too close.

The needle was sharp, the pain piercing. Suddenly weak, she tried to break loose, but couldn't. She struggled to remain conscious, hoping whatever he'd shot her with wouldn't kill her.

She tried to get up, but couldn't. She felt so weak.

Darla raised her head. "Take—take care of Jason," she gasped.

"I will," Sheila promised.

Nate grabbed her shoulders. He had her in his power now. She felt herself blacking out, sliding to the floor. She fought the weakness and lost.

❧

"Got the Marshal bitch," Nate growled into the phone. "Don't worry no more about that S.O.B. bean counter. He'll come looking for her, and then I'll take care of him. A nice little accident in her own Mustang should finish them off, don't you think?"

"Be careful," Sheldon urged in his gravelly voice. "Someone could be listening in."

"Don't be paranoid. I'm using a cell phone."

"I'm not worried about your end. This is a prison, damn it. We can bloody well kiss our privacy rights goodbye in here."

"Okay, I'll contact you in a few days after I take care of the witness and this Sheila bitch."

"Do it today." Sheldon paused. "If you can't get through, leave a message. Say, 'the mustang and the stallion won't run anymore.' Then you'd better get the hell away from Dallas."

"Not so fast. What about the money?"

"Call Carl's girlfriend, Kathy Brandon, in Austin. She's got power of attorney, as long as she doesn't take more than nine grand out in a month."

"You promised twenty for each."

"Okay, but ask for nine now. If she doubts you, tell her to check with me. When it's done, tell her to contact me, and I'll okay the rest. Uh oh, guard's coming. Have to get off the phone."

Nate looked at his sleeping charge. Sheila was still out, but she twitched from time to time. He'd better give her something sweet before her sugar got too low. She mustn't die yet. He opened a can of orange juice, raised her up and tried to force her to swallow.

After taking a few sips, she seemed to rally and grabbed the can. He couldn't let her have too much. She'd come to. He had to pry the can loose from her grasp. She lunged toward him, and then fell back. Good. He'd given her just enough. Now if she would stay in that comatose state long enough, he could stage a believable accident.

He needed someone to watch his charge while he worked on her car. He picked up the phone and called his half-brother.

"Hello. Who's this?" his brother said.

"It's Nate. I need a favor."

"Depends. I have to keep a low profile now."

"You don't have anything to fear from me, but Sheldon's another story."

"What do you want?"

"I've got an unconscious U.S. Marshal bitch that Sheldon says I need to get rid of. All I need is someone to keep an eye on her while I sabotage her car. I have to make it look like an accident, so it might take a while."

The line was silent for a moment. "You've got a female Marshal?" Dobson asked.

"What difference does the sex make?"

"There's one supposed to be watching me, a tough one."

"Well if it is, and she has an accident, you can get a male guardian, one who'll protect you better. This one puts up a good fight. Went straight for the balls."

"Ouch."

"You goin' to help or not? Don't forget all the fights I helped you win when we were kids."

"I'd better not chance it. If someone ties me to that so called accident, they might kick me out of the program. Then one of Sheldon's goons will get me for sure."

"Damn it! Some help you are. I'll get someone else." Nate slammed the phone down.

Carl would have been perfect, but he was locked up. Now Kathy just might help, especially if he gave her half a grand. He'd lost her number, so he dialed directory assistance for Austin.

He was scribbling down Kathy's number when he heard Sheila's phone ringing.

❧

Brent held his cell phone to his ear and counted the rings. Why didn't she answer? Maybe she had caller ID and was refusing to answer because she knew it was he. She'd said she was going to visit Darla and her son today, but she'd agreed to pick him up and take him to the hospital to visit his father because Joe was out of town again. Visiting hours were almost over. Why didn't she answer?

After the incident with Dobson, Sheila had insisted he not go to the hospital alone. He tried her number again. Still no answer. An uneasy feeling haunted him.

Not knowing what else to do, he dialed Joe's cell phone. Joe would want to know if something had happened to Sheila.

Joe answered on the second ring. "What's up?"

"It's Brent. Sheila took me to see my father in the hospital yesterday. Good thing she did because Dobson was there, and he attacked me."

"Yeah, she told me. Maybe I should have given Dobson to someone else, but she asked to trade, and he was the only witness I had that was suitable. Did Dobson find out where you live?"

"No. Sheila called last night. She told me Dobson was fired from the hospital and has gotten a part-time job keeping books for a group of doctors. I'm calling because Sheila promised to take me to the hospital today, but visiting hours are almost over, and she doesn't answer her phone. I'm afraid something's happened."

"Let me call Dobson, see if he knows anything. Bye."

Brent sat on the couch, then stood and paced the floor. Sheila claimed she could take care of herself. She had to be all right. But he couldn't help imagining her knocked out and moaning on some cold floor — not cries of satisfaction like he'd heard in Hawaii, but because she'd been beaten.

Dirk Dobson checked the figures again. He was missing ten cents somewhere. Those doctors who paid him to do their books might not miss ten cents, but it was a matter of pride. He added the figures again, wishing he'd brought more than a simple calculator with him when he went into hiding. He'd been so flustered when Marshal Berg had picked him up, he'd just grabbed the bare necessities. Maybe he could ask Sheila to get his financial calculator out of storage.

His phone rang. The caller ID said Berg. Wondering what Joe wanted, he picked up the phone.

"Have you done anything to Sheila?" Joe's harsh tones assaulted Dobson's ear.

"Hell no."

"What's this I hear about you assaulting a guy at the hospital?"

"He's the reason I'm in this position."

"Wait a minute. You're the one who kept two sets of books for Sheldon."

Traffic noises sounded in the background. Joe must be driving somewhere. Dobson wondered if Sheila had told Joe where he lived now. "So I engaged in creative bookkeeping; that's small potatoes. And if I testify, they might let me off with probation."

"But you knew about Sheldon's illegal activities and didn't report them. And you asked to be in the Witness Security Program. Nobody forced you."

"I'm not afraid of Sheldon's main enforcer. I know him, but Sheldon might get someone else to silence me."

"Do you know where Sheila is?" Joe asked.

"I thought she was supposed to be keeping tabs on me."

"She promised another witness to take him somewhere, but she hasn't shown up. Just want to be sure you weren't responsible for her being missing."

"Hell no." After moving him from that Latin neighborhood where his blonde hair and blue eyes made him stand out like an albino pigeon, she'd kept him safe so far. "Joe," he asked,

"How many female Marshals work in the Witness Security Program in Dallas?"

"Sheila's the only one. Why do you ask?"

"Uh, oh." He'd been afraid of that. Nate hadn't said it in so many words, but he probably did in Darla's husband because he welshed on a gambling debt under Sheldon's orders. Had he been ordered to do in Sheila?

"What's that mean?" Joe said. "Do you know something I should know?"

Dobson hesitated. If he ratted on Nate, his brother could face the death penalty. And Sheldon might put a contract out on him. But if he didn't say something, Sheila would die. Except for the hospital incident, she'd been good to him so far. No matter what he chose, there'd be trouble.

"Well?" Joe asked.

Dobson rubbed his neck. What the hell was he going to do now?

Chapter 19

Her cell phone was ringing. Sheila forced her eyelids open. She could barely see out of one eye. Beneath it her cheek felt swollen, but she couldn't reach it. Damn, her hands were tied.

She ached all over. Why did she feel so weak? And why was she lying on the floor beside a bed? She tried again to reach the phone in her pocket. By the time she got it out of her pocket, it stopped ringing.

This wasn't Darla's house, but where was she? She vaguely remembered Nate, the man who'd injected her with insulin in Hawaii, had surprised her at Darla's house. Must have found a sharp lawyer to get out of the Honolulu jail so fast.

She hoped he was sporting a few bruises, too. She'd been about to get the best of him this time when the damn brute had grabbed a syringe from the table and stuck her with a needle again. Still groggy, she couldn't tell if it were insulin or something else.

Was Darla dead? Sheila hoped not. Had Jason made it to the house next door?

Was her son on the bed? She craned her neck and winced from the pain. She was too close to see.

Her feet were tied. Straining to sit upright, she toppled over the first time, then held her breath. Trying again, she managed to pull herself up. Her muscles cried out for relief.

No one lay on the bed. Thank goodness he wasn't here. She

wanted to beat Nate to a pulp, but she wasn't in any shape to do that now.

No one else knew where she was. It was up to her to save herself. Hearing footsteps, she lay back down. The hard floor pressed against her backbone. The musty odor of dust threatened to overwhelm her. Feeling a sneeze coming on, she crammed her tongue against the roof of her mouth to stifle it.

The clomp of boots vibrated the floor, making her head ache even more. She turned her head. A blinding pain forced her eyes shut, but she opened them enough to see the heavy-set man who'd abducted her in the doorway.

Nate stepped closer and kicked her. She let out a quiet moan. He'd expect that. Then he grabbed her shoulders, raised her to a half-sitting position and shook her. He smelled of cigars and sweat. She looked at his unshaven face and willed herself not to gag.

Wincing from the pain, she let her head droop and looked down. That made her neck ache, but she didn't want to appear alert. She let her head loll, forcing her expression to remain bland. All the while, her mind raced, trying to think what she could do.

"Look at me, slut."

That did it. "You bastard. You're a coward to pick on women and a little kid. What's the matter? Afraid to face me in a fair fight?"

"Why you—" His huge hand covered her face. She couldn't breathe. One of his fingers slid over her mouth. She bit it.

He let go, howled in pain, and cursed. She gulped in air.

Using the heel of his hand, he shoved her down. Sporting an evil grin, he rose and left the room. His footsteps made the floor vibrate, jarring her already aching body, but she was alone.

Somehow, she'd have to get out of here.

"Well, Dobson?" Joe's voice on the phone sounded insistent as he repeated his question. "Do you know something or not?"

Nate had said things would look like a regular accident, but Sheila hadn't done anything to deserve that. On the contrary, she'd done everything to keep him safe, even told him where to apply for a job. He couldn't let Nate carry out his plan.

Dobson took a deep breath. "Think one of Sheldon's men kidnapped her… he called me to help."

"What did you say?"

"Told him no."

"Did you call the police?"

"No. Don't know where she's at. Cops would laugh at me with a story like that." And besides, they'd want to know the identity of the kidnapper. He couldn't just throw his brother to the wolves.

"What else can you tell me?" Joe asked.

"Sheila stopped by earlier, to check on me she said. Said she was visiting a girlfriend with a kid. Heard her asking directions from here on the phone. Sounded like Pinella Court."

"Did you get the house number?"

"Hell, no. Didn't think it important."

"What's this guy's name? Know where he lives?"

"No," Dobson lied. "Only know his nickname…Tiny." He grinned. Nate would hate that, but he had to tell Joe something.

"Thanks. I'll get on it. Got to go now."

❦

Brent grabbed the phone on the first ring. "Hello," he barked.

"It's Joe. I called the cops, but they won't do anything since Sheila hasn't been missing twenty-four hours yet. Got two Deputy Marshals on standby until I hear something."

245

Brent gripped the phone, its hard plastic cover warm from his touch. "Damn it, we've got to find her."

"Cool it, man. Any idea where she went?"

"Only that she was going to her friend Darla's house before she came to pick up me."

"Know where this Darla lives?"

"On some court about a mile from here."

"Was it Pinella Court? I'll look it up."

The sound of brakes being applied came over the phone. Brent hoped Joe wasn't on a busy highway.

"Damn it. My GPS won't work, and I'm sixty miles from there."

"I'll ask my landlady."

"Find out. I'll stay on the line. Sheila's tough, but I think something's happened to her."

Brent raced down the outside stairs of the house, and pounded on the front door. "Mrs. Simmons, I need your help."

The door opened a crack. A chain limited the opening to four inches. Two blue eyes peered at him. Her wrinkled face, framed by salt and pepper curls spoke of wariness. He couldn't blame her for that after the way he'd pounded on the door and yelled.

She squinted. "Oh, it's you. What do you want?"

He stepped back. No use frightening her. "Where's Pinella Court?"

Her face relaxed. With a sweet smile, she said, "Oh, you need directions. Go down this street three blocks and turn left at the next corner—or is it right, I'm not sure, but that's Market Street. Pinella is a little street that runs into it."

"Thanks," he said. He told Joe what he'd found out and took off running.

Three blocks later he had to admit he was out of shape. As soon as this was over, he'd start jogging again. Stopping for a minute to catch his breath, he dialed Sheila's number again. He hoped he'd find her drinking coffee and laughing with Darla, maybe holding her son in her lap. Must be hard to give your child away and let someone else raise him.

The phone rang nine times, and then a voicemail message kicked in. "Damn." Stuffing the phone in his pocket, he pounded the pavement again.

He looked at the street sign, Market Street. Well, at least the old lady was right about that. He turned left, ran down the street. It dead-ended just ahead. He was about to turn and go the other way when he saw the opening. No wonder he hadn't seen it before. The street sign was bent almost to the ground.

He raced around the corner, looking for a two-story house. Sheila had said the living room had a cathedral ceiling with two skylights.

Nearing the circle at the end of the court, he saw only three two-story houses, and they all had skylights. Damn. He couldn't remember if it was the middle house or one of the two beside it. Hopefully, he wouldn't have to knock on all three doors. The motor of a lawnmower roared to life on the house on the left, and a brawny man pushed it along the edge of the yard. Sheila had told him Darla's husband had been found dead in an alley. That ruled out one house. Both of the other houses had skylights on the roof.

He strode up to the door of the middle house and knocked. A slender teenage girl in jeans came to the door. "Yes?" she said.

"Uh, does a woman named Darla live next door?"

The girl nodded and shut the door, her single blonde pigtail flapping against her shoulder.

He took a deep breath, then ran to the other house. The door was cracked open, but he knocked anyway. No one answered. Then he called. Still no answer.

He smelled he coppery odor of blood. His pulse raced. Wary of calling out, he pushed the door open. He trod across the gold carpet, well lit by the skylight. An eerie silence lay over the house. Even the sound of the lawnmower had ceased.

If someone had attacked Sheila or Darla, they'd be gone by now, wouldn't they? The hairs on the back of his neck rose.

He peeked in the kitchen. The smell was stronger. Things looked normal—clean dishes stacked in a dish drainer, a fresh towel hanging over the sink, but the back door was open. A breeze flapped the pages of a calendar tacked to the side of the cupboard. A highchair stood beside the table. A child's mug tipped on its side lay on the tray. Something spilled on the floor. Tomato juice? Catsup? Or blood?

Then he saw the woman's body. He swallowed a lump in his throat. He hoped to hell it wasn't Sheila.

Leaning over, he smoothed matted blonde hair from her face. It wasn't Sheila, thank the lord. He checked her neck for a pulse, but his sinking spirits told him she was already dead.

His fingers confirmed what he'd suspected. She had no pulse. Pulling his phone from his pocket with shaking fingers, he dialed 9-1-1 and reported what he'd found. He ran upstairs and checked the bedrooms. No sign of Sheila or the kid.

The sound of a car engine startled him. Sheila's Mustang roared out of the curved driveway. Must have been parked in back of the house. He hadn't seen it from the street. A man was driving it. He didn't see anyone in the passenger seat. Was Sheila lying on the back seat or in the trunk—perhaps unconscious or dead? His heart pounded. He ran outside. "Wait!" he yelled, but the car kept on going.

Maybe there was another car in the garage. He ran outside. No car, but a motorcycle leaned against the back steps.

A helmet hung from the handlebars, and a key was in the ignition. He grabbed the key and mounted the bike.

It took precious seconds to start it, but he managed to zoom down the street before the blue Mustang drove out of sight. He passed a black pickup truck parked near the corner.

Stopped at a red light, one car behind the guy, Brent tried Sheila's number again. After several rings she answered. Her "Hello" sounded weak and reedy.

"Are you all right?" he asked, his heart pounding in time to the rock music of the car beside him.

"No. I'm tied up. Don't know how long I've been here. Barely managed to get the phone from my pocket. I've been drugged."

"Where are you?"

"Some house where Nate took me. He killed Darla, then kidnapped me. He said something about planning an accident for me."

Brent gulped. "Did he take Jason too?"

"No. I told him to run next door."

"I just saw him drive your car away from Darla's house, but I didn't see anyone else in the car."

"He must have gone back for my car," Sheila said, her voice sounding weak. "I'll try to call the police, but you'd better do it too. I'm in a house with a weeping willow outside the bedroom window. It's on Austin Street just before the light at Garland Road. I remember driving by this place before on my way to check on you."

"I'm following him." The light changed to green. Cars surged forward. "Got to go now."

At the last minute Brent realized the Mustang had turned right. He zipped around the corner. A few blocks later, he heard the clanging of a railroad signal and the whistle of a train. If he could beat it, he could get to that house before Sheila's captor.

Holding his breath, he zigzagged around the cars in front. The crossing guards were lowering. He hoped to hell he had enough time to get through.

The sound of the train blended with the clanging. The beam of its bright light called like a beacon to death.

Heart pounding, pulse racing, he zoomed through, almost blinded by the engine's bright light. A whoosh of air cooled his back. The clackedy clack of the wheels and metal bars hooking the cars together resounded in his ears. But he'd made it. And the man in Sheila's Mustang was back on the other side. Now if he could only find Sheila in time.

Later, stopping for a red light, he was tempted to run it. Then he glanced at the street sign, Austin Street. The light changed. He turned right and raced down the street, the wind chilling his face and hands. He gripped the wheel. His gaze raked the row of houses. Two blocks later he saw it: the house with a weeping willow.

Braking, he turned in the driveway. Saw a partially open window. "Sheila," he yelled.

"In here," came a reply.

Sheila lay trussed on the floor. He caught his breath and fingered his pocket knife in his pocket. "Are you okay?"

"I think so."

Sound of a car screeching to a stop was followed by the rattle of a key in the door.

"He's back. Hurry," Sheila begged.

Frantic, Brent tried to squeeze through the window.

The door opened and Nate stood in the doorway. After whipping out a Glock, he aimed it at Brent. "Don't come any farther or I'll shoot."

Realizing he wouldn't be any help dead, Brent pulled his head and arms back from the narrow opening.

A siren wailed in the distance. Thank goodness. Now if only the cops got here in time.

Holding the gun to her head, Nate cut the rope around her ankles and pulled her up. "Walk out with me, and I won't shoot your boyfriend." He hustled her out the door.

Seconds later, the sound of a car drew Brent's attention. Sheila's Mustang zoomed by and careened around the corner. The big guy was driving. Sheila was in the front seat beside him. Damn. He should have done something to stop him.

Chapter 20

Gut twisting, Brent watched the car speed away. Sheila was slumped inside. Had he drugged her again? Brent shook his fist at the departing car, dialed 9-1-1, and reported what had happened. Pulse pounding, he waited for the police. They had to catch that pervert before he hurt Sheila.

Life had been simple. Before. All he'd wanted was to run his own life again. Now it would be empty without her. Loving Sheila changed everything. If something happened to her, he didn't know what he'd do. More than anything else, he wanted to go after Sheila and punch the daylights out of Nate for hurting her, but the cops were better able to deal with him.

Inside the Mustang Sheila squirmed, trying to get her hands free. At least he'd tied them in front of her. "What kind of sick bastard are you to drug an innocent woman?"

"Never mind that. I'm betting your witness has the guts to come after you."

"He's a real man. He doesn't pick on women and little kids."

Nate scowled. "A real man's tough, like me."

"Yeah, so tough, you had to beat me up and drug me."

"Didn't want you getting away and spoiling my plans," he snarled.

"What makes you think you can get away with kidnapping a U. S. Marshal?" she taunted, hoping he wouldn't notice she was trying to get her hands loose.

"Besides being strong, I'm clever."

"Your ego's humongous."

He pointed his gun at her. "Don't try to impress me with big words. I could shoot you right here and now."

"You hear those sirens. The cops are coming. They'll catch you. Killing a U.S. Marshal gets you the death penalty in Texas."

He zoomed around a corner and ran a red light. The car picked up speed. "I won't get caught. That's LBJ Freeway ahead."

She looked at the speedometer. It said sixty. Even if she got her hands free, she didn't dare jump out. Not at this speed. Maybe she could cause him to crash, but at sixty, she had a good chance of being killed.

She looked behind, hoping to see a patrol car. Nothing. It was up to her.

Her wrists were raw from trying to get loose. The access ramp to LBJ Freeway lay ahead. It was now or never.

She leaned toward him, bit his right arm.

"Ow." He yanked his arm free and shoved her face away, his finger jabbing into her eye.

The pain overwhelmed her so much she could hardly think. By the time she could focus, they were on the freeway. He wove in and out of lanes. She focused on the speedometer with her other eye. It showed eighty-five. She didn't dare attack him now. They'd both be killed.

"Why are you doing this?" she asked.

"Shut up."

"It's for the money, isn't it? What good will that do if you get caught?"

"I'll get twenty grand with each of you dead, and they won't catch me."

Oh, no. He planned to kill Brent too. She had to stop him somehow.

With his meaty hand, he adjusted the rear view mirror and then glanced at the side mirror. He talked big, but he looked worried.

Sirens sounded closer. She could only hope the police caught him before they wrecked.

After he reached Highway 80, the speedometer hit ninety, then one hundred. She held her breath as he pulled around an eighteen-wheeler.

❧

Back in Garland Brent saw the police cruiser, its sirens screaming, come down the street.

The police cruiser pulled into the driveway. Brent explained how the killer had driven off with Sheila in her Mustang.

The cop's female partner, a black woman, asked, "Did that guy hurt the woman?"

"I don't know, but he drugged her."

The male officer, a stocky white man whose name badge said Lt. Stapleton, said, "Which way did he go?"

Brent pointed to the right. "I'm coming with you." He started walking toward the cycle.

"Leave it to us. You could get killed yourself." Stapleton turned to his partner. "We're losing time, Jo. Let's go."

The female cop said, "You stay here, sir."

Stapleton's scowl deepened. "Jo, call for backup." He slid behind the wheel of the cruiser.

Jo scribbled down Brent's cell number. "We'll call when we have the kidnapper under control." She was speaking into a microphone as they zoomed off.

Brent jumped on the motorcycle and roared down the street. Thank goodness they were still blowing the sirens. He ran a red light and finally caught up. He followed them to the freeway, almost choking in the exhaust of the cop car. His heart pounded.

They had to get to her in time. He gritted his teeth. Hoped against hope she'd be all right. She had to be. He didn't want to go through life without her. Even listening to her telling him what to do would be music to his ears.

Pulse racing, he kept pace with the patrol car. The Crown Vic pulled onto the freeway. His heart sank. More chance of accidents with all that traffic. With luck it would slow down that maniac who had Sheila. He kept his eyes straight ahead, trying to catch a glimpse of her blue Mustang. Thank the lord, there hadn't been time for the bastard to switch cars.

❧

Jolted by the impact, Sheila heard a terrible scraping noise and the sharp blast of a horn. Nate had cut it too close. The eighteen-wheeler moved to another lane, but her car was knocked against a guard rail. A siren sounded in the distance.

Her captor scowled and swerved down an exit ramp, then to the side of the road. The car plowed through the grass and into underbrush, barely missing a tree. It knocked down a skinny sapling and came to a halt.

Nate jumped out and ran around the car. He jerked the door open. Yanked her out. She stumbled, nearly knocking him down. However, with her hands still tied, she couldn't do much. Thank goodness, he hadn't had time to tie her feet again. Maybe she could run for it.

He pulled her behind a tree and held a gun to her head. She felt rough bark against her back, a cold metal rim against her temple. Her heart beat a staccato rhythm. Would he shoot her now? Suddenly she found it hard to breathe.

His hot breath heated her face. "Don't even think of running. I'm an excellent shot."

The sirens sounded louder now. If only the police could follow their trail, and she could stay alive long enough for them to catch him. Her pulse raced. Her mouth grew dry. He was too close to kick.

*

Weaving in and out of lanes behind the police car, Brent marveled at the way cars parted. He'd enjoy this ride if only he weren't so desperate to get Sheila back.

After following Nate onto Highway 80 and traveling several miles, the patrol car pulled to the side of the road. Why were they stopping?

Then he saw a flash of blue, lit by the sun. Sheila's Mustang. It sat mired in underbrush. Woods loomed beyond. His heart jerked. Was she hurt?

He jumped off the bike and let it fall. Took a few steps toward the Mustang.

"Get back," shouted an officer.

Brent halted. Strained to see if anyone still were inside the Mustang. It looked empty. Might be a trap.

Guns drawn, the two cops approached the vehicle.

*

Twenty yards from the highway Sheila stumbled. Nate pushed her ahead of him. "Look," she said, "it's not me you want, but my witness. I can show you where to find him."

He scowled. "And have you two gang up on me? Forget it. I don't need a stupid bitch telling me how to do my job."

The cold metal of the gun chilled her back. This wasn't the time to argue. Not if she wanted to stay alive. "Where are you taking me?" she asked, trying to sound meek. Maybe if he thought she felt helpless, he might be less vigilant.

"Shut up and walk."

She tried to head back toward the highway.

"Not that way, stupid."

Obediently, she turned and headed deeper into the woods. With him walking beside her, she couldn't work on getting her hands loose. Too risky to try anything with a gun at her back. She'd hold out until he moved the gun to another position. Then she'd make a move.

Surely, the police would find her Mustang beside the road and follow their trail. She trudged on, ignoring the scratches from twigs and branches. She had to stay alive until then for Jason's sake.

❧

Brent halted a few yards behind the patrol car. They were about twenty yards from Sheila's Mustang. The female cop was crouched behind a squad car, gun in hand. Stapleton, megaphone in hand, said, "Come out with your hands up or we'll shoot."

Brent moved closer to get a better look.

"Get back," shouted the female cop.

He stopped in his tracks. She was right, damn her. He needed to use his head, not listen to his heart. He hoped Sheila wasn't lying dead or injured in the back.

Other cop cars pulled up. Two male officers got out. Officer Stapleton approached the Mustang. "Step out with your hands up," he barked.

No sounds came from the vehicle. Stapleton walked over to the window on the driver's side. "No one inside."

Brent drew a sigh of relief. At least Sheila wasn't lying dead inside. But where was she? Picturing her captor walking her through the woods at gunpoint, he cringed.

The cops followed a trail of broken undergrowth through the woods. They were armed. He wasn't. He should let them handle the search. He paced back and forth, clenching his fists and wishing the motorcycle could penetrate the brush.

If he followed the cops at a distance, he could see what was happening. The officers would probably nail the bastard if they could get a clear shot.

Brent wanted to be near when they did, to hold Sheila, to tell her that he loved her and that he'd see her son was safe. If she were fatally wounded, at least he could give her that.

He wasn't going to think about that. He had to keep hoping she'd be all right. His eyes watered, blurring his sight. He scrubbed at them. He needed to be able to see clearly. He swallowed. Couldn't stand here doing nothing. He followed the trampled path the officers left behind.

As Brent headed for the woods, the female cop shouted, "Don't follow us. Stay back."

Brent ignored her. He had to get to Sheila.

A brisk breeze chilled his skin as the sky clouded over. A few drops wet his face. The rain might beat down the weeds so no one could see which way that guy and Sheila went. They needed to find her soon.

A bobcat came barreling down the path. The cops must have scared it away. He'd heard there'd been several sightings in Dallas of the big cats knocking over garbage cans and pawing through the contents. Pulse racing, he stepped off the path onto a large rock and picked up a stone. Did bobcats attack humans? Better not to provoke it. He tensed, ready to fight.

The cat snarled, but ran on by. Then he noticed the brush slightly dented off to one side of the rock. Had Sheila and that scum branched off that way?

Only one way to find out. He followed the trail. A broken branch lay across the path. He dropped the rock and grabbed the branch.

He was making too much noise. Needed to surprise the kidnapper. He slowed, trying not to step on any twigs.

Up ahead, Sheila and Nate tussled over a gun. Brent worked his way around the pair, hoping the man wouldn't see him. It seemed to take forever to get in position. First Sheila seemed to have the gun, then the kidnapper.

"You won't get away with this," Sheila shouted as the kidnapper yanked the weapon from her grasp.

Her foot darted out, striking him with a karate kick to the groin. Her captor bent, one hand going to his crotch, but he kept his grip on the gun.

Brent took one more step. Now in position, he sprang forward, raised the branch, and conked the guy on the head. The branch broke, but it stunned Nate enough so Sheila could snatch his gun.

"Freeze," she ordered. Glancing up at Brent, she let out her breath. "Grab him," she said.

Quickly, Brent grasped the man's arms and pinned one behind him.

The policemen came crashing through the underbrush, guns drawn. "We'll take it from here," said Stapleton, pointing his weapon at the kidnapper.

Brent released first one arm, then the other to the officers. A tall lanky one snapped handcuffs on Nate.

Brent hugged Sheila, then cut the cord binding her wrists. He took her cold hand in his and rubbed it. Her face looked swollen, and her lip was cut. "You okay?" he asked.

She nodded. "I'll be a little stiff, but I'm all right. I only hope my son's okay."

Behind them, Stapleton recited the Miranda warning to the handcuffed man, then asked his name.

"I ain't telling you nothing," Nate said belligerently.

"I didn't see Jason at Darla's house," Brent said.

"I sent him to a neighbor next door. I hope he made it."

Brent kept his arms around her. "Thank goodness I got here in time."

Stapleton walked up to Sheila. "Do you know his name?"

"Nate is all I know."

"He claims his brother is a government witness and that

you were supposed to be protecting him."

Glancing at Nate, Sheila saw the resemblance now. She said, "I'm a U.S. Marshal, and it could be his brother I'm responsible for. I was visiting my friend, Darla, when this man broke in and killed her, then kidnapped me from her house."

"What's his brother's name?"

"I can't release his name. He's under government protection."

Stapleton turned to the other two male officers. "Question him about killing the Marshal's friend, and then take him to Lew Sterrett Jail. I'll order a crime scene task force there." He turned to Sheila. "What's the address of your friend's house?"

She rattled it off. "Hope you get enough evidence there to nail him."

Even with handcuffs, it took two of them to hustle Nate into the back seat of the second squad car.

Brent took hold of Sheila's hand, surprised to find it trembling. "You sure you're okay?"

She nodded. "Yes, but I need to get back to Jason."

He glanced at her Mustang. "I don't think your car's drivable. You want me to call a tow truck?"

"Would you please?"

"Sure. And Sheila, after things cool down, we need to talk."

Leaving Nate cuffed and sitting in the back seat of the Crown Vic, Stapleton walked back to Sheila, who was rubbing her wrists where the rope had been. "I need you to come to the station and fill out charges against him. We also need you to make a statement so we can keep him locked up until his trial."

"I'll be glad to as soon as I get my son back."

Officer Stapleton looked at Brent. "Thanks for helping us capture him. You can follow us on the bike. We can pick up her son on the way to the station."

Brent nodded and mounted the bike as the two cops and Sheila got in the squad car.

She was safe, thank goodness. She'd want her son with her,

but would she want him, too? He didn't know if he was ready for instant fatherhood, but if that's what it took, he was willing. He started the motorcycle and took off after the squad car. It held his best chance for happiness. Now all he had to do was convince her.

❦

When they got to Mary's house, Sheila jumped out and ran toward the neighbor woman sitting in a yard chair and jiggling Sheila's son on her knee.

Shivering at the realization they'd barely escaped death, she took a deep breath and held out her arms to her son. With the papers Darla had signed years ago in case she and Bill died, Jason was her future now. He was smiling, but his face was tear streaked.

"Jason, thank heavens you're all right," said Sheila.

Her son let her pick him up. She hugged him and breathed a silent prayer of thankfulness.

"Sheila," Jason said. "We go home now, wake up Mommy."

She knelt down in front of Jason. "Your mommy's…she's gone to live with daddy and the angels in Heaven. She'll blow you a kiss at bedtime."

Jason had a puzzled look. "Where's Heaven?"

Sheila hugged him. "It's a very nice place with lots of sunshine and flowers."

"And swings? Like my house?"

Sheila nodded. "Yes. Your mommy could be having fun on a swing right now." A tear coursed down her cheek. She turned her head to hide it.

"But-but," Jason asked. "Who's pushing her?"

"I think it's God," said Brent.

"Who's God?" Jason asked.

Brent looked at Sheila. "Your turn."

"He's—he's sort of like your father."

Jason frowned. "Daddy went away. Mommy said he's not coming back."

Sheila smoothed back his hair from his face. "Maybe your daddy is pushing mommy on the swing."

"Can he blow me a kiss, too, when I go to bed tonight?"

"Yes, dear."

The kid looked at her, wide-eyed. "Sheila, will you tuck me in, okay?"

"Yes, I will, every night." She hoped he would soon adjust to having her take care of him. She hugged him tighter.

Footsteps sounded on the gravel driveway. Stapleton's partner, Jo, approached. "We need you to come to the station now."

Sheila glanced at Brent. "May we ride in the squad car?"

Stapleton nodded. "Since our back-up took him to jail, we have room, but since Brent was the last one to see the crime scene I want him to meet the CSI at that house in case they have any questions he can answer."

Sheila took Jason's hand and urged him into the rear of the patrol car. "I'm not letting him out of my sight."

Brent said, "When I'm through, I'll call a cab and meet you at the station."

Sheila grasped his wrist. "Afterwards, you should go to your new apartment. I can take a cab from the station."

Brent frowned, then nodded. "Okay, but if you don't show up in two hours, I'm coming after you, wherever you are."

"Is that a threat?"

He blew her a kiss. "No, it's a promise."

Sheila climbed in the police car, buckled Jason in the seatbelt, then fastened her own.

The session at the police station was long and grueling. A female officer took Jason to her desk. Once he came in to the room where they were questioning Sheila. He asked if they could go home and see his mommy again.

Sheila bent down and took his hand. "I'll come get you in just a little while. Now please go with the nice policewoman."

Jason stuck his thumb in his mouth and let the woman lead him out of the room. Sheila hoped she'd be better able to deal with his questions later.

When they finished, Jo called her a cab, and Sheila took Jason out and settled him beside her. After arriving at Brent's place, she paid the driver and got out. Jason's head lay on her shoulders.

As she climbed the steps, her burden seemed to get heavier and heavier. When Brent opened the door, she held a finger to her lips, stepped inside and laid the sleeping child on one end of the couch.

Brent walked over beside her and took her hand. "Sit down," he said. "I have something to tell you." His voice quieter now, had a determined tone.

She sat. Was he going to give her a hard time about letting herself get captured? Then she looked into his eyes and saw him smile.

His expression turned serious. "I wanted to do something memorable and romantic, but everything I think of seems trite after what you've been through." He took her hand and squeezed it. "You don't know how scared I was that you would die, and I might never have a chance to hold you tight and tell you I love you."

She held her breath and gazed into his earnest brown eyes.

He grasped her other hand and pulled her to her feet. He wrapped his arms around her and kissed her long and hard. Pulling away just the barest amount, he met her gaze. "I love you because of what you are and in spite of what you are. You always seemed to be ordering me around, and I resented that. I realize you were only trying to keep me safe. I appreciate the risks you took for me."

He smoothed a lock of hair from her face. "More than that, I love the way you gave yourself to me, wholehearted without holding anything back. You have become the most important person in my life. And bossy or not, I want to marry you."

She'd found someone who loved her unconditionally. She could hardly believe her ears.

He grinned. "Surprised you, didn't I?"

"I don't know what to say."

"You better say, 'I love you, too' — or I won't marry you."

Her heart swelled, but she couldn't resist saying, "Now who's being bossy?"

He tipped up her chin and kissed her gently. "Well?"

She grasped his face in her hands and pulled it close. Meeting his mouth more than halfway, she kissed him heartily. She let her hands rove through his hair, loving the feel of his thick waves.

His hands caressed her breasts, making them tingle. Her senses sizzled as his hands slid to her waist. "I'd like to make love with you right now, but Jason's taking up the bed. More than that, I want to hear your answer. Will you marry me?"

She nodded.

He blinked. "And they say men are the ones who beat around the bush and don't talk about their feelings. I need to know if you love me."

She raised her hand to his mouth, placed her fingers over his lips. "You don't need to say anymore. Yes, I love you, and if you can stand my being bossy on occasion—"

"On occasion? Lately it's been most of the time?"

"Okay, I admit it, but it was all for your best interests."

"That's what my mother always says."

"Well, I'll try to remember to say 'please.'"

"There's something else."

Sheila gazed into his eyes. He looked determined. She was willing to give him her heart. What else could he want?

"I want to be a cop again."

She breathed a sigh of relief. "I can handle that—unless you wanted to go undercover again. I mean, I'd hate to be constantly worried about your safety."

He took her hand, raised it to his lips. "There's always danger for a cop, unless he has a desk job, which I'd hate. But you can bet your bottom dollar, if I have you to come home to, I'll make darn sure it will be in one piece."

"And when you do, I'll remember to say, 'please,' most of the time."

"There's one exception I think I can live with."

"What's that?"

"Don't think I'll mind if you command me to make love to you—but it would be much sweeter if you beg."

She swatted the air as he ducked back. "I'm not begging you for that or anything else."

"Well, then I'll just have to seduce you, and I plan to do a lot of that." He reached over and unfastened the top button of her blouse.

"We can't, not here with Jason."

He grinned. "Think it's time you took a shower, and had someone wash your back."

"If you're suggesting what I think you are."

His grin grew. "And what if I am?"

She took his hand. "What are we waiting for?"

She left the bathroom door open a crack to listen for Jason. Brent undid her clothing, pausing after removing her blouse to caress her breasts and kiss the tips. Her nipples firmed instantly, and her breasts swelled as he suckled each one. A hot feeling suffused her body and spread to the area between her thighs, making her ache for completion. His fingers slid downward, massaging her there. She tingled, instinctively rubbing against his roving fingers.

He whispered in her ear. "We could skip the shower, you know."

"What if Jason wakes and comes in?"

"Okay, we'll do the shower, but hurry."

She reached behind him to turn on the water. "But you're not even undressed."

"You going to order me—?"

The sounds of the shower drowned out the rest of his words. She turned to protest, but saw all he had on were his boxer shorts and socks. In short order he removed them, and then stood before her, his masculine desire obvious. Hands on her bottom, he pulled her against him, and then urged her toward the rushing water. She took a step back. He followed her into the shower. Her heart beat faster in anticipation and he pulled her against his hard body.

She wasn't even wet all over when he pushed inside her. His hard thrusts filled her again and again. She met him stroke for stroke. Inside a tightness was bursting to capacity. Faster and faster he thrust. He held her so close that her breasts seemed to meld with his chest. He showered her with wet kisses, as if he couldn't get enough.

She felt the climax building and leaned into it. She savored the excitement and the closeness as they both exploded within.

He kissed her gently and whispered, "I love you. I'll always love you."

She felt his hands caressing her breasts, and then he placed a gentle kiss on each before meeting her gaze.

"Ummm, nice," he said. "Have to do that again sometime, real soon I hope."

Someone pounded on the frosted glass door of the shower.

Sheila froze. Had Nate gotten out on bail?

Then she heard a tiny voice. "What are you doing, Sheila?"

Jason. She pulled away from Brent.

"I—I—" What could she say?

Brent answered, "I'm scrubbing her back. Do you want yours washed?"

"No." He mumbled something else Sheila couldn't quite understand, then shuffled out of the bathroom.

"What did he say?" she asked.

"Daddy always say makin' baby."

Sheila felt her face grow hot.

Brent turned off the shower and pulled her close. His skin warm and moist, felt comforting against her.

Brent whispered in her ear. "Could be that kid's smarter than we think he is."

Sheila smiled. "Guess Darla and Bill were still trying to have one of their own."

Brent held her hand next to his heart. "I'm sure you'll tell him all about them when he gets older, but I wouldn't mind trying for one of our own, and if it doesn't happen, well, we'll sure enjoy the trying." A broad grin spread across his face.

She was about to say she'd like that, but his kiss stopped her. Now, all she could concentrate on were his lips, the tender way he caressed her, and that he'd promised to love her for the rest of his life.

Epilogue

Sheila walked with Brent out of the courtroom. Although Brent had just arrived after a quick trip to Detroit, he'd done a good job of testifying about how Dobson had falsified Bart Sheldon's books and sent incorrect returns to the IRS. Dobson had detailed all of Sheldon's shady business ventures and listed the contacts he knew of.

Since Sheila and Brent were getting married, Marshal Joe Berg took over Dobson's case. Dobson had been put on probation and sent off to a town in another state to make a new life for himself, but never again as a CPA. Sheldon had been given two terms of twenty years, and Nate's bond had been set at a million. The federal attorney told Sheila he was sure Nate would be convicted on the basis of the testimony Sheila would give at his trial next month. As she and Brent walked out beside Joe, her partner whispered, "Your defense attorney for the hearing on your unapproved trip to Hawaii is sure agency charges against you will be dropped because you brought the witness back safely and got him to testify."

Sheila and Brent walked to her car, now fixed and repainted. Sheila unlocked the door, but Brent took her hand. "I want to tell you what happened in Detroit."

She waited, knowing he'd gone to get his name cleared.

Brent grinned. "I had the upper hand. Maynard, the guy who screwed up on that raid that went bad and blamed me, is chief now. He's vulnerable to public opinion. I told him I'd call in a reporter and tell her exactly what happened and why the raid went wrong unless he pulled all mention of blame from my file and told the Fort Worth Police I'd been a good cop."

"And he gave in, just like that?"

"I reminded him that Dorrie, my dead partner Smitty's wife, was trying to raise two little boys by herself. Guess he felt responsible after all."

"So did he agree then?"

"Better than that, he took the sample letter I'd written listing my accomplishments, gave it to his secretary to type and signed it. He faxed it to the Human Resources Department in Fort Worth. I stopped there on the way here from the airport. That letter cinched the job. I report for work on the first of next month."

"That's wonderful. Now get in. We don't want to be late."

He grinned. "You're right." He got in the car.

She drove to Cleburne where a wedding gown, a preacher, and a church soon to be filled with his parents and her grandparents and friends, waited. She thought about Jason waiting to begin life with her and Brent in their house in the country and hoped she'd be a good mother.

Brent took Sheila's hand and pressed it to his lips. "I'm looking forward to a whole new life with my fellow officers in Fort Worth and best of all, my favorite woman."

She smiled. The sun had never seemed so bright nor the air so clear.

Dear Reader: If you enjoyed *Tempted by Love, Witness Protection Series, Book Three*, a review on Amazon (or other retail sites) would be appreciated, and you'll want to read the other books in the Witness Protection Series.

HIDING FROM LOVE
Witness Protection Series, Book One

Auburn-haired Laura Lee, won't let her ex-boss continue running his miniature mafia. Laura trusts the Witness Security Program to set up her new identity in the small town of Grandville, Texas. There, she not only hides from him, but from love and marriage until she meets handsome Alexander Brandon. When her ex-boss's thug shows up, Alex helps her escape. Wary, she resolves not to get involved with him.

Available Now in print and digital formats

PROTECTED BY LOVE
Witness Protection Series, Book Two

Fashion designer, Elizabeth Leventhal, Lee's sister, wants to escape her abusive ex-husband, who works for The Elites, a Texas crime ring. When he beats down her door, she calls U.S. Marshal Joe Berg to put her in the Witness Security Program. Handsome and muscular, he swears to protect her, but insists her evidence is thin. He asks her to learn more by attending an Elite's party at a huge honky tonk. That fills her with dread.

Joe Berg's sympathies and his heart are drawn to the plucky Elizabeth. He struggles with his obstinate boss, his forbidden attraction to Elizabeth, and the Elite's attempts to turn her over to her ex-husband.

Available Now in print and digital formats

———————

Also by Carolyn Rae

ROMANCING THE GOLD
MuseItUp Publishing 2014

Adventurous Megan McKinley finds searching for gold more exciting after hunky, bearded photographer, Joseph Logan, a man with a hidden past and a secret agenda, arrives at the dig.

When Megan's archaeology professor boasts he found the terra cotta bowl she dug up, she suspects he's not the benevolent mentor she'd thought him. Then she discovers the photographer is actually Josh Seward, the clean-cut high school teacher she had a crush on years ago.

Available Now in print and digital formats

———————

Check my website at Carolynrae.com and Carolyn Rae Author / Facebook for excerpts from *Romancing the Gold.*

About the Author

As a teenager, Carolyn Rae told stories to kids she babysat. On a long road trip, she entertained her younger sister with stories she made up.

Later she taught home economics, family living, and English in Michigan, Illinois, and Texas, where she earned a master's degree. She worked as a researcher for a mincemeat company and met her neighbors by bringing samples of mincemeat pies. At the Fort Worth Federal Correctional Institution in Texas, she taught ironwork, painting, and carpentry residents. While there, she also wrote and directed videos on nutrition and fair fighting for married couples

Carolyn Rae wrote the text and many recipes for *There IS Life After Lettuce* (Eakin Press, Fort Worth, Texas), a cookbook for heart patients and diabetics. Her profile and travel articles have appeared in the *Romance Writer's Report, Fort Worth Star Telegram, The Dallas Morning News, Positive Parenting,* and *AAA World, Hawaii and Alaska.* She has worked as a paralegal and follows her passion, writing romantic suspense where bullets are flying, people are dying, and lovers are resisting attraction until they can escape the danger following them.